DEATH BY BLUEBERRY

I watched as the ride attendants helped people unstrap themselves and disembark. But Porter remained slumped forward even after the halter strap was released. Sloane sat next to him, and I saw her give him a brief shake to get him to move. I wondered if he had passed out drunk.

When the attendants couldn't rouse him, I became fearful. Porter had taken his insulin shot minutes ago. What if the combination of insulin, beer, and all the junk food he had eaten sent him into shock?

"Wait here," Ryan ordered. He ran over to the small crowd gathering around the ride.

The crowd grew larger as fairground employees and Blueberry Blow Out workers came on the scene. Within minutes, EMS arrived. When paramedics put Porter onto a stretcher, Sloane grabbed his hand and kissed it.

Ryan raced back to me.

"Has he gone into insulin shock?" I asked him. "A diabetic coma?"

"Neither."

"What do you mean? What happened?"

"It looks like the Blueberry Hill Death Drop has earned its name . . ."

Books by Sharon Farrow

DYING FOR STRAWBERRIES

BLACKBERRY BURIAL

KILLED ON BLUEBERRY HILL

Published by Kensington Publishing Corporation

Killed on Blueberry Hill

Sharon Farrow

KENSINGTON PUBLISHING CORP.
www.kensingtonbooks.com

KENSINGTON BOOKS are published by

Kensington Publishing Corp.
119 West 40th Street
New York, NY 10018

All Kensington titles, imprints, and distributed lines are available at special quantity discounts for bulk purchases for sales promotions, premiums, fund-raising, educational, or institutional use. Special book excerpts or customized printings can also be created to fit specific needs. For details, write or phone the office of the Kensington sales manager: Kensington Publishing Corp., 119 West 40th Street, New York, NY 10018, attn: Sales Department; phone 1-800-221-2647.

ISBN-13: 978-1-4967-0490-0
ISBN-10: 1-4967-0490-8

First printing: November 2018

10 9 8 7 6 5 4 3 2 1

Printed in the United States of America

First electronic edition: November 2018

ISBN-13: 978-1-4967-0491-7
ISBN-10: 1-4967-0491-6

For Barry
Who hopes to spend all his days along the lakeshore

Acknowledgments

My heartfelt gratitude to everyone at Kensington for their support of the Berry Basket series, especially John Scognamiglio, Michelle Addo, and Arthur Maisel. A special thanks to the art department for their delightful fairground cover. I also want to thank my agent, John Talbot, a stalwart champion of the cozy mystery. Finally, a nod of thanks to The Blueberry Store of South Haven, Michigan. Their blueberry-themed shop inspired me to write these mysteries.

Chapter One

As owner of The Berry Basket store in Oriole Point, Michigan, I'm regarded as an expert on all things berry related. My involvement in two murders this summer tacked on *amateur sleuth* to my résumé. Now I prepared to add *glutton* to that list of accomplishments. Of course, I first needed to win the blueberry pie–eating contest to earn the title, but I felt confident I had the determination—and the appetite—to pull it off.

Adjusting my rain poncho, I sat down at the picnic table.

"You can win, Marlee. I know you can."

I glanced up to see the concerned blue eyes of my fiancé, Ryan Zellar.

"But what really matters is that you beat Porter's wife. The Gales can't defeat us twice in one morning." Ryan seemed genuinely pained by the prospect.

Fifteen minutes ago, his brother had been beaten in the men's pie-eating contest by Porter Gale. Ryan's family ran Zellar Orchards, and the Gale family, led by Porter, owned Blueberry Hill, the largest blueberry farm in the state. To Ryan's dismay, Blueberry Hill exceeded them in sales and global reach, resulting in a rivalry between the two families. I didn't understand the enmity. After all, Blueberry Hill sold only blueberries, while Zellars grew everything from peaches and apples to four kinds of berries. It seemed silly to turn a healthy commercial competition into an orchard blood feud. But a feud it certainly was, and the reason I wore a plastic poncho on a sunny August day, readying myself to dive into a blueberry pie.

"The odds are in my favor. I didn't eat breakfast or lunch today, so I'm starving. And blueberry pie is my favorite. Last year, I finished off half a pie at the Fourth of July picnic."

"I remember. I swear, I don't know where you put it." His appreciative gaze swept over my trim body, visible beneath the transparent poncho. "I only wish I'd volunteered to compete in the men's contest instead of Richard. Even if I don't like the taste of blueberries, I couldn't have done any worse than my brother."

"Don't blame Richard. He did his best." Indeed, Ryan's youngest brother made a valiant attempt to bolt down his pie but broke out in a coughing fit midway through.

"Give me a break. How does someone snort blueberry pie up his nose? And for Porter to win makes it even worse." Ryan glared at the man who stood at the end of the table. "The man's a diabetic, for God's sake."

"What!" I looked over at Porter with alarm. Like Ryan, he appeared to be giving last-minute encouragement to his wife, Sloane, one of my fellow contestants. "If he's diabetic, he shouldn't be eating sugar, especially not an entire pie. What if he goes into insulin shock?"

"Don't get my hopes up. The man looks as healthy as an ox. He's as dumb as one, too."

Ignoring Ryan's sarcasm, I observed Porter more closely for signs he might become ill. But he appeared remarkably robust. I knew he was the same age as Ryan—thirty-four—but his powerful, stocky frame made a sharp contrast to Ryan's lanky physique. Not that Ryan wasn't muscular, but he didn't give the impression of brute force like Porter did. I didn't find it surprising Porter had eaten a whole pie in record time. He seemed like a person who wouldn't let anything stand in his way, including a pie-eating contest at the fairground. Still, as a diabetic he should steer clear of sugary pie. He might not be dumb, as Ryan claimed, but Porter had proven himself reckless where his health was concerned.

My attention turned next to Porter's wife, Sloane, who looked more like a cast member of *The Bachelor* than a pie-eating contestant at the county fair. Although a pretty girl, Sloane wielded her cosmetic brushes with such zeal that she often brought to mind a Kabuki performer. Today was no exception. Since the contest required that she stick her face in a pie, I didn't understand why she wore cherry-red lipstick, a shimmery bronzer, and false eyelashes. I thought her an unlikely candidate for such a contest. No doubt her husband "volunteered" her for the event, as Ryan did me.

I watched as Sloane tucked her shoulder-length mass of perfectly highlighted blond hair beneath a shower cap to prevent it from getting covered in pie filling. My fellow contestants did likewise. I should have followed their example. Instead, I skimmed my long hair back into a ponytail. Bad enough to be photographed with a face covered in blueberry pie. Doing so while wearing a shower cap *and* a rain poncho ranked too high on the cringe meter.

Two women acting as the contest judges covered the picnic table with a white plastic tablecloth. A moment later, volunteers delivered our blueberry pies, each one set before us with a flourish. My empty stomach growled at the delectable sight and smell of fresh-baked buttery crust and blueberry filling. The flies agreed, and I shooed them away.

"Don't let Sloane Gale win," Ryan reiterated.

"Don't worry. She's probably never taken part in a pie-eating contest before."

Actually, I had no way of knowing what Sloane Gale might enjoy. Oh, we'd exchanged a few words at Oriole Point county events. Our lakeshore village numbered only four thousand residents, so none of us were strangers to each other. But I didn't know much about her aside from the fact she married Porter Gale a little over a year ago, and that they had no children. I judged her to be a good decade younger than Porter, but her *Vogue* photo shoot makeup made it difficult to gauge her exact age. A younger millennial, for sure. And one unprepared for the indignity of taking part in a pie-eating contest.

When a loud electronic hum rang out, all eyes turned to an elegant blond woman who surveyed the crowd from the nearby outdoor stage.

Ryan groaned. "Why is Piper announcing your

contest? Isn't it bad enough she runs everything in town? Now she's barging in on county business."

"You know the Blueberry Blow Out involves everyone in Oriole County. That includes the villagers." I grinned at him. "Don't forget I'm from the village, too."

"Not for long. As soon as we get married, you'll be out in the country with me."

"That's still up for discussion," I reminded him, but his attention had shifted to Piper.

"I need everyone to quiet down now," Piper said in a tone demanding obedience.

As the crowd near the stage grew silent, Piper frowned in the direction of the carnival midway, where a cacophony of bells, whistles, and calliope music could be heard. When it became apparent she had no control over the din coming from the rest of the fairground, she rolled her eyes. To Ryan's consternation I liked Piper, despite her air of entitlement, which she wore as easily as a cashmere stole. Yes, she sometimes tried my patience, but since she was nearly twenty years older than me, I allowed her some leeway. Ryan did not.

He was right about Piper getting involved in everything. Piper ran the Oriole Point Tourist and Visitor Center in town. And as a descendant of Oriole Point's founding family, Piper Lyall-Pierce managed to take control whether the event took place at city hall or a tractor pull. Her social standing rose even further after she married retired executive Lionel Pierce, also known as our mayor. These things, along with her enormous wealth, put Piper at the top of the Oriole County food chain. Only I wouldn't have thought Piper cared to take part in something as slapstick as a pie-eating contest. Then again, Piper couldn't bear to be left out of anything.

Tapping her microphone, Piper said, "Attention, everyone. It is time for the women's blueberry pie–eating contest. Before we commence, how about another round of applause for the victor of the men's event: Porter Gale, owner of the world-famous Blueberry Hill."

Whistles and cheers rang out as Porter took a bow. Oriole Point not only sat along the beautiful shores of Lake Michigan, our surrounding countryside was known as Michigan's fruit belt. Tourism and the orchards provided much of the employment in the village and the county. The biggest of these commercial enterprises, Blueberry Hill enjoyed the grateful support of its workers, evident in the reception Porter now received.

Ryan swore under his breath, increasing my worry. What if I didn't win? I looked at the women who sat at the table with me. Could I beat all of them? Sloane, probably. But the others hailed from farms and orchards out in the country. As the only contestant who lived in the village, I had no idea what their eating capacity might be. Perhaps they ate more pie than I did. And faster, too.

Maybe I shouldn't have agreed to take part in the contest when Ryan asked me. I needed to say no more often. Especially to him. Only I felt I had little choice. Ryan's sister-in-law Emily had won this contest four times. This summer a pregnant Emily suffered from morning sickness, and her sensible doctor disapproved of the mother-to-be gulping down an entire pie in a few minutes. Even the highly competitive Adam Zellar thought Emily should refrain from fairground contests this year. Of course there were four other Zellar brothers whose respective wives and girlfriend could have been drafted for the event. Ryan decided my two years as owner of The Berry Basket qualified me as the best woman to pig out on berry pie. Besides, the Zellars already regarded me as one of them, even if Ryan and I wouldn't exchange vows until January. If I won today, the Zellars won, too.

I smiled at the assorted Zellars waving at me from the crowd of onlookers. When Ryan's dad gave me a big thumbs-up, I sent a silent prayer to the pie gods.

Piper tapped the microphone once more, which brought the cheers and hoots for Porter to a close. I wondered what had happened to Walter Kluyper, owner of Kluyper Feed Store. He'd presided over the men's event with lusty enthusiasm. Certainly, Walter seemed better suited as a pie contest emcee than Piper, who wore a black sundress covered with huge sunflowers that I suspected came from the latest RTW collection of Dolce and Gabbana. I'd spent several years as a producer at the Gourmet Living Network in New York City and knew my designers.

"For those who have just joined us," Piper said, "let me welcome you to the opening day of our annual Blueberry Blow Out. Because this is the height of tourist season along the lakeshore, many of you might be from out of town. If so, you will be interested to learn that Michigan leads the nation in highbush blueberry production. Every August, Oriole Point County celebrates the bounty of our blueberry harvest with seven days of festivities here at the fairground. We hope you enjoy the many activities we have scheduled, which include live musical performances, amusement park rides, vendor booths, and a variety of competitions. This brings us to the women's blueberry pie–eating contest."

She pointed a blue air horn at the twelve of us in our plastic ponchos. "As soon as my air horn blasts, these ladies will race to see who can finish eating an entire blueberry pie first. And they must do so without using their hands. Before we proceed, I'd like to thank the Cooking Circle members of Oriole Point's First Presbyterian Church for baking the pies."

A smattering of applause greeted this acknowledgment.

Piper continued, "The first woman to eat her pie wins fifty dollars, along with the title of Women's Champion Blueberry Pie Eater of Oriole County."

I made a face. There were lots of things I'd like to be known for instead of stuffing myself with pie. But I'd never turn down a blue ribbon. And because I hadn't eaten a thing all day, my appetite for that pie grew every second. However, my thirst outweighed my hunger pangs. The afternoon sun beat down, causing my bare legs and arms to grow damp beneath the poncho. Reaching for the water bottle each contestant had been given, I let out a cry of protest when someone yanked the bottle out of my hand.

"No drinking until after you've eaten the pie," a familiar voice hissed in my ear. "Water cuts down on your appetite. You need to stay ravenous."

I lifted an eyebrow at Andrew, one of three retail clerks I employed at The Berry Basket. "It's like a sauna out here and I'm dying of thirst. If my mouth is too dry, how do you imagine I'll be able to eat an entire pie?" Snatching the water bottle away from him, I unscrewed the cap and took a long swig.

"That's enough." He took it from me once more. "Dean and I bet twenty dollars you'd win this contest. I have no intention of letting you blow this thing right before it starts."

"You and your brother shouldn't be betting on the contest at all. And why are you here? You're supposed to be manning our Berry Basket booth right now. Or did you convince Dean to take over for you? His shift doesn't start for another hour."

"Don't be silly. Dean isn't about to miss this. He's right there." Andrew nodded at his older brother, who waved at me from among the crowd.

People who saw the Cabot brothers for the first time often assumed they were twins. Both were tall, attractive, auburn haired, and as concerned with style and fashion as Piper, but without her disposable income. Despite their striking similarities, they were eleven months apart in age—actual Irish twins, given their Celtic ancestry. They also were the bearers of every snippet of gossip in town; their knowledge surpassed only by the rumor-spreading talents of their mother, Suzanne Cabot, who worked as receptionist at the local police station. Between the three of them, Oriole Point had no need of a newspaper or Twitter feed.

Luckily, I'd grown quite fond of both brothers in the two years they had worked for me. There were times I felt more like their big sister than their employer. They were often as hard to control as kid brothers, too.

My best friend, Tess, stood beside Dean, holding up her phone to let me know she was about to film my pie-eating efforts. Dean fished his own phone out of a back pocket and held it up, too. While I expected Tess to be here to give moral support, I should have known neither Cabot brother would miss the chance to watch their boss make a public spectacle of herself.

"If neither of you are at our booth, who is? It can't be Gillian. She's working at the store today. Please don't tell me you left our merchandise *and* the cashbox unattended."

"Do I look that irresponsible?" Andrew threw me an injured look. "I spotted Theo at the fairground today, so I asked him to watch the booth while I came here."

"Theo? Theo's a baker. He doesn't know anything about sales." I didn't need to add that Theo suffered from crippling shyness. Andrew knew my Berry Basket baker grew anxious and uncomfortable when surrounded by too many people.

"Theo will be fine," Andrew replied. "You baby him too much."

Ryan crouched down beside me. "Concentrate, Marlee. The contest is about to start."

"He's right." Andrew massaged my shoulders, as if I were a boxer about to go into the ring. "Keep your head down. Focus. And eat like a pig."

Taking a deep breath, I readied myself. Except I couldn't get rid of the image of a panic-stricken Theo left alone at the store's booth. Now I had another reason to gobble up that pie. As soon as I did, Andrew could be sent to relieve my skittish baker.

The blare of the air horn made me jump. As shouts rose up from the crowd, I looked at the blueberry pie before me. I'd taken part in pie-eating contests at summer camp and knew exactly what to do. Clamping the side of the aluminum pie plate with my teeth, I flipped the contents of the pie onto the table. It spread before me in a gooey blue mass. Like a human vacuum cleaner, I started to slurp up the blueberry filling.

The sticky filling coated my face and lashes; some got into my eyes, but I continued to eat, running my tongue along the tablecloth to scarf up as much as possible. Turning my attention to the crust next, I reminded myself to chew the pieces a few times before swallowing. The woman next to me hadn't and began to choke, just as Ryan's brother had.

With Ryan and Andrew cheering me on, I quickly devoured what was left of the pie. Smeared with blueberries, I raised my head and sat back. The crowd hooted and yelled. The judges who stood at the end of the table signaled to Piper, who once again blared the air horn.

"We have a winner!" Piper yelled into the microphone. "Marlee Jacob, owner of The Berry Basket, is this year's women's champion of the Blueberry Pie–Eating Contest!"

Relief washed over me, accompanied by a wave of nausea. I hoped I wasn't about to be sick. Andrew clapped me on the back, which didn't help.

"Fantastic!" Ryan grabbed my face and gave me

a jubilant kiss. When he pulled away, I giggled to see his own face now smeared with blueberry filling. "You're the best, Marlee. The best! No one else came even close."

When I glanced over at the pillaged pies on the table, I saw he was right. I could have eaten much slower and still won. At least, everyone had a good time. My fellow contestants, covered in varying amounts of blueberry pie, laughingly extended their congratulations to me. Except for Sloane Gale. As soon as I had been declared the winner, Sloane ripped off her plastic poncho. A stony-faced Porter shook his head. I didn't know why they seemed upset. Sloane's pie looked like she had taken all of three bites out of it. More like nibbles, actually.

While I wiped my face clean with a wet towel, Sloane got to her feet. Tossing her shower cap to the ground, she marched off into the crowd.

"It's not over, Zellar," Porter snapped at Ryan.

"You got that right. In an hour, we'll be humiliating Blueberry Hill in the tug-of-war." Ryan gave a playful tug to my ponytail. "And my victorious girlfriend is going to help beat the crap out of the Gales one more time."

I stopped cleaning my face. "Wait a second. I'm in the tug-of-war, too?"

Porter shot Ryan a disgusted look. "How pathetic. Leave it to a Zellar to expect his girlfriend to do all the work for him. You're a loser, Ryan. Always have been. Always will be." He turned his attention to me. "I've heard you're a smart woman, Marlee. If so, you should know better than to marry someone like him. Get out while you can."

"You're the one who's pathetic!" Ryan shouted at Porter as he left to join his wife. "Can't even handle losing one little contest."

I looked up at Ryan. "You never said I was supposed to be part of the tug-of-war."

Ryan reacted as if I had spoken gibberish. "Of course I expect you to take part. All my sisters-in-law have begged off. Emily can't this year because she's pregnant. Adam would deck me for even suggesting she take part. Amanda has no upper body strength, so she'd be as little help to us as her husband was at the pie-eating contest. Barry's wife sprained her ankle in the tug-of-war last year. Now Melissa flat out refuses to do it again. And Jim told me that Beth has cramps today, which is the worst excuse ever. But it doesn't matter. You're in much better shape than they are. You're strong, too. I've seen you carry around heavy crates of berries. You'll be fine. Only I wish you'd worn jeans instead of those shorts. Your legs might get scraped pretty bad."

My mouth fell open.

"I'm with Porter on this." Andrew put his hand on my shoulder. "Let Marlee sit out the next contest. She won't have time to digest all that pie before then."

Ryan laughed. "You're both overreacting. If we pull hard enough, the contest will be over in seconds. No time for her to get sick. And what if she does? It will be worth it if Marlee helps us beat Blueberry Hill."

Another wave of queasiness swept over me. This time I wasn't certain if it was the blueberry pie I had wolfed down—or the suspicion that Ryan cared more about his feud with Porter Gale than he did about me.

Chapter Two

Gluttony has its rewards and drawbacks. The fifty-dollar check counted as a reward, as did the fervent gratitude of the Zellar family. The entire Zellar clan had to be prevented from hoisting me on their shoulders and parading me about the fairground in a victory lap. The drawbacks included too many photos of me slathered in pie. A local news station from Grand Rapids had filmed the event, which would allow the rest of west Michigan to witness my victory on the six-o'clock news. The worst drawback: a nasty stomachache to accompany my blue ribbon. I swore to never let Ryan sign me up for another pie-eating contest.

I felt relieved when Ryan and his family left to check out things at the Zellar Orchards tent set up at the fair. I also ordered both Cabot brothers back to work at our vendor booth. And I managed to escape after only a five-minute conversation with Piper, most of it filled with her complaints about the disorganized behavior of the Blueberry Blow Out volunteers.

That left only Tess, who waited until everyone was gone before coming over to give me a friendly hug. "Congratulations," she said. "You and Porter Gale have proven yourselves to be Oriole Point's most eximious pie eaters."

"I don't know if I'd call our achievement either distinguished or excellent. But I'd describe my current state as crapulent." Tess Nakamura and I became best friends back in fifth grade when we tied for first place in the regional spelling bee. Since then, we'd kept our spelling skills in shape by using the occasional uncommon word.

Tess pulled a bottle of Tums from her purse. "I figured you might be feeling sick."

"You're a lifesaver. Now I need to get out of the sun. Otherwise I may faint or throw up. Possibly both."

Tess looked around for a shady spot. "Follow me."

A few minutes later we sat down at an umbrella table near the kiddie pony rides.

"All right, what's going on? You don't look happy. And I'm betting it's not just from gorging on pie." Tess waited while I chewed three fruit-flavored Tums.

"It's Ryan," I said finally. "He entered me in the pie-eating contest without asking me. And that was okay. After all, I do love to eat, especially anything with blueberries. But now I learn he signed me up for the tug-of-war, too. A contest scheduled to take place in less than thirty minutes. My stomach will not be ready."

"That was presumptuous of him. And rude."

"It's not just him signing me up for contests. Ryan won't stop pressuring me to put my family's lake house up for sale. He's determined to have us live at the Zellar Orchards. And he wants to break ground on a house there before the end of the month. I'm afraid he'll build the house no matter how much I protest."

I held up my ponytail to allow what little breeze there was to reach the back of my neck. The lakeshore felt like a rain forest today. Not for the first time I envied Tess her short, asymmetrical haircut. "And last week, I discovered the ceiling fan on my back porch had vanished. Without a word to me, Ryan hauled it off to the county dump."

"What!"

"Ryan hates fans. He always complains about them. But it was my fan and he removed it from my house." Although Ryan spent a lot of nights at my lakeside home, we maintained separate residences. I resented him treating my possessions as if they already belonged to him.

"He needs to stop making decisions for you. It's disrespectful." She frowned. Tess in a disapproving mood brought to mind a fierce female samurai. "If this is any indication of what your life with Ryan will be like, maybe you should reconsider your decision to marry him."

This startled me. "I thought you liked Ryan."

"I do. However, there are lots of people I like whom I don't think you should marry. And until recently you seemed happy to be his future bride, so I never said anything. But for weeks you've joked about bridal jitters and getting cold feet. Maybe it's time to stop joking." She paused. "I wish you'd follow the example of David and me, at least for a couple of years."

David Reese and Tess met as eighteen-year-old art students and quickly became a romantic couple. Twelve years later they were still together, with their partnership also a professional one. Oriole Glass, their studio shop in the village, had become one of the most successful art glass galleries in Michigan. But even after a dozen happy years together, the pair had no intention of walking down the aisle.

I nervously tapped the bottle of Tums on the table. "My parents told me to postpone the wedding if I'm having doubts."

"Sounds like good advice," Tess said. "Although I doubt Ryan will agree."

"I did suggest we slow things down a bit. After all, he has one bad marriage behind him. A longer engagement would really be for his benefit. He didn't buy that excuse. Instead, he accused me of refusing to grow up, being afraid of commitment. And he could be right. After all, I'm thirty and never been married."

She shrugged. "Same here."

"But you and David share the same view about marriage. And the two of you are perfect for each other. I'm not so sure about Ryan and me."

"Marlee, I love David, but no relationship is perfect. Trust me, we fight and get on each other's nerves sometimes. But we also like and respect each other. Neither of us would dare make a decision without talking it over with the other. Ryan seems to be doing that more and more lately. Not a good sign. You're too strong a person to put up with a controlling husband."

"I know." I watched the children being led around on ponies in the adjacent ring. I remembered doing just that at the Blueberry Blow Out when I was growing up. I suddenly missed being eight years old, with nothing to worry about except trying to convince my parents to let me have another pet bird. Even though I had recently seen them, I also missed my parents, who now lived in Chicago. Fortunately, they were only a two-hour drive away.

Tess scrunched up her nose. "We need to move. This is way too close to the ponies."

I took a deep breath. "Perfect for me. I've always loved the smell of horse manure."

"I remember. Maybe you should marry the owner of a horse farm, not an orchard." Tess took my hand. "Or maybe you shouldn't be getting married at all. At least not to Ryan."

This conversation hadn't made me feel any better, even if the Tums had. And I needed to find Ryan. Tess had convinced me to make at least one decision this afternoon. My stomach felt awful, and I dreaded what might happen if forced to pull on a rope with all my might. No matter how much Ryan insisted, I refused to take part in that tug-of-war.

I found Ryan huddled with his brothers, like a football team before the kickoff. Intent on the upcoming contest, they ignored everyone in the vicinity, including me. I had little choice but to mingle with the Zellar women, who instructed me on the finer points of tug-of-war competition. Too bad Tess left the fairground to go back to work at her studio. When she was around, I always had at least one person in my corner. At the moment, I even missed the Cabot brothers.

A sizable crowd had gathered along the stretch of field marked off for the tug-of-war contests. In an hour, potato sack races were scheduled to start here. I prayed Ryan hadn't signed me up for that as well. Although I'd missed the first three tugs-of-war between other fruit growers in the region, I did catch the start of the latest contest between the O'Neill Blueberry Farm and Janssen Blueberries.

Evenly divided between male and female, the O'Neill and Janssen teams comprised family members and employees. While taking their places for the tug-of-war, they yelled insults to each other, but the mood felt playful. And if I had to bet on the outcome, I gave the edge to the O'Neill team led by the farm's husband-and-wife owners, Brody and Cara O'Neill. In their forties, Brody and Cara boasted sturdy muscular frames, a product of long days spent working on their farm. Their hardy physiques came in handy as they dug their heels in and leaned back as far as possible while straining on the tug-of-war rope. If I tried to do the same in my current queasy state, my stomach would probably explode.

Rallied by Brody and Cara, the O'Neill team soon dragged the Janssen team toward them with one great pull. When the white bandanna hanging from the middle of the rope edged over the bright red line painted on the ground, everyone collapsed in a heap of sand and laughter. Cara O'Neill laughed the loudest. Since Cara was also the sister of Porter Gale, it appeared the Gale siblings shared a healthy competitive drive.

I scanned the area for Porter and his team. Like the Zellars, the Gales stood close together talking;

no females were part of the group. A few yards away, Sloane sat cross-legged on the ground, fanning herself with a carnival program. She looked bored to death.

An unattractive young man I recognized as Cara's son, Wyatt, joined her. When he crouched down and kissed her on the neck, she shoved him hard and he fell backward onto the dirt. Sloane wore an angry expression, but Wyatt merely laughed before ambling away. What was that all about? I knew Sloane and Wyatt were close in age, but nuzzling your aunt on the neck ranked as creepy. I also wondered why he hadn't competed with his family in the tug-of-war.

"There you are." Ryan trotted over to give me a hug. "Your stomach feeling any better?"

"A little, but I don't think it's wise for me to pull on a rope right now."

"Don't worry. We found out the Blueberry Hill team will be men only. I guess Porter got spooked about going up against my pie champion fiancée. Marlee, I'm sorry I volunteered you for the tug-of-war, but I forgot it began so soon after the pie-eating contest. And I should have asked you first. I guess you're engaged to a stupid, selfish idiot. One who doesn't deserve you." He kissed me, making me feel a bit guilty about my conversation with Tess. "Forgive me?"

"Yes." I kissed him back. "But I haven't forgiven you for taking my ceiling fan."

He chuckled. "You don't need it. That's why God invented air-conditioning." Ryan gestured at the Zellar tug-of-war team. "The contest might get rough.

So me and my brothers asked J.J., Tommy, and Boblo to join us." J.J. was Ryan's teenage nephew, while Tommy and Boblo were Zellar cousins who worked at the orchards.

I looked over at the Gale team. "I assume most of those guys work for Blueberry Hill."

He snorted. "Yeah, Porter has to literally pay to put together a team."

"Not every family is as big as your own. You can't blame him for including employees."

"I blame him for everything."

"I don't get this hatred of Porter Gale. Blueberry Hill is much bigger than Zellars. They're a national brand, like Dole. It doesn't make sense to be so competitive with them. Why can't Blueberry Hill and Zellar Orchards peacefully coexist? Like Kosovo and Serbia?" I put my arms around his waist and pulled him closer. "Or Taylor Swift and Katy Perry."

"Because we can't. At least Porter and I can't. And now it's time to whip his ass."

With a sinking heart, I watched as Ryan ran to join his brothers and cousins. This whole thing promised to be even more absurd than the pie-eating contest.

Porter and his team now busied themselves with kicking at the sandy ground where the previous tugs-of-war had taken place. Ryan yelled at them, prompting an angry response from Porter. I wondered what happened last year at the tug-of-war. I missed the entire Blueberry Blow Out when my dad broke his leg and I spent the week helping him and my mom in Chicago. During the rest of the year, I was too busy at The Berry Basket to keep tabs on any disputes out in the orchards. However, Ryan and I had been dating since last summer, and this was the first I'd heard about his personal animosity toward Porter.

Cara O'Neill walked up to me. "Hi, Marlee. Looks like the next one is boys only."

"I'm glad they decided to go stag. My name was on the original team roster. But I did my part today." I tapped the blue ribbon pinned to my BERRY BASKET T-shirt. "And congratulations on winning your tug-of-war. I thought your son would be taking part."

"You know kids. He thinks all these games are juvenile. But we didn't need him. And congrats on the pie-eating win. Porter should never have entered Sloane. The girl hates pie."

"Surprised you didn't compete again."

She took a sip from her water bottle. "I'm forty-two, past the age anyone should be embarrassing themselves in a pie-eating contest. Also your soon-to-be sister-in-law Emily has beaten me every time. Who knew she'd let a little thing like pregnancy stop her this year?"

"Doctor's orders." I watched while the guys lined up for the tug-of-war. In a show of machismo, all of them decided to remove their tank tops and T-shirts. The sight of sixteen tanned and muscled men elicited raucous whistles and cheers from the growing crowd.

"Now they're showing off," Cara said with a wry expression. "Men."

Half-naked, Ryan and Porter made an even more contrasting pair. Tall, sandy haired, lean, and muscled, Ryan reminded me of movie star Ryan Gosling; how ironic they shared the same first name. Although much shorter than Ryan, Porter boasted the confidence and the physique of a champion of the World Wrestling Federation. I wasn't certain who would come out a winner in an actual fight. I hoped we never had to find out.

"You and the O'Neills did great in your contest. The Janssens never had a chance."

She chuckled. "The Janssens spent too much time in the beer tent at lunch. They were lucky to last as long as they did. But we fielded a pretty tough team this year." A look of pride came over her face. "We O'Neills stay in good fighting condition."

"You've also got the competitive Gale genes."

Her smile vanished. "I consider myself an O'Neill now. After all, I've been married to Brody for over twenty years."

We watched as Porter did a few stretches; all of them highlighted his bulging biceps.

"Your brother stays in good fighting condition, too."

"Don't let his muscles and strutting around fool you. I'm in much better shape than Porter, even if I am eight years older. He's also diabetic. It runs in the family. Our dad had the disease, along with two uncles." She bit her lip. "My son was diagnosed with diabetes last year right around the time my dad died. That knocked the wind out of me, let me tell you."

Wyatt was only twenty. "I'm sorry to hear that."

"Like I said, it runs in the family. I've been lucky. And I pray my daughter is, too. Meanwhile, I'm trying to get Wyatt to take better care of himself. But he's as bullheaded as his uncle." She shook her head. "I'm the one who's tough. A damn sight tougher than they are."

I gave her a sideways look. Cara's sleeveless green blouse and cut-off jeans let me appreciate her toned, sunburned arms and muscled legs. Like Porter, Cara gave off an aura of strength, but without his pugnacious attitude to accompany it. Brother and sister also boasted similar features: round faces, straight brown hair, piercing slate-blue eyes. Those eyes narrowed now as she watched the men take their position along the rope.

"I wish the O'Neills had gone up against Blueberry Hill in the tug-of-war," she said. "I'd love to have beaten my brother. But Porter insisted he wanted to compete against the Zellars."

"When did this feud between the two families start?"

"The rivalry started with the grandfathers. Typical business competition, but after Blueberry Hill went national thirty years ago, the Zellars couldn't hope to catch up. Now the feud primarily involves my brother and your fiancé. I know they never liked each other growing up. But things have gotten worse lately. And I wouldn't be surprised if Porter is to blame. When in doubt, always blame Porter." Her voice rang with bitterness.

This gave me a start. Ryan said almost the same thing to me only minutes ago.

She drained the rest of her water. "I'll let you cheer your boyfriend on while I grab another water bottle."

"I guess we'll be rooting for opposite sides," I said.

Cara lifted an eyebrow at me. "Don't know why I'd cheer for Porter. He's won too often already. It's time he lost."

She ran off to join her husband and friends, leaving me to wonder at the state of affairs between Porter Gale and his sister. Normal sibling rivalry, or something deeper?

I hurried to join the Zellar women as both tug-of-war teams took their places; sixteen pairs of muscled arms gripped the thick rope with iron determination. Ryan took up the last position, as did Porter for his team. According to the short lecture Ryan's family had given me on tug-of-war strategy, the strongest person on each team should be last on the rope line, with the rest of the line alternating with the weakest and strongest competitors. Everyone gripped the rope underhanded, arms extended. Apparently, leg muscles were what won a tug-of-war, and I watched as the men planted their bare feet in the sand, shoulder width apart.

Unlike the O'Neill and Janssen contest, no one wasted time yelling challenges or insults. And no one laughed. The air vibrated with tension. Thank heaven I wasn't part of this challenge.

Both teams remained frozen in place while the judge positioned the rope's white bandanna. The scream of the whistle shattered the tableau as the men began pulling in opposite directions. Shouts and cries rose up all around me, and I held my breath as the men bore down. Sweat glistened on all those bare chests as they grunted and heaved.

"It's too hot for a tug-of-war." Emily Zellar stood

beside me, watching the contest with a furrowed brow.

"I agree," I told her. "Especially with guys that take it this seriously."

"I checked the weather app on my phone. It's ninety-seven degrees."

I suddenly felt even hotter.

Just when I thought the tug-of-war would remain frozen indefinitely, Porter's team took one baby step backward. Ryan responded by yelling, "Dig in! Dig in!"

Another long minute passed when the teams did nothing but strain and pull. Finally, Ryan's team took one tiny step back. Another. And another. *Please let this contest end soon,* I prayed. *And let Ryan win.* His body dripped with sweat, his arms trembled, and his face had turned an ominous scarlet. Did people die of heart attacks during a tug-of-war?

Now it was Porter's turn to shout commands to his team. They stretched so far back to resist the pull of Ryan's team, they almost lay flat on the sand.

"Maybe we can ask the judge to call it a draw," I suggested to Emily.

She shook her head. "The guys would never agree."

I heard Ryan shout out another command, spurring his team to pull like never before. The crowd noise grew to a roar when Ryan's team began to take larger steps, all in unison.

"They're power-walking." Emily grabbed my hand. "It's almost over."

Inch by tiny inch, Ryan's team pulled Porter's men closer, the white bandanna almost at the red line painted on the ground. So close. I smiled. There was no way Ryan would lose now.

Suddenly, Ryan's nephew J.J. cried out in pain. His right knee buckled and he loosened his grip on the rope. This not only stopped the Zellars' power walk, it allowed Porter's team to regain lost ground. They did more than regain it. Now on the offensive, Porter's team inexorably pulled the Zellars toward them. No matter how much Ryan shouted at his brothers and cousins to resist, the men of Blueberry Hill kept pulling them to their side.

The white bandanna not only approached the red line, but was yanked across it. The Zellars collapsed forward, the rope finally released by an exhausted but victorious Blueberry Hill team. Porter fell back on the sand, arms upraised.

Emily sighed. "I need to sit down in the shade. All this heat and excitement isn't good for me or my baby."

I thought about joining her. Ryan was sure to be in a foul mood, and I dreaded having to deal with it. But I needed to give him moral support. If only both teams would get up and leave the contest area so life could go on. However, Ryan now bent over J.J., who clutched his foot. When I saw the blood staining J.J's foot, I broke into a run.

"How did you get hurt?" I heard Ryan ask his nephew.

"I stepped on something sharp," the boy replied.

Ryan dug around in the sand. His brothers crouched down and did the same.

I knelt beside Ryan. "What do you think J.J. stepped on?"

"This." Ryan held out a jagged piece of glass, covered in sand and stained with blood.

"The judges should have checked the sand," I said. "Maybe there's more broken glass."

Ryan pointed at Porter and his team, who were congratulating each other. "Porter, you're a slimy cheating bastard! You planted glass in the sand!"

Porter looked at him with a scornful expression. "What are you talking about?"

"You were kicking at our sand before the contest started." Ryan took a few steps toward Porter. "That's when you dropped the glass there. Knowing one of us would gash our feet on it."

"You're crazy, Zellar." Porter shook his head in obvious disgust.

"My brother's right," Jim Zellar said. "One of you sabotaged our side of the sand."

"Get over yourselves," Porter said. "Zellars lose, Gales win. That's the way it's always been. Accept it and move on. And try not to whine when you get beat."

Ryan lunged at Porter, knocking him to the ground. Porter lay stunned for a moment, allowing Ryan to land two solid punches to his face. Blood gushed from Porter's nose.

Shouts rang out as both teams attacked each other. The scene reminded me of a baseball fight that empties the benches. Within seconds, I got knocked down in the resulting furor. By the time I struggled to my knees, I found myself in an honest-to-God brawl. Men wrestled, shoved, and yelled all around me. I had to duck to avoid getting hit by punches being thrown by both sides. Ignoring his injured foot, J.J. gripped one of the Gale team members in a headlock. I pushed my way through the melee to where Ryan and Porter wrestled on the sand.

"Stop, Ryan!" I made a futile attempt to pull Ryan off Porter. It was a mark of Porter's sheer strength that he was able to prevent Ryan from pummeling him nonstop. "You're hurting him! Stop!"

Ryan ignored me. Maybe his rage was so great, he could focus on nothing but the man lying on the ground beneath him. When Porter at last managed to free one arm and smack Ryan on the head, Ryan reacted as if he had been seared by a hot poker. With an angry cry, he wrapped his hands around Porter's throat and began to strangle him.

I screamed. "Someone help me! Please! He's choking him!" Frightened Porter might die, I pounded at Ryan's arms.

A second later, I was pulled away as three security police separated Ryan and Porter. This brought the brawl to a halt. Alarmed friends and family rushed in to keep the respective team members apart. I saw Ryan's mother and father try to calm down their enraged son. The other Zellar boys were surrounded by their wives. Sloane had now joined the group, helping a bruised and bloodied Porter sit up. I felt sick to my stomach, but this time it had nothing to do with the pie I ate.

I shoved my way out of the crowd. No matter how the glass had gotten in the sand, Ryan should never have flown off the handle like that. He might have choked Porter to death! And over something as meaningless as a tug-of-war contest.

As I stomped off the field, I passed a couple with two children in tow.

"What's going on?" the father asked me as he pointed to the mob scene I had just left. "We're looking for the tug-of-war contests between the fruit growers."

"The contests are over now," I said.

"Who won?" the woman said as she picked up the youngest child.

"No one." I glanced back at Ryan and Porter, surrounded by security and an agitated crowd of onlookers. "No one won."

Chapter Three

After the tug-of-war brawl, I worried they might rename the festival the Blueberry Blow Up. How embarrassing to have Zellars and Blueberry Hill involved in such a melee. It had spoiled the whole day for me. My first instinct was to take refuge in work. It had always helped me deal with personal problems in the past, especially those of a romantic nature. But if I went back to my Berry Basket booth here at the fair, Ryan would know where to find me. And I didn't want to be found. At least not until I could process what I'd just witnessed.

I thought about leaving the fairground and heading to my store in the village. Except my business revolved around all things berry. I had a responsibility to be an ongoing part of an annual event dedicated to blueberries. The Berry Basket booth at the fairground would be operating every day, with the Cabot boys, Gillian, and myself taking turns working at the shop and here. A good business decision, too. The first three hours we had been open today had seen record sales of most of the items I had brought, including blueberry-flavored coffee, candy, pancake mixes, muffins, jams, jellies, and syrups.

With the booth currently overseen by the Cabots, I decided to explore the rest of the fairground. After watching Ryan nearly choke a man to death, I needed frivolous distraction. When I reached the carnival midway, the aroma of fried elephant ears and funnel cakes helped to raise my spirits. Perhaps no one could stay depressed when surrounded by carousel music, laughing children, and vendors holding aloft clusters of colored balloons.

While my stomach made me forgo any of the concession treats, the many prize booths called out to my natural competitive drive. An hour later, I'd won five plastic necklaces, a hand puppet, a giant blueberry ring, and two yo-yos. As soon as I won a prize, I gave it to the first child I saw. The games were only a welcome mindless activity, although if I'd won the stuffed blue parrot, I might have kept it.

I'd just given away my last plastic necklace when a tall ginger-haired man waved at me. "Hey, Marlee! Take a ride on my bumper cars."

Feeling my mood grow even lighter, I walked over to the Blueberry Blow Out Bumper Cars where my friend Max Riordan stood guard.

Max seemed eternally boyish. His hat crowned with foam blueberries only added to that impression. He brought to mind the character of Ron Weasley in the Harry Potter novels.

I had a tendency to associate people with fictional characters since I had been named after one. My mother, an English literature professor, happened to be rereading *A Christmas Carol* when she went into labor. I entered the world a few hours later on Christmas Eve. With the last name of "Jacob," my Dickens-loving mother couldn't resist naming me after Jacob Marley from the Christmas tale. Given the unpleasant backstory of Mr. Marley, I wished she had been reading *Little Dorrit* that night. But it had inspired me to imagine what fictional character other people reminded me of. The fun-loving Max belonged at Hogwarts. House Hufflepuff, most likely.

A line of people waited to board the cars. "You chose the perfect ride to sponsor, Max."

Every summer, local businesses and farms sponsored rides at the Blueberry Blow Out, with half the proceeds going to a charity of their choice. I sponsored the Bounce House this year; it seemed maintenance free and safe, unless some child accidentally bounced their way out of the inflatable structure. Max, owner of Riordan Outfitters in downtown Oriole Point, signed up for the bumper cars. Not a surprise. We dated during our senior year in high school, and I had white-knuckle memories of driving around with Max in his beat-up Ford, a car that was beat up because he rarely paid attention to the road and got in one fender bender after another.

He laughed. "Yeah, I do have experience bumping cars. Why don't you give it a try? But this time you can be at the wheel. I'll even let you cut in line."

"Maybe later. My stomach is finally starting to settle. I don't want to rile it up again by crashing into cars."

"That's right. I heard you won the pie-eating

contest." He eyed my blue ribbon. "Congratulations, marzipan."

"Marzipan" had been his nickname for me since high school. I found it an endearing name and liked it, as I did Max. But because he and I had once been romantically involved, his affection for me did not sit well with Ryan, who had a jealous nature. I had no patience with jealous men, and Ryan knew it. He also knew Max and I only dated a few months before I ended the relationship when Max asked me to marry him right before prom night. And with his grandmother's ring, no less. Luckily, I soon went off to college in New York. By the time I moved back years later, any awkwardness over the proposal had vanished. I regarded Max as a loyal and true friend, even if I suspected he still harbored romantic feelings for me. I also had no intention of giving up his friendship merely to calm Ryan's unwarranted fears.

"It appears I'm a pastry-eating monster. I finished my pie before the other contestants got halfway through theirs."

"Doesn't surprise me. You were also the girl who ate two large boxes of Jujyfruits whenever we went to the movies back in high school."

"Please don't remind me. I paid for that with a half dozen cavities. My parents banned sugar from the house until I went to college."

His smile faded. "I heard a fight broke out at the tug-of-war between Ryan and Porter Gale. Is it true security had to be called?"

Shifting my gaze to the midway, I chose to watch the carousel spin rather than meet Max's penetrating gaze. But the carousel only reminded me of

Ryan. The Zellar family had chosen to sponsor the ride this year. Luckily, none of the Zellars were there at the moment.

"Things got a little heated." I had to speak louder to avoid being drowned out by the calliope music. "Porter's team won and Ryan accused him of cheating." I briefly explained about the piece of glass buried in the sand.

Max wore a disapproving expression. "Getting into a fight over something that stupid is uncalled for. Is Ryan always so quick to fly off the handle?"

"Not at all. When he gets irritated, he usually shuts down and says nothing. I've never seen Ryan come close to punching someone out before. Let alone choking a man! But he has this thing about Porter Gale. It's making him act crazy today."

He put his hands on my shoulders. "Marzipan, you know I love you. Always have. Always will. And I'm glad we've remained friends all these years. As your friend, I need to be honest with you. I don't like Ryan. And not because you accepted his proposal after turning down mine."

"Let's not talk about this." I tried to pull away, but he held me tight.

"He's not the one for you, Marlee," he went on. "Yeah, he's good-looking and all the girls in the county trip over themselves trying to get his attention. But is his attention really worth having? What has he done to make you willing to marry him?"

"I love him. Why else would I agree to marry him?" I sighed. "What has he done to make you dislike him so much?"

"I don't trust him." Max finally released me. "And I don't think you should, either."

* * *

My conversation with Max troubled me almost as much as Ryan's attack on Porter. Everyone thought highly of Max. I doubted he'd ever made a single enemy, notwithstanding Ryan's jealousy. He never spoke ill of anyone. So why the warning about Ryan now? Despite what he said, was Max jealous that I agreed to marry Ryan after turning him down?

Still in need of distraction, I headed for my Blueberry Bounce House, which shook with the movements of the children inside. I relied on the fairground's seasonal carnies to watch over things, but all sponsors were expected to spend some time at the rides they were responsible for. While we didn't actually operate the rides—although a few experienced growers did—many of us took tickets, allowing us to socialize with Blueberry Blow Out visitors.

Since my "ride" was only an inflatable bounce house, I signed up for a two-hour shift this afternoon. When I arrived early, the young carny taking tickets went from bored to excited in five seconds. He immediately took off into the crowd, leaving me in charge of the bounce house's leaping inhabitants. Two hours later, I felt just as excited to see another carny relieve me. As adorable as my bouncing children were, their nonstop shouts made my ears ring.

I resumed my walk along the midway, hoping Ryan's family had been able to calm him down after the brawl. Perhaps the unseasonably hot temperature had pushed Ryan to the edge. Our lakeshore summers rarely saw days above ninety degrees.

When it got this hot, Oriole Point residents headed for the beach or open water. Those who couldn't escape to the lake tended to become cranky. Maybe in Ryan's case, crankiness veered a little too close to violence.

I stopped in my tracks as terrified screams rent the air.

Heart racing, I looked up in time to see the riders on the drop tower hurtle toward the ground. The biggest thrill ride at the carnival, the drop tower was even more popular than the roller coaster. Once riders were strapped in, the ride slowly lifted the gondola skyward three hundred feet. There they paused for a heart-stopping moment, legs dangling in midair. Then without warning the ride released and sent everyone plummeting toward the ground.

We had always had a drop tower ride at the Blueberry Blow Out, but this looked to be a bigger and better variation. Not only did it carry more people, the ride climbed to a higher level, increasing the excitement. Given the size and expense, such a ride required a sponsor with deep pockets. A number of businesses often went in together, but this year the drop tower had only one sponsor: Blueberry Hill. And it had been renamed the Blueberry Hill Death Drop. The Blueberry Hill name shone in big white bulbs at the top of the tower structure.

"Gaudy, isn't it?" For the second time today, Cara O'Neill joined me. She pointed at the big illuminated sign above. "Porter asked the event coordinators to print an image of the ride on every ticket. Along with the Blueberry Hill name and logo. They almost agreed until I got wind of it. I convinced the sponsors to make a formal complaint. After all, someone has to stop my brother. Otherwise, he'll make them change the festival name to the Blueberry Hill Blow Out."

"At least it's for a good cause. Half the ticket proceeds go to charity."

"Don't be too impressed. Porter picked a charity working for a diabetes cure. Research he hopes to benefit from one day. Nothing Porter ever does is selfless."

"Given his condition, I'm surprised he entered the pie-eating contest," I said. "Unless they gave him a sugar-free pie to eat."

"My fool brother loves sugar. Real sugar. I'm amazed he takes his insulin shots. We probably have Sloane to thank for that. From what I've seen, she is conscientious about treating his diabetes. I'll give her that much."

"Where did he meet Sloane? She's not from around here."

"Porter met her at a fruit growers' convention in Baltimore. She was some intern or college student they hired to help with registration. I'm guessing Sloane stood out. I've been to those conventions. Sexy young women are in short supply there. And she's certainly his type: a living, breathing Malibu Barbie."

"Then she's from California?"

"I have no idea. She just looks like a Malibu Barbie I had when I was younger. But she's not brainless. Sloane had to be one shrewd blond cookie to not only catch Porter's attention, but keep it." Cara shook her head. "After he met her, Porter spent the next two months flying to Baltimore to see her. Without a word to any of us, they got married in Vegas. By an Elvis impersonator, no less. Don't know why we were shocked. My brother was ripe for the picking."

"Why?"

"He'd been divorced for a while and missed not having a woman around to listen to him brag. His first wife, Madison—another blonde—could only put up with so much bragging. She left after two years." Cara smirked. "I wonder if Sloane likes being Mrs. Gale more than Madison did. Porter's a lot richer since our dad died. That's probably convinced Sloane to stick around. A shame. I'd love to watch another wife walk out on Porter. It's what he deserves."

Although I had known Cara O'Neill a long time, we qualified as only casual friends. Most of our dealings involved business. O'Neill Blueberries made the best blueberry butter and jam in the region, and I ordered these items from them every month. While grateful the O'Neill products sold well in my shop, I didn't think she should be telling me how distasteful her brother was. Even if it were true.

"Did you and your brother have a falling-out?" I asked.

Cara's mocking expression grew serious. "We were never close, but our dad didn't help matters. He only had two children, and I'm the firstborn. Only I wasn't the son he longed for, and he never let me forget it. When that son finally did show up, I became a footnote in the Gale family. Didn't matter how hard I worked helping to run the orchard business. I wasn't Crown Prince Porter, so none of it mattered."

As an only child, I had no experience of sibling rivalry. Even so, her family situation sounded heartless.

"I realized he valued his son's opinion about the business more than mine," she continued, "even though Porter hadn't even reached his teens. The day I married Brody and left Blueberry Hill felt like a release from prison. Only I'd been imprisoned by my own foolish hopes. Hopes that my father would show me a tenth of the respect and love he gave to Porter."

"I'm sorry."

"My mom tried to make up for his treatment of me. But there was only so much she could do. Especially since Dad was such a strong personality." Her voice hardened. "Porter enjoyed being our father's favorite. He took advantage of it constantly. And didn't he love it when my father's will left everything to him: the business, the investments, all the money. Not a dime to me or my children. Imagine that. Eric Gale didn't so much as mention the only grandchildren he has. While Blueberry Hill is dropped into his son's lap. A son with no children of his own. Don't you think that's awful?"

I thought it was indeed quite awful, but didn't want to make her feel worse. "Porter and Sloane will probably start a family at some point."

Cara remained silent for a long moment. "I'm sure they will," she said finally. "He and Sloane have been trying for months to have a child." She pointed at the young woman making her way toward us. "Speaking of Barbie . . ."

I noticed men of all ages ogling Sloane as she walked past. And why not? She was pretty, tanned, well endowed, and wore a clingy red tank top and matching shorts. Had she entered a swimsuit competition rather than a pie-eating contest, she would have won.

"Hi." She smiled. "I'm glad I caught you two together." Up close, her contoured blush, multi-hued eye shadow, and glossy red lips seemed runway ready. It must take her an hour to apply her makeup. "Marlee, I saw you leave right after the big fight at the tug-of-war. You looked really upset. I wanted to let you know Porter has no hard feelings against Ryan."

"Are you serious? Ryan attacked your husband. Before I left, I saw he'd given Porter a black eye and a bloody nose. And he choked him. My God, he might have killed Porter."

She waved her hand at me, and I got distracted for a moment by her gorgeous manicure. "Porter's bragging about how he got Ryan Zellar mad enough to attack him after he lost the tug-of-war to Blueberry Hill. It's the kind of thing Porter enjoys." She giggled. "He acts like a ten-year-old boy sometimes."

"That's an insult to ten-year-old boys," Cara remarked.

Sloane kept her attention on me. "The two of them have made peace."

I stared at her in disbelief. "No way. When did that happen?"

"Soon after security arrived. To be honest, if they hadn't shaken hands, the cops would have kicked both of them out of the fairground and banned them for the rest of the Blow Out. Especially after

Ryan's team accused Porter's of putting glass in the sand. Neither of the guys wants to be banned from the festival. Ryan found us at Trappers Corner later on and apologized. There was no security around, so he must be genuinely sorry."

I felt a little bit better. At least Ryan realized he'd acted like a fool.

"The guys even cracked open a few beers," she went on.

"Let's see how long this lasts," Cara said. "All of us fruit growers are going to be at the Blueberry Blow Out until the weekend. I can't believe Porter won't try and get back at Ryan."

Sloane threw her sister-in-law an irritated look. "I think I know Porter better than anyone else. And he's put the fight behind him."

Cara laughed.

Sloane now regarded Cara with a sly expression. "Aren't the O'Neills sponsoring the Ferris wheel this year?"

"Yeah. We've sponsored it every year for as long as I've been married to Brody. In fact, we've done it so often, all of us know how to operate it. Not that it's rocket science. Wyatt should be running things right now."

"Really? Well, I just walked past the Ferris wheel." Sloane lifted her perfectly shaped brows. "There was a long line of people waiting to board, but no one there to operate it."

Cara's face darkened. "Are you serious?"

She nodded. "I hope nothing's happened to Wyatt. Then again, Porter always says your boy's not good with responsibility. Looks like he was right. Maybe you should let the carnies handle everything. At least they have a work ethic." Sloane flipped back her golden mane of hair. "I have to get back to Porter. But we should be happy to know the boys have called off their feud, Marlee." Sloane waved those perfectly polished nails at us. "And I hope Wyatt turns up."

Cara watched as her sister-in-law sauntered off into the crowd. "I haven't spent a lot of time around Sloane. Until now, I didn't realize how lucky I was. Although I haven't been lucky where my son is concerned. He is beyond lazy." She spotted something over my shoulder. "What is that boy doing at the roller coaster? Wyatt!"

It didn't surprise me to learn Cara's son, Wyatt, blew off his assigned shift at the Ferris wheel. Twenty-year-old Wyatt O'Neill had a reputation as a stoner and party animal. I visited the O'Neill orchards to do business every month, and Wyatt was the only O'Neill I had never warmed up to. My feelings also extended to his gang of male friends. As usual, they were with him now. All of them, including Wyatt, ignored Cara's shouts to get their attention as they hurried to board the roller coaster.

"Sloane's right. He's supposed to be at the Ferris wheel," Cara said as the roller coaster began to climb the track. "Brody and I are trying to get Wyatt to take on more responsibility. He doesn't do anything except work at the orchard part-time. That's why we put him in charge of the ride. Instead, he's running around with those friends of his." She shook her head. "My son better grow up soon. His father isn't as patient as I am."

"Do Wyatt and Sloane get along?" I remembered how Wyatt had nuzzled Sloane on the neck earlier—along with her angry reaction. "They're almost the same age."

Cara looked even more dispirited. "Oh, he likes her. Far too much. Even before she came on the scene, Wyatt was jealous of Porter and his money. But when Barbie joined the family, Wyatt literally turned green with envy. He shares his uncle's taste in women: young, blond, and decorative. My son thinks it's unfair that Porter gets to be rich *and* have Sloane. I told him to start working harder and make a lot of money. That's how he'll get a woman like Sloane."

"Is Wyatt interested in taking over O'Neill Blueberries one day?"

"He's interested in having fun and spending money. Only he doesn't want to work for it. Well, I'm not letting that boy slip away again. When he gets off that ride, his mama is going to be there to greet him. And she won't be happy."

While I didn't have children of my own, I thought part of the problem might be that she still referred to someone no longer in their teens as a "boy."

"At least Ryan and your brother are no longer at each other's throats," I told her.

"It won't last. But tell Ryan the next time he hits Porter, to swing much harder." She shot me a harsh smile. "With luck, the blow might kill him."

Chapter Four

Disturbed by the dynamics in the Gale and O'Neill families, I returned to the Berry Basket booth on the midway. The Cabot brothers were as thrilled as the bounce house carny to be relieved early. I felt relieved to be selling merchandise, talking with customers, and joking with the vendors on either side of me. As usual, work often became the only thing that made sense. Business grew so brisk, I sold out of all my jams, jellies, coffees, and cookies. Looking over my depleted stock, I reminded myself to bring more products tomorrow. I'd have to close early. There was little left to sell today.

I also must have finished digesting that blueberry pie because I was ravenous. A glance at my watch told me it was after seven thirty. Although the summer sun hadn't set, all the lights had been turned on, making the fairground even more festive. Time for dinner. First, I had to pack up what was left and take it out to my SUV in the parking lot. And the very thought of my brand-new SUV with THE BERRY BASKET printed on the sides brought a smile to my face. After loading up my vehicle, I stopped at my empty booth one last time to make certain I had taken everything away.

"Hey, Marlee." Loretta Janssen beckoned me from her own vendor booth. "Ryan was looking for you. I told him you were about to leave. He says if you came back for me to tell you to meet him at the Zellar tables at Trappers Corner."

A section at the fairground near the animal pens had long been known as Trappers Corner. Set apart from the rest of the activity, a huge white open-air tent was reserved for vendors, fairground employees, and performers. Sawhorses placed around the tent kept everyone else away. It offered a much needed respite from the din and hubbub, especially since we had our own picnic tables and a nearby food concession stand called Midway Café.

After I thanked Loretta, I set off for the area with mixed feelings. I'd hoped to enjoy my dinner without an intense emotional conversation to accompany it. But I couldn't avoid my fiancé forever. Nor could I ignore my conflicted feelings about our relationship. What I wasn't conflicted about was my appetite. My stomach growled in response to an air laden with the smells of the unhealthy but delicious items offered at the concession stands. I was trying to decide if I wanted pizza or hot dogs for dinner when I caught sight of yet another Gale.

Jacqueline Gale hurried past me, head down. This was the first I'd seen of her all day. She hadn't been at either the pie-eating contest or the tug-of-war. Like Piper Lyall-Pierce, Jacqueline seemed an unlikely carnival attendee. I took her to be in her early forties—the same age as her stepdaughter

Cara—but there was nothing else similar about the two women. Cara had the no-nonsense demeanor and robust figure of a farmwoman accustomed to long hours of outdoor labor. Jacqueline reminded me of Mia Farrow's vulnerable heroine in *Rosemary's Baby*, even to the closely cropped, golden brown hair.

Aside from a charity function at Blueberry Hill, I'd had no interaction with Jacqueline Gale. She seemed a demure, intelligent, but somewhat uncertain woman—a mix that must have appealed to Porter's father Eric. She'd been his first wife's nurse before she died of a long terminal illness; there had never been any reason to suspect foul play. However, given the wealth of Eric Gale and his age, most of Oriole County assumed Jacqueline married the much older man for money and security. Jacqueline may have regretted her decision now that Eric had left everything to his son. At least, Porter allowed her to continue living in the main house at Blueberry Hill. He and Sloane resided in a much newer house on the property. But I wondered how long before Porter decided it was time for his stepmother to move on.

As I watched Jacqueline's retreating back, two men jostled me aside.

"Excuse me," I said. "Watch where you're going."

They ignored me. "Honey, don't run away," one of them called out. "Come back."

"Sexy lady, get back here," the other chimed in. "Don't make us chase you."

I realized they were harassing Jacqueline, who now quickened her pace.

Both men increased their own speed. "Baby, stop

running," the taller guy shouted. "You can't get away from us. We're gonna catch you, honey. We're stronger and faster."

Incensed, I took off after them. The men were carnival workers, their shirts marked with the distinctive BBO letters and employee name tags. I planned to grab those name tags and report these jokers to the event coordinators. Because they weren't aware of me, I was able to run past them and catch up to Jacqueline. She turned a frightened face in my direction when I touched her elbow. A look of relief came over her.

"Miss Jacob, isn't it?" she asked in her soft, reedy voice. "From The Berry Basket? I'm so glad you're here. Those awful men are following me."

I spun around as the two oafs caught up to us. "Back off!"

Both men jumped back. They seemed as startled to see me as Jacqueline was.

"Who do you think you are, bothering this woman?" Hands on my hips, I stared them down. "Why are you chasing after her? Do you enjoy scaring women? Well, you don't scare me. And I'm going to see you don't scare her any longer. Security! We need security here!"

The people in the surrounding area cast worried looks in our direction; some of them pulled out cell phones.

The carnies backed away, too far for me to now read their name tags. "No reason to call security," the shorter man said. "We're just trying to be friendly."

"Yeah, right," I said with as much scorn as possible. "Security!"

The taller man scowled. "We only wanted to speak to the lady."

"Since she was trying to get away from you, it looks like she doesn't want to speak to you. So I suggest you leave her alone."

He glared at me. "We got a right to speak to anyone we want. Because we work the carny don't make us bums."

"I don't care where you work," I shot back. "You don't have a right to harass women."

His partner looked around nervously. "Let's go. There are friendlier bitches on the midway than these two."

The taller one peeked over my shoulder to wink at Jacqueline. "Hope to see you again, honey. Maybe next time, Wonder Woman won't be around to spoil our fun."

I swore under my breath as they disappeared into the crowd. While I had inherited my love of berries from my fruit-growing paternal Dutch ancestors, my quick temper had been handed down by my mother's Italian family.

"Thank you, Miss Jacob," Jacqueline said. "That was kind of you. And brave."

"Please call me Marlee. Are you okay? Do you know those men?"

She shuddered. "I never saw them before. They started to follow me right after I left the restroom. Calling out for me to stop and talk to them. Saying all sorts of suggestive things." Her hazel eyes widened. Unlike Sloane, Jacqueline never wore makeup, which enhanced her pale, waiflike appearance. "What kind of men do that right in the middle of a crowd like this?"

"Psychopaths and losers. I'll walk you to wherever you're going to make sure those guys don't bother you again."

"Thank you. What just happened makes me miss my husband even more. A woman alone is fair game. I don't think I'll be spending a lot of time at the fairground after today. Not without a man to protect me."

I didn't want to remind her that it was a woman who had come to her rescue. If Jacqueline Gale chose to see herself as a helpless female, I doubted anything I said would change her mind. "I'm glad to see you here. Your husband always loved the Blow Out."

"I know. So does his son Porter." She pointed at the white tent up ahead. "That's where I'm headed to. I'm eating dinner with Porter and Sloane. To be honest, there isn't anything at the concession stands I care to order. And Sloane didn't pack a single healthy thing to eat in the coolers. Although Porter probably made sure she didn't. But I did want to make an appearance today. To show my support for Blueberry Hill."

We pushed through the crowd. "Were you here earlier for the pie-eating contest?"

"No. I arrived about ninety minutes ago. It was too hot to come earlier." She fanned herself with what looked like a crumpled sun hat. "I know my stepson won. Foolish of him to eat an entire pie with his condition. I wish Sloane could talk some sense into him."

"I've heard she takes good care of him."

She shrugged. "When he lets her. Sloane may be young, but she's far more levelheaded than he is.

I'm afraid Porter's like his father. Some men can't be reasoned with. They want their own way, no matter how much you wish they'd compromise, even a little. Most of the time, it's easier to give in."

I thought about Ryan signing me up for the two contests today. And how he got rid of my ceiling fan without telling me. Then there was his insistence I sell my family home. I feared I had already been too accommodating to Ryan.

"At least Porter does remember to take his insulin shots," Jacqueline continued. "He's been diabetic for so long, it's become second nature to him. And he remembered to pack them in one of the coolers. Unfortunately, the cooler is also crammed with bottles of craft beer, something else Porter should avoid. It's maddening. I work in health care and there's more to treating diabetes than insulin shots. Porter's diet is appalling." She sighed. "Eating an entire blueberry pie at one sitting. Sometimes, I think my stepson has a death wish."

While I doubted that, I knew Ryan would be ecstatic if it was true. "Did you hear about the tug-of-war?"

"No. Did Porter's team win?"

"Yes." I hesitated. "Although there was a bit of a disagreement."

Our conversation ended there. We had reached the picnic tables beneath the tent at Trappers Corner. I spotted only one empty table. The others were filled with people eating, laughing, drinking. I recognized all the fruit growers and their families, along with several game booth vendors, the man who made balloon animals, and the trio of women slated to perform country and western songs later tonight on the fairground stage.

Ryan spotted me at the same time I saw him. Jacqueline waved at a table of people holding Porter, Sloane, and several Blueberry Hill employees. I also noticed a red cooler on a bench beside the table, the one that no doubt contained all the craft beer and insulin.

Jacqueline gave my hand a quick squeeze. "Thank you again for helping me with those men. I don't know what I would have done if you hadn't shown up."

I wanted to tell her not to automatically assume she was helpless, but I only smiled and said, "Thanks. But I bet you're tougher than you know."

While Jacqueline went to join her family, I made my way to where Ryan sat. Although we hugged, I felt the tension between us.

I looked around at the picnic tables reserved for Zellar, all marked by pieces of paper taped to the tables bearing the family name. One table held a pair of adolescent Zellars texting on their phones. At the table next to them, an exhausted Emily slept against the shoulder of her husband Adam, who spoke with a burly man standing beside him. I thought it was time for Adam to take his pregnant wife home. I wondered if all the Zellar men were as thoughtless as I now suspected Ryan was. Maybe the heat was getting to me, too, because I felt cranky and out of sorts. Or maybe I was just hungry.

"Why didn't you answer any of my calls or texts?" Ryan asked after I sat down.

"I needed time to think. That brawl was pretty upsetting." I was glad we had this table to ourselves, although an empty cooler sat on one of the benches. My stomach growled again as I noticed Ryan had been in the middle of eating a plate of French fries and two hot dogs. "I guess you didn't wait to have dinner with me."

Ryan got to his feet. "I wasn't certain you would show up. What can I get for you? The family brought sandwiches for lunch, but they're long gone."

When Ryan went to buy the two slices of pizza and Diet Coke I asked for, I turned my attention to the Gale party several tables over. Other friends and employees sat at adjoining tables, which made one corner of the picnic area Gale territory. They were a rowdy bunch, and a hard-drinking one. I now noticed more than one cooler from which bottles of iced craft beer were hauled out. I'd been here only five minutes and Porter had drained one bottle and opened another.

After the brawl, I wouldn't have thought Porter and Ryan wanted to be anywhere near each other. Then again, Sloane swore the two had kissed and made up. Or shaken hands at least.

The sight of Wyatt sitting in the Gale section did surprise me. Laughing with two of the Blueberry Hill employees, Wyatt reached into the nearby cooler for a beer as if he belonged among them. I wondered how this sat with his mother. Cara, Brody, and daughter Courtney ate tacos at a picnic table far to my left. The last time I saw Cara, she'd been headed for the roller coaster and a confrontation with her slacker son. Things were probably tense between them at the moment, which might explain why Wyatt had forsaken his parents and sister for his uncle.

Although I did suspect Wyatt had another reason for hanging out at the Gale tables. He never took his eyes off Sloane, who seemed to avoid looking at him.

Ryan returned with my food, and all was forgotten while I devoured my pizza and soda. When both of us finished eating, we pushed away our paper plates and looked at each other.

"Well?" I asked him.

"Well, what?"

"Exactly what happened after the security people showed up? I heard you and Porter shook hands. So it's safe to say no one got arrested."

"Marlee, no one gets arrested at the fairground because some guys get into a fight. Especially when the fight involves two of the biggest fruit-growing families in the state."

"You make it sound as if Zellars and Blueberry Hill are Apple and Microsoft."

"In a way we are. We're important to the local economy. Important enough that people should think twice about arresting one of us." Ryan glanced over at Porter, now eating chips with one hand and knocking back a beer with the other. "Good thing the security guys got there when they did because I wanted to beat the hell out of him. I still do. It was my parents who finally got me to calm down. But I had to go home for a couple hours to really cool off."

"Relieved to hear that. I've never seen you so angry. Or violent. When I saw you choke him, I thought you'd gone crazy." I shook my head. "I never want to see that behavior again."

"So I gathered." He regarded me with an offended

expression. "You didn't think twice about leaving me after the fight. And you never bothered to check your phone or try to look for me. I stupidly hoped my fiancée would be on my side."

"Not if you're wrong, Ryan. And you were wrong to attack Porter."

We stared at each other, and I grew nervous. Should I end it now? Should I tell him how uncertain I felt about our upcoming marriage and whether we were really suited to each other? Should I admit my cold feet had become positively frozen? Should I dare confess there were times I felt I didn't really know him? Before I could say any of this, a round of applause went up from the Gale table, followed by a wave of laughter.

Ryan and I watched as Porter got to his feet. Even at this distance, he appeared off balance. *Drunk and diabetic,* I thought with chagrin. Jacqueline must be feeling as frustrated as Sloane, who tried to take the beer bottle out of her husband's hand. Only Porter held it out of her reach. She sprang to her feet and snatched the bottle away. Wearing a sheepish grin, Porter swept her up in a tight bear hug. After he released her, he walked over to the cooler and retrieved what looked like a plastic bag.

I turned my attention back to Ryan. "We need to have a long talk. A serious one."

But Ryan continued to watch Porter as he took something out of the plastic bag, then rubbed it between his hands. It must be his insulin shot. No one at the Gale tables gave him more than a passing glance as Porter lifted up his shirt and injected himself in the abdomen. They must be accustomed to seeing him to do that, but it made me wince.

"Ryan, are you listening to me? This is important. We've been arguing too much lately. And there are too many things we don't see eye to eye on."

"What is this?" Ryan finally turned to me, this time with alarm. "Are you breaking up with me?"

"Please, we need to take a deep breath and think about our future."

"I've done nothing but think about our future since I realized I was in love with you."

"I love you, too. But I'm not sure that's enough."

"Are you crazy? What's more important than that? Marlee, we love each other. And I'm tired of being alone. It's time I had a family. I want to build something for us and our children. They'll be part of Zellar Orchards one day. We should start working on that future together."

"But you never listen to me. You don't seem to care at all what I want for the future."

"I thought we wanted the same thing. Why else would you agree to marry me?"

"Because I love you." I felt tears well up. "But is that enough?"

"Enough?" He took my face in his hands. "I know you're uncertain about marriage. So am I. My first marriage was a disaster. But I'm not uncertain about my feelings for you. Don't destroy what we have. Not over minor things we can fix. Because what we have is important." Now his own eyes filled with tears. "It's the most important thing there is. I can't imagine my life without you." Ryan kissed me. "You're my berry girl."

After I kissed him back, we kissed again for much longer, and I remembered why I was with him. Why I loved him. Why I had agreed to marry him. When we finally stopped kissing Ryan pulled me close, and we nestled together beneath the white lights strung along the tent.

Too soon, the moment ended when Porter shouted, "Hey, Ryan and Marlee! Break it up! If you two lovebirds want some real thrills, follow me." He walked toward us, even more unsteady than before.

"What is he doing now?" Ryan muttered.

Porter stopped before our table. His nose was swollen and he had a black eye. "No fighting," I said quickly.

"Nah, we've fought enough for one day. Now it's time for fun. That's what a Blow Out is all about. And if you two want some real excitement, hop on my Blueberry Hill Death Drop. Unless you're afraid. Maybe all you're ready for is an inflatable bounce house. Or a safe little carousel ride." He smirked at Ryan. "That's probably all a Zellar can handle. A ride that goes 'round and 'round but ends up nowhere. Just like you, Ryan."

I felt Ryan stiffen as Porter walked away, laughing. "Ignore him," I said. "He's trying to get a rise out of you. Don't give him the satisfaction."

Ryan took a deep breath. "Let's get out of here."

Relieved, I threw our plates in the trash. Arm in arm, Ryan and I went to the midway, hopefully en route to the parking lot. But first we had to pass all the rides, each one filled with screaming fairgoers, flashing lights, rides swooping and spinning in the darkening sky.

"I love carousels," I said to Ryan, and he chuckled. "Bounce houses, too."

Although we both looked the other way as we reached the Blueberry Hill Death Drop, Porter shouted at us as he took his seat on the ride. "Hey, Zellar! I'm King of Blueberry Hill, baby. That means I'm King of the World around here!"

With that, the ride slowly rose into the night sky. As it did, the sound of Porter's mocking laughter faded away. Ryan bristled with anger.

"There's no reason to stay here," I said. "He's only going to say something again."

But Ryan's attention now focused on the gondola of people high overhead, legs dangling. A moment later, they fell with dazzling speed. Screams—filled with delight and fear—accompanied the drop.

"It's time to confront him," Ryan said, his voice tight. "No punches, but no fake handshakes, either. This has gone on long enough."

My heart sank at the same speed as the Blueberry Hill Death Drop.

I watched as the ride attendants helped people unstrap themselves and disembark. But Porter remained slumped forward even after the halter strap was released. Sloane sat next to him, and I saw her give him a brief shake to get him to move. I wondered if he had passed out drunk.

When the attendants couldn't rouse him, I became fearful. Porter had taken his insulin shot minutes ago. What if the combination of insulin, beer, and all the junk food he had eaten sent him into shock?

"Wait here," Ryan ordered. He ran over to the small crowd gathering around the ride.

The crowd grew larger as fairground employees and Blueberry Blow Out workers came on the scene. Within minutes, EMS arrived. When paramedics put Porter onto a stretcher, Sloane grabbed his hand and kissed it.

Ryan raced back to me.

"Has he gone into insulin shock?" I asked him. "A diabetic coma?"

"Neither."

"What do you mean? What happened?"

"It looks like the Blueberry Hill Death Drop has earned its name." Ryan stunned me by laughing. "The king is dead."

Chapter Five

"Can you fly?"

Slouched at a bistro table near the ice cream counter, the Cabot brothers shot weary looks at the African gray parrot who sat atop a four-foot-tall wooden perch near the shop window.

"Why does your bird keep asking if we can fly?" Dean said, removing the paper holder from his blueberry muffin.

"Maybe she wants to make us feel bad about not having wings." Walking over to where Minnie sat fluffing her gray feathers, I filled one of the two attached metal bowls with the fresh veggies I'd brought from home.

"I think she needs to be the center of attention," Andrew piped up as he went through the store mail scattered before him.

"Takes one to know one," I murmured.

"What did you say?" Andrew asked.

Minnie whistled, followed by her perfect imitation

of my cell phone ringtone. "How are ya? How are ya?" she asked.

"Fine, sweetie." I scratched the back of her feathered head and she closed her eyes in bliss. Being around Minnie put me in a more relaxed state, something I needed after yesterday's shocking death at the fairground.

"Kiss for Mommy," Minnie murmured.

I leaned closer and gave her a kiss. She responded by making several lip-smacking sounds. I'd only had Minnie two months, but it felt like she and I had been lifelong companions. Certainly her conversation never lagged.

Indeed, I had adopted the most talkative rescue bird in the state—maybe the country. So far I'd counted three hundred words in her vocabulary, not including the phrases Minnie had picked up since living with me. I'd fallen in love with the beautiful parrot who often spent hours perched on my shoulder when we were home. But with tourist season in full swing, I had little opportunity to keep my gregarious bird company at my house on the beach. I now brought her with me to work, even if it meant keeping an extra perch on the premises, along with a sleep cage for the naps she took in my back office.

She and my customers enjoyed the interaction, except for a couple from Ohio who took offense when Minnie told them to, "Move your ass, people." I blamed Andrew for that phrase; he loved to mutter it whenever the store became too crowded.

Minnie's presence also convinced my bird-loving baker, Theo Foster, to remain on the premises each morning after finishing his pre-dawn baking shift. Theo did not possess the best social skills due to a head injury he suffered as a child. But he'd recently come to trust me, Minnie, and the three other employees of The Berry Basket: Dean, Andrew, and college student Gillian Kaminski. All six of us were now at the store an hour before opening.

Because the Blueberry Blow Out required added shifts at both the shop and the fairground booth, we agreed to meet at the store to figure out what schedule we could live with for the remainder of the event. Gillian worked full-time at The Berry Basket when on college break, but Dean and Andrew had other commitments. Dean ran *The Dean Report*, a highly successful blog describing life along the lakeshore. The blog's amusing and gossipy observations recently earned it a place on *Chicago Magazine*'s Top 25 Midwest Blogs. *The Dean Report* garnered so much online attention, I placed ads for The Berry Basket on the site.

As for Andrew, he worked part-time for a florist named Oscar in nearby Saugatuck. Andrew had no interest in flowers and only applied for a job at Beguiling Blooms because he thought it might be amusing to work at two places with the same initials. This kind of thing made sense only to Andrew. Given how attractive Oscar the florist was, it also made sense when he and Andrew became a romantic couple.

All of us managed to keep The Berry Basket running smoothly, even during the busiest of times. But the Blueberry Blow Out was one of the largest summer events in the region, and the next few days promised to be hectic. Opening day had turned far more stressful than expected. I hoped if I buried myself in work, I could ignore further unpleasantness. However, the image of Porter Gale's lifeless body being removed from the ride last night haunted me. Along with Ryan's gleeful reaction.

"Here's what I was looking for." Andrew held up the *Oriole Messenger*, one of two local newspapers our small town supported. The headline read: PORTER GALE DIES ON BLUEBERRY HILL RIDE, with a photo of a smiling Porter beneath it. "Can a death get any more ironic? Dying on a ride named after your own business. Unbelievable."

"And one named a Death Drop, too." Dean finished off his muffin. "Not good news for the Blueberry Blow Out. Someone dying on a ride the first day is bad for business."

"No way. I bet even more people will want to ride the Death Drop now," Andrew said.

"If so, they're nothing but ghouls." I straightened the bags of dried raspberries stacked near the window. "And I agree with Dean. Porter's death may put a damper on things, at least for a day or two. But Piper probably feels better about not being part of the planning committee now. Her feelings were hurt at not being included."

Actually, Piper had been outraged she'd not been asked to help organize this summer's Blueberry Blow Out. But no one had forgotten how the Blow Out souvenir T-shirts she ordered last year bore the lettering: BLUEBERRY BOW OUT. Since they arrived the day before the event began, the misspelled shirts had to be sold at the fairground until new ones arrived by express mail. I thought it turned out well in the end. The BOW OUT tees had become collector items, even if it did mortify Piper.

Andrew read aloud the account of Porter's untimely death. I'd already read it, relieved it was basically a long obituary, with an emphasis on the success of Blueberry Hill and its products. It seemed unlikely the paper even realized Porter's death was due to a foolhardy indifference to his diabetic condition.

I preferred not to think about Porter Gale and turned my energy to counting the money in the cash register. Gillian opened shipping boxes beside me, pulling out an assortment of oven mitts decorated with cranberries. To my left, Theo Foster laid out the pastries he had baked early this morning. Today's selections included blueberry cobbler, blueberry muffins, lemon blueberry cheese tart, and blueberry spice whoopie pies. Berry Basket pastries contained a variety of berries, but during the Blow Out festivities, I preferred an emphasis on blueberries.

Oblivious to all the activity around them, Andrew and Dean relaxed at the bistro tables, apparently conserving their energy for the day ahead. In the background, Minnie sang a chorus of "Ba-ba-ba ba-ba ba-ran" on repeat. When Andrew finished reading the article, he sat back with a heavy sigh. "I don't see how I managed to miss the tug-of-war fight *and* Porter dying on the Death Drop."

Gillian stopped removing oven mitts. "Why would you want to see either one? The fight must have been embarrassing."

"That it was," I said.

"And Porter Gale dying on a ride—one named after the family business!—is horrifying." She shook her head at Andrew in disapproval. Younger than both Cabot brothers, twenty-one-year-old Gillian possessed a far more mature view on life. "A man died, Andrew. No one wants to see that."

Andrew and Dean exchanged skeptical looks. "I bet your dad disagrees," Dean told her.

As editor of the other local paper, the *Oriole Point Herald,* Gillian's father no doubt would have liked to witness Porter's death. As he would have liked to have made it his own paper's headline. His bad luck that the weekly *Herald* came out on Friday, which meant he'd once again been bested by the *Messenger,* whose weekly issue arrived in county mailboxes on Tuesday morning.

A scowling Gillian marched into the back room with the remaining box of oven mitts.

"You know Gillian is sensitive when her dad's paper gets scooped," I chided the brothers.

"Maybe he should put the paper out more than once a week," Andrew said.

"We don't have enough news to fill even one weekly paper, let alone two."

"You have to admit it's been a newsworthy tourist season so far, Marlee." Dean sipped his cup of blueberry coffee. "More than enough for a daily paper."

He had me there. This summer's Strawberry Moon Bash and Blackberry Road Rally had been marred by murder, lies, and scandal. And I'd found myself smack in the middle of it all. Indeed, I'd been lucky to survive the festivals.

"Let's be grateful Porter's death is untimely but not suspicious." I shut the cash drawer with a satisfying bang, its bell ringing out. Minnie immediately imitated the sound.

"How do you know that?" Andrew turned to look at me. "I've never paid much attention to the farmers out in the country. In fact, I don't think I ever met Porter Gale. But I heard him and his sister Cara didn't get along."

"Our mom said Cara was cut out of their dad's will last year. So were her kids. And Porter's stepmother, Jacqueline, didn't inherit much, either." Dean lifted an eyebrow. "Revenge is one juicy motive for murder."

"Peeky boo, I see you," Minnie said by the window.

"And what about the young widow?" Andrew asked. "Sloane might be capable of other crimes aside from her over-use of blusher and Urban Decay eyeliner."

This finally got the attention of Theo, who stopped cutting slices of cobbler by the pastry case. "Did Sloane Porter kill her husband?"

"Of course not," I hurried to answer. Theo took things literally, including the Cabot brothers' sarcastic humor. I didn't need rumors of murderous Gale family members to be traced back to my Berry Basket staff. The store and I had been front and center in local crimes far too much. "Porter died of diabetic shock, caused by an overload of sugar. Compounded by alcohol."

"Who says?" Andrew persisted.

"The newspaper article you just read."

"Not really. The reporter claims the probable

cause of death might be complications due to diabetes." He gave me an impish grin. "But what if Sloane killed him so she could inherit the Blueberry Hill business? It's worth millions."

Theo's eyes widened in alarm. He, too, had seen his share of murder and didn't need to be upset again.

"That's enough, Andrew. Porter wasn't killed by his wife, his sister, or anyone."

Dean ignored me. "Lots of people might be happy he's dead. He inherited one of the most successful businesses in the state. And he never let anyone forget it. Jealousy is as strong a motive as revenge. I mean, everyone knows the Zellars and Gales haven't gotten along for generations. Look what happened at the tug-of-war yesterday."

Andrew grabbed his brother's arm in mock alarm. "Omigod. Ryan did it!"

"Maybe they're all guilty, like *Murder on the Orient Express*," Dean said with a laugh. "I hope so. A story like that would get a lot of hits on my blog."

Refusing to let the Cabots' teasing provoke me, I glanced at the red strawberry-shaped clock on the wall. Thirty minutes until we opened. Time to send the Cabots off to the fairground. I only hoped they didn't continue with this topic of conversation after they left.

"The tug-of-war fight occurred due to a misunderstanding," I said. "Ryan thought Porter buried a piece of glass in the sand so one of the Zellars would cut their foot during the contest. I'm sure it was an accident. An unfortunate one."

"It wasn't an accident, Marlee," Theo said. "I saw the muscular man, the one they called Porter, put something in the sand. I don't know what it was. Except it was small."

"You were at the tug-of-war yesterday?" I asked.

He nodded. "I've never been to a Blueberry Blow Out. I thought I should go because I work at a berry store. I was there all day. I saw you eat the pie." His solemn expression lightened momentarily. "You ate it really fast. I was proud."

Andrew chuckled. "Our Marlee can eat. Especially anything with berries in it."

I walked over to the pastry case and faced Theo, but decided not to mention that he was supposed to be manning the Berry Basket booth at the time of the pie-eating contest, according to what Andrew had told me yesterday. "I didn't see you at the tug-of-war."

"I didn't see you, either. At least not until the boy on Ryan's team got hurt. It was really crowded. And I wore a hat and sunglasses. But I liked the tugs-of-war. I watched the players all the time. That's how I saw the Porter man put something in the sand."

"It looks like Ryan was right." I frowned. "Porter did cheat."

"Uh-oh." Andrew put on a sad face. "Your boyfriend is now the prime suspect."

"Will you stop? Porter died a natural death caused by his unnatural food and drink choices."

"Don't worry, Marlee," Dean said. "If Ryan is charged, his lawyer can get him off with the tug-of-war defense. Applicable only during the Blueberry Blow Out. Or any season of *Survivor*."

"Okay, guys, off to the fairground," I said. "The booths open at ten, and you still need to transport everything there and set up." I snatched up the mail from their table, along with Dean's half-full cup of coffee.

"I'm not done yet." He reached for the cup, but I held it out of his reach.

"Yes, you are." I gave the brothers my steeliest "boss" look, which propelled them to their feet. "We're done talking about murder. The Berry Basket will focus on nothing but fruit and festivities for the rest of the summer. And confine your gossip to what you love best: making fun of everyone's fashion choices, and rumors about Old Man Bowman's sex life."

"We can do that." Andrew smoothed down his blue BERRY BASKET T-shirt. "But after the murders we've been involved with this summer, it will be a dull way to end the season."

"Fingers crossed, it will stay dull all the way to Christmas." When I remembered my January wedding date, I added, "And beyond."

"Move your ass, people!" Minnie shrieked.

As always, Minnie had the last word.

Eager to put thoughts of Porter Gale's death out of my mind, I opened the store fifteen minutes early. After placing the OPEN flag in its iron holder outside my door, I took a moment to enjoy the beautiful morning. Shortly before dawn, a storm moved in, bringing an hour of heavy rain accompanied by thunder and lightning. The system had moved inland, leaving behind hazy skies and much lower temperatures. I took a deep breath, savoring the breeze blowing up the street from the water.

The weather app on my phone informed me the temp was a delightful seventy-six degrees. Perfection. Tourists would divide their time between the beach, the village shops, and the festivities at the fairground. It promised to be a busy, lucrative day.

Fellow shopkeepers began to appear, putting out their OPEN flags or sandwich boards. I spent a moment appreciating the scene from my shop door. The Berry Basket had a prime spot on Lyall Street, our main shopping thoroughfare. Over sixty galleries, stores, and restaurants comprised downtown Oriole Point, which benefited from the Oriole River running right through the center of the village. But Lake Michigan was the heart and soul of Oriole Point, as it was for every lakeshore town along the coast of western Michigan. A mere four blocks from my shop door glittered my favorite Great Lake. I loved to look down the street toward the water, the vista veering from shops and boutiques to the marina, then out past the channel markers where the blue expanse of Lake Michigan never failed to impress. To make it more picturesque, the white Oriole Point lighthouse stood at the mouth of the river, its red rotating light pulsing like a steady heartbeat.

Born and raised in Oriole Point, I had traveled extensively and spent almost a decade in New York City. Yet the beauty of this lakeshore seemed to grow each year, along with my deep appreciation of it. I couldn't imagine living anywhere else.

Denise Redfern, owner of the Tonguish Spirit Gallery next door, came outside with her flag. "Morning, Marlee. Gorgeous day. I couldn't take much more of that heat. So humid, too."

"I know. If I wanted to live in the Everglades, I would have moved to Florida."

She reached up to hang her flag, beautifully decorated with the Algonquian thunderbird symbol. Not only was the Tonguish gallery devoted to Native American artwork, but Denise herself was a full-blooded Potawatomi, one of the tribes of the Algonquian nation. While the OPEN flags of most storeowners simply said OPEN in colorful letters, some of us ordered flags specific to our businesses. Strawberries were stitched onto my OPEN flag; the flag of the Wiley Perch restaurant displayed a giant leaping fish; Tess's Oriole Glass flag boasted a splendid orange and black oriole. I did have reservations about the flag for the Gouda Life cheese shop, emblazoned with a chunk of cheese crowned by wavy fumes. Limburger, no doubt.

"Terrible news about Porter Gale," Denise said. "And the paper said his wife was sitting next to him. What a painful thing for her to witness. She's so young, too. Only twenty-four." She shook her head, the movement causing her long silver earrings to sway. "I was only a little older myself when my husband died. I remained in shock for nearly a year."

I looked over at Denise with surprise. A striking woman in her late thirties, Denise always seemed as unflappable and serene as the carved totems she sold in her gallery. While I knew she'd been widowed, Denise guarded her privacy and I wasn't privy to much else. She moved here from the Charlevoix area several years ago, which meant the locals didn't know much more about Denise aside from her remarkable good humor and reliability.

For Oriole Point, that was sufficient . . . at least for people we liked and respected.

Denise sighed. "Poor Sloane. Do you know her?"

"Not really. She rarely comes to the village. I think she spends most of her time at Blueberry Hill. I went there for a big charity event before Eric Gale died. The place seemed like a compound: stables, swimming pool, tennis courts, guesthouses. Sloane probably had little reason to leave. Although I did see her a few times at the malls in Grand Rapids. And I'm sure she made shopping trips to Chicago."

"Wonder what the girl will do now."

"No idea. Maybe go back to Baltimore. Porter's sister said that's where he met her."

"I also wonder what will happen to Blueberry Hill."

That gave us pause. A national brand, Blueberry Hill had to be worth over a hundred million. I'm sure there was a board of directors, investors, and all sorts of other people who were an integral part of the Blueberry Hill empire. Yet, Porter Gale had owned and controlled a big chunk of that enterprise. So who inherited Blueberry Hill? Maybe Cara O'Neill would finally get a share of her family's fortune and legacy. I couldn't imagine a business such as Blueberry Hill being handed over to Sloane. As Andrew implied, the young woman seemed to devote a lot of energy to experimenting with makeup. A shame she wasn't in line to inherit Sephora.

Denise stepped to the curb, staring down the street. "Officer Davenport is out and about early. I don't usually see her on Lyall Street until after lunch.

After patrolling the beach access roads, she spends the rest of the morning at Coffee by Crystal." She chuckled.

"I wonder if taxpayers realize they're paying her to ticket drivers and drink iced mocha lattes."

My grin vanished when I saw Officer Janelle Davenport turn in our direction. Although she was a good two blocks away, there was no mistaking the officer for anyone else. First, she was the only policewoman on Oriole Point's small force. Second, she always wore aviator sunglasses, even indoors. It was either an affectation or a nod to what I knew was her favorite movie, *Top Gun*. Regardless, Janelle was not my favorite person in the village—not by a long shot—and I had a funny feeling she was on her way to see me. And that it had something to do with Porter Gale's death. I wished now I had scheduled myself to work at the fairground this morning.

I breathed easier when she stopped to speak with Sheila Sawyer, one of the cantankerous owners of the Sweet Dreams candy shop. Maybe Janelle was on Lyall Street this early on some other business. If so, I planned to stay out of sight. After a few more friendly words with Denise, I ducked back into the store. I thought about closing the door behind me, but when the weather was this mild, I preferred keeping it open. An open door encouraged foot traffic. I hoped part of that traffic didn't include Officer Davenport.

Three customers followed me inside. The ladies were regulars, here for their morning berry smoothies. Tying on her chef apron, Gillian greeted the trio by first name as she took her place behind the ice cream counter. I smiled as all three ordered their usual smoothies: Strawberry Peach, Triple Berry, and Blueberry Blast.

Because my poster on the wall extolling blueberries looked slightly askew, I spent some time trying to get it to hang straight. Not only were blueberries my favorite berry, they were also the healthiest. The bright colorful poster listed all their benefits, especially the fact that they contained more antioxidants than any other fruit or vegetable. Blueberries also boost brain function, reduce DNA damage, and help prevent heart disease. And since his world revolved around blueberries, I assumed Porter had known that the anthocyanins in blueberries possess anti-diabetic effects on a person's insulin sensitivity. Sadly, no matter how many blueberries Porter ate, they couldn't counteract a diet packed with sugar and alcohol.

Once satisfied the poster hung straight, I did a circuit of my shop: rearranging bags of blueberry pancake mix, restacking tins of wild berry tea, and making a note to reorder more bags of blackberry granola. I noted how well the berry jams and jellies were selling. And every berry-flavored syrup was currently on backorder. Since I made all the syrups, I felt a tiny swell of pride. My newest creation, a raspberry ginger syrup, had sold out within three days. I planned to whip up another batch as soon as the Blueberry Blow Out was over. This summer had seen a bump in tourism, and Oriole Point already ranked as one of the most popular resort areas along the lakeshore. Thank goodness the recent murders hadn't turned tourists away.

When more customers entered, I looked up

from counting how many strawberry hullers and slicers remained on the shelves. One woman walked over to the table of berry-flavored coffees, as the others made their way to the pastry counter. I spent the next few minutes waiting for them to decide which berry pastry they wanted. And I agreed that all of them looked sinfully good. I'd just finished handing the last of them her lemon blueberry cheese tart when I heard Minnie say, "What's up, punk?"

Officer Davenport stood in front of Minnie's perch, staring at the one-foot-tall gray and white bird as if she were an avian suspect. Trying to keep a smile on my face, I made my way over there. She'd better not tell me I couldn't keep a bird in the store. I'd already okayed everything with city hall, but I wouldn't be surprised if Janelle had found some obscure, punitive ordinance about parrots in berry-themed shops.

"Is there something I can help you with?" Maybe if I treated her like a customer, she'd act as civilly as one.

I wanted to roll my eyes when she turned her attention from Minnie to me. Her omnipresent sunglasses reflected the irritation on my face.

"Your bird has quite a mouth on her," she said. "She's already called me a punk and told me to move my ass."

"Don't take it personally. She's a parrot, not a perp."

"A couple times she sounded Australian. Exactly where did you acquire this bird?"

For the love of Woody Woodpecker, did Janelle think I got Minnie on the black market?

Taking a deep breath, I replied, "She's a rescue bird. An African gray. And you're right about the Australian accent. She's mimicking her original family, who were from Australia. They bought her three years ago when they were living in Niles. Minnie was little more than a chick then. The family was apparently quite fond of her, but they ran into problems during their move back to Melbourne this summer. Something about taking an exotic pet through customs. That's how Minnie ended up as one of my aunt's rescue animals." I scratched Minnie's head and she closed one eye. The other remained fixed on me. "I love birds, so Aunt Vicki knew I'd adopt her. How could I refuse? Minnie's the best. Aren't you, sweetie?"

Minnie gave a piercing whistle before repeating, "Minnie's the best. Minnie's the best."

"Any more questions?" I asked Janelle. "Would you like to know about her diet? Expected life span?"

"Any more questions?" Minnie said, then launched into a chorus of "Ba-ba-ba ba-ba ba-ran."

"That bird would drive me nuts. I don't know how you can stand to listen to her all day. Don't your customers complain?"

"Not at all. They're animal lovers." I gave her a forced smile. "In fact, the only thing I hear the tourists complain about are the speed traps the local police set up. Is there anything you can do about that?"

Now it was Janelle's turn to take a deep breath. "Very funny."

"Not to them. Look, is there a reason for the visit today? Something you're interested in buying?"

"No thanks. I have no desire to waste money on a bottle of elderberry wine." She jerked her hand in the direction of the shelf behind her. "Or raspberry oatmeal."

"I'm glad my customers don't agree with you. We live in Michigan's fruit belt, surrounded by orchards. That's why I thought a store devoted to all things berry was a perfect business to open. And I was right."

She smirked. "As P.T. Barnum allegedly said, 'There's a sucker born every minute.'"

Tired of the pretense, I stopped smiling. "What do you want?"

"I want you to come with me to the police station. The chief wishes to speak with you."

My stress meter inched upward. If the police chief wanted to talk to me, it couldn't be good. Fortunately, I had a great deal of respect for Gene Hitchcock, who had headed our village police force since I was a baby. With the exception of Hitchcock, Janelle, and Bruno Wycoff, the rest of the police force was part-time. And their inexperience showed. I dreaded the day Chief Hitchcock retired.

"Where are the cashews?" Minnie asked.

I fished out a cashew from the stash I kept for her in my apron pocket. "Why does he want to see me?"

"He needs to ask you about Porter Gale's death," Janelle replied.

"I was nowhere near Porter when he died on the ride. What could I possibly say? I assume some complication of his diabetes caused the death. I'm not a doctor."

"I'm not a doctor," Minnie repeated. "Hi ho. Hi ho."

"We already spoke to the doctors at the hospital. Along with the techs who ran preliminary results on the deceased. Porter Gale didn't die of natural causes." At long last, Janelle whipped off her sunglasses. "He was murdered."

Chapter Six

The walk from my shop to the white clapboard building that housed the police force measured only a few short blocks, but it felt like a mile. Officer Davenport refused to give me any further information on Porter Gale's death. Or murder, as she had informed me. Unless someone confessed, I didn't believe it. Porter had been in clear view of everyone as he rode to the top of the tower. And the ride was over in the blink of an eye. How could he be murdered in such a short amount of time?

This was not only further bad news for the Blueberry Blow Out, but confirmed the Cabot brothers' joking suspicions about how Porter died. And their egos were inflated enough.

When we entered the village police station, several tourists milled about, all of them sporting flip-flops and beachwear. Ringing phones, a blaring radio, and the tapping of a computer keyboard filled the air. The voice of the police receptionist, Suzanne Cabot, added to the cacophony. Animated and gossipy, Suzanne could have been no one else but Andrew and Dean's mother. Certainly, all three of them spent a great deal of time on personal grooming, even if her sons didn't approve of her love of jump-suits and "statement piece" jewelry.

Speaking on a phone headset, Suzanne held a mirror in one hand while smoothing her teased, reddish-brown hair with the other. When she caught sight of me, she pointed at a side office. "The chief wants to see you," Suzanne mouthed.

"She knows, Suzanne." Janelle shook her head as I followed her to the office.

The office door had been left open and we peeked in. An empty desk greeted us. "Wait here," Janelle said. "I'll see where he went to."

I sat down on the metal chair facing the desk. I doubted the search for Chief Hitchcock would take long. Built in 1903, the police station initially housed the Oriole Point Apothecary, and the small building had never been renovated. What little space there was seemed crammed with ancient filing cabinets and stacks of manila folders. I wondered again why the chief wanted to speak to me. What could I possibly tell him about Porter Gale's death?

"There you are. We've been waiting for you." Detective Greg Trejo of the Michigan State Police entered the room. Although the state police and the sheriff's department had arrived at the fairground after Porter died, Trejo hadn't been among them. Also missing last night was the head of Investigative Services at the sheriff's department, Captain Atticus Holt, known as "Kit" to his friends.

Craning my neck past Trejo, I felt disappointed to see that Kit wasn't behind him.

Both Trejo and Holt investigated the Blackberry Art School murder last month, which also involved me. I first met Detective Trejo during a previous murder, and I had been put off by a brusque manner that outweighed his good looks. I was relieved to learn a real human being existed behind Trejo's chilly outward demeanor. I thanked Kit Holt for that, who told me Trejo was not only his brother-in-law, but the doting father of three children. Since then, Trejo occasionally permitted me to see a friendlier side to his guarded personality.

However, I preferred the company of Kit Holt. I thought he enjoyed mine, except I hadn't seen him since returning from a trip three weeks ago. Probably a good thing. There were times last month when we seemed to drift away from friendship and edge too close to romance. And I didn't need anything further to confuse me about my upcoming marriage. But I missed Kit. We had a lot in common. For example, he, too, had been named after a fictional character; his mother christened him after her favorite character from *To Kill a Mockingbird*, Atticus Finch. He also had a disarming smile, and the warmest brown eyes seen on any creature since Bambi.

"How are you doing, Marlee?" After moving a spider plant to the side, Trejo sat on the ledge by the window. "You're looking nice."

Dressed in my usual work attire—a BERRY BASKET T-shirt and jeans—I thought he was simply being polite. "Thanks. I expected to see you at the fairground last night."

"I took my family to Mackinac Island for a few days. We didn't get back till after midnight. But I am looking into what happened to Porter Gale. That's why I'm here."

"Is Kit working on it, too?"

"Not at this time."

"Is he all right? I haven't seen Kit since I left on my trip to Illinois. He even gave me a book to read on vacation."

Trejo glanced at the door, as if making certain no one could overhear. "Marlee, you know I'm married to Kit's sister. He's family. And I don't want to see him get hurt."

"I don't want to see him get hurt, either."

He remained silent a long moment, allowing me to hear Suzanne tell someone about the best place to eat sushi in Grand Rapids. "Kit likes you. He likes you a lot. It might not take much for those feelings to get stronger. And you're engaged. Someone may get hurt if this continues." Trejo gave me a warning look. "We talked about this while you were gone."

"We?" I felt as if I'd been excluded from something important.

"Yes. I convinced him to keep his distance. Otherwise it's not fair to Kit. Or you."

That last part sounded insincere. Then again, Kit and Greg had been family for almost a decade. Who was I to upset their lives? A silly shopgirl who got involved in too many risky things—like murder. "I only want the best for Kit. And I consider him a friend. Nothing more." I hoped this was true. I honestly didn't know.

He nodded. "It's better for all concerned. Especially with what we've learned so far about the Porter Gale case."

Before I could ask him if it was true Porter had been murdered, Chief Gene Hitchcock and Janelle walked in. The room suddenly seemed smaller. Our strapping, six-foot-five police chief took up a lot of space. Having a police chief of such imposing size probably helped to discourage criminals in our little village. Having the same last name as the famous movie director of thrillers didn't hurt, either. Who wanted to mess with Chief Gene Hitchcock? Not me.

"Hi, Marlee. Hope your parents are doing well." Hitchcock gave my shoulder an affectionate squeeze before he sat down at his desk. I'd known him since I was a child, and his wife was my aunt's best friend.

"They're great. And they're coming to town for Labor Day."

"Good to hear." Hitchcock's attention turned to the paperwork on his desk. "We should all get together for a picnic that weekend."

Janelle let out an exasperated breath, which luckily her boss didn't hear. A divorced mother of two, Janelle had moved to Oriole Point from Green Bay, Wisconsin, eight years ago. Coming from a big city, she seemed baffled by what a tightly knit community Oriole Point was. And she openly resented how residents left their cars and homes unlocked. I was the exception to that; ten years in New York City taught me caution. With time, she might understand the dynamics of a small village, but I thought it was taking her a little too much time. Nonetheless, Officer Davenport had become Hitchcock's favorite on the force. No surprise, given her competence and the casual policing of the remaining officers. But she needed to acquire a little of Greg Trejo's Vulcan-like professional demeanor. I found her way too easy to read.

Right now, I sensed her impatience. Janelle leaned against the wall, her sharp, angled face revealing nothing. Of course she still wore her aviators. But her foot tapped the floor, impatient for questioning to begin. I didn't blame her. I wanted to know why I was here. The sooner, the better.

I cleared my throat, making Chief Hitchcock look up from his papers. "Officer Davenport said you wanted to ask me about Porter Gale's murder."

"What?" Trejo stood up. "Why are you calling it a murder?"

"Excuse me." Hitchcock straightened. "Who told you Mr. Gale had been murdered?"

I pointed at Janelle.

Hitchcock shot her a look so disapproving, Janelle actually withered, like a time-lapse film of a dying plant. "Officer Davenport, I instructed you to bring Marlee to my office. You were told to say nothing else about the case."

"Sorry, sir," she said, a flush creeping across her face. "But Miss Jacob asked why you wanted to see her. I assumed you would tell her as soon as she got here, so—"

He cut her off. "Enough. When I give an order, I expect it to be followed." Hitchcock shook his head. "And take off those sunglasses, Davenport. This is an office, not the beach."

Janelle removed her sunglasses, revealing a face crimson with embarrassment.

Trejo and Hitchcock exchanged irritated looks. "At this time, Porter's death is officially being viewed as suspicious," Trejo told me. "Unofficially, we're treating it as a homicide. We're waiting for further test results before we make the announcement. Officer Davenport should not have said anything until then."

"I don't understand why you think Porter may have been murdered," I said. "I assumed he died of something related to his diabetes."

"Why do you say that?" Hitchcock narrowed his eyes at me.

"After Porter won the men's pie-eating contest yesterday, Ryan mentioned how stupid it was for a diabetic to eat that much sugar. That was the first I heard about his diabetes. I thought Porter was lucky not to have gone into insulin shock there and then."

"Do you have family members or friends who are diabetics?" Trejo asked.

"Not that I'm aware of, but I know enough about diabetes to realize eating sugar isn't wise. Especially an entire pie. Then an hour later, I watched as Porter took part in the tug-of-war. It was almost a hundred degrees, too. I can't imagine all the exertion was good for his health."

"Ah, the tug-of-war." Chief Hitchcock pointed at the open door, and Janelle quickly shut it. "We've been told the Gales beat the Zellars. This led to a physical altercation."

"Yes. But not simply because the Zellars lost." I explained about the piece of glass that triggered the brawl. "Theo Foster, my baker, told me that he saw Porter bury something in the sand. So Ryan may have been correct to accuse Porter of cheating." I held up my hand before he could respond. "Not that I think attacking him was called for. Ryan should never have touched Porter. But there's a longtime rivalry between the two families, and Ryan and Porter obviously didn't like each other." My voice died away. I'd seen enough legal dramas to know I was volunteering too much information. To do so in a murder case could prove disastrous.

"The situation seems to have been cleared up once security officers arrived," Trejo said. "And Porter Gale refused to bring charges of assault against your fiancé."

"I left right after the fight, but Porter's wife, Sloane, told me the guys even shook hands."

Hitchcock pulled out one of the papers on his desk. The pile must be a printout of last night's police report. "Witnesses agree the two men shook hands shortly after the fight. A few hours later, they were seen at a table drinking a beer together at Trappers Corner."

"Is there a reason they call it Trappers Corner?" Janelle asked. "Seems a funny name for the middle of the fairground."

"A long time ago, raccoons overran the area. After a bounty was put on the animals, trappers came from all over Michigan to take part. To collect their money, the trappers brought their skins to that part of the county, and it became known as Trappers Corner." Hitchcock leaned forward. "Marlee, did you visit Trappers Corner at any point yesterday?"

"I met Ryan there a little before eight o'clock. I'd just closed up my Berry Basket booth, and I hadn't eaten anything in hours. When I arrived, a lot of the fruit-growing families were having dinner at the tables. The Janssens, the Ramakers, the O'Neills, the Gales. Most of Ryan's family had eaten, then went off to enjoy the rides."

"Was Porter there?" Hitchcock obviously knew the answer but wanted to see if I could confirm it.

"All the Gales were there, including Sloane and Jacqueline. There were three or four tables of Blueberry Hill employees. Oh, and Porter's nephew, Wyatt, sat with them."

"Wyatt O'Neill?" Janelle asked.

I nodded. "I was surprised to see that. But only because his mother Cara wasn't on good terms with Porter. Of course that doesn't mean Porter never saw Wyatt. Or his niece Courtney."

"Did you notice anything else unusual?" Trejo asked.

I shrugged. "It looked like Porter had been drinking. There were several coolers around the table and he kept pulling bottles out." Since they continued to stare at me, I thought back to last night. "I watched Porter give himself an insulin injection. In the abdomen."

"That confirms what everyone else observed," Trejo said. "We've learned Mr. Gale required up to six shots a day. And he preferred receiving his injections by syringe, rather than by the newer NovoPen. Apparently it's what he's been used to since he was a kid."

"Where did Porter Gale take the insulin from?" Hitchcock asked me.

"A red cooler that sat on the picnic bench. The same one a lot of people pulled beer from. He took out his shot and rubbed it between his hands."

Trejo looked at Hitchcock. "Getting the medicine to room temperature," he said.

"Soon after that, he teased Ryan and me for acting so lovey-dovey."

Trejo threw me a sharp look, which made me uncomfortable.

"Porter told us to follow him to the Blueberry Hill Death Drop," I went on, "He was being a little obnoxious so Ryan and I left to go to our cars. On the way we passed the Death Drop just as Porter strapped himself in. He yelled something about being King of Blueberry Hill, then the gondola rose to the top. A minute later, it came down and Porter was unconscious. Ryan ran over to see what was going on. That's when we learned he had died."

"I see." Hitchcock drummed his fingers on the desk. "Are you certain you do not know anyone with diabetes, Marlee? Think."

More bewildered than ever, I went through a list of relatives and friends in my mind. "No one, aside from Porter Gale. Although his sister told me yesterday that her son, Wyatt, is diabetic. Otherwise, I can't think of a single person in my life who has diabetes. Is this relevant?"

"It might be." Hitchcock moved a desktop photo of his family a few inches to the right. He seemed distracted. No, not distracted. Troubled.

"I don't see how it could. And I don't know why there are any suspicions about Porter's death. His sister told me that he took dreadful care of himself. His stepmother, Jacqueline, said the same. And I saw some of his reckless behavior yesterday. It seems obvious Porter died as a result of too much sugar, too much alcohol, and too much exertion in the blistering heat. I don't understand why I'm here. Or what you think I can tell you."

"You can tell us where Ryan Zellar is." Hitchcock fixed me with an unnerving stare.

"Ryan? He left on a fishing trip early this morning around six thirty."

"Tuesday seems a strange time to go off on a fishing trip," Trejo remarked. "I assumed Ryan would be helping out at the orchards and the Blow Out."

"There are a mob of Zellars to help run the business. And weekends are even busier at the orchards because of U-Pick. Besides, his fishing trips never last longer than two or three days."

"He does this often?" Hitchcock wrote something down on a piece of paper. This felt too much like an interrogation.

"Yes. Ryan has a college buddy who lives in Muskegon. His name is Joshua Edelman. Josh owns a boat, and the two of them go out on the lake about every eight weeks. Like I said, they're gone no more than three days. They even fish in the dead of winter, but of course they can't take out the boat then. They go ice fishing, usually near Traverse City." Because Ryan preferred to socialize with his relatives, I welcomed these fishing trips. Ryan needed to spend time with people who weren't part of his family. The Zellars had such strong family bonds, it verged on tribalism.

"When we called Ryan's parents at the orchards, they said the same thing," Hitchcock said. "They also claim he spent the night at your house. It looks like you are the last person in Oriole Point to see him."

My heart skipped a beat. "Are you saying something happened to Ryan?"

"No, Marlee. We're saying it looks suspicious.

Ryan left town only hours after Porter Gale died. Earlier, he accused Porter of cheating and physically attacked him. In fact, if security hadn't arrived when they did, reports claim he might have choked Porter to death."

I didn't know how to defend such indefensible behavior. "But they made up later."

"True," Hitchcock said. "Afterward, he and Porter were seen drinking beer together at Trappers Corner at approximately three thirty in the afternoon. Witnesses claim Ryan sat at the Gale table for nearly an hour."

"Next to the red cooler containing Mr. Gale's insulin," Janelle added.

I looked at them with growing dread. "I don't understand. Was there something besides insulin in the shot Porter gave himself?"

Hitchcock took a deep breath. "The medical examiner looked over Porter's records and heard accounts from the two people who sat on either side of him during the Death Drop; one of whom was his wife. During the short duration of the ride, Porter is reported to have complained of a racing heart and heart spasms. He died within seconds of the ride coming to a halt. The M.E. initially assumed Porter Gale died of a heart attack."

"This doesn't seem like murder to me," I protested.

"Porter's personal physician, Dr. Wheeler, disagreed. He's head of endocrinology at Oriole Point Hospital, where Porter's body was brought last night. Dr. Wheeler's been treating Porter since he was twelve, which is when he diagnosed Porter with type one diabetes. He took a much closer look at the first toxicology results and discovered high levels of potassium in the blood." Hitchcock sat back, arms crossed over his chest. "That's to be expected in a sudden cardiac death. But Dr. Wheeler had given Porter a complete physical one week ago and found his heart to be in excellent condition. So what else could account for the high amounts of potassium in Porter's system?"

"You suspect something besides insulin was in the injection." I still didn't understand how this concerned Ryan.

"The state police confiscated the cooler holding the syringes and vials of insulin," Trejo said. "Inside they found a plastic bag filled with emptied vials, and a separate bag containing those which hadn't been used yet. Samples from all the vials were tested. All but one contained insulin or its residue."

"And the one that didn't?" I asked.

"Lab results showed residue in an emptied vial contained potassium chloride, not insulin," Trejo said. "The effects mimic a heart attack. And a heart attack raises potassium levels in the blood. We're lucky Porter's doctor got suspicious."

"What does this have to do with Ryan?"

"The red cooler sat at the Gale table for hours in Trappers Corner," Hitchcock said. "It is highly unlikely Porter Gale switched his own medication. Which means someone who wanted Porter dead did compromise one of the vials."

"It appears likely the murderer found an opportunity to place a vial of potassium chloride in Porter Gale's cooler," Janelle said. "A vial the victim would eventually use to inject himself with. If not that night, sometime in the next twenty-four hours. That means any person in close proximity to the cooler yesterday is a possible suspect." She paused. "Assuming that person has a motive to want Porter Gale dead."

I didn't like where this line of questioning was headed. "The cooler probably sat at the table for hours. Anyone could have gotten into it. When I was there for dinner, a whole gang of Gale employees was at the table. All of them pulled beer bottles out of the cooler." I tried to remain calm. "Has the vial been tested for fingerprints?"

"Of course," Trejo said. "The only prints belong to Mr. Gale. But we assume the murderer would have made sure not to leave their own prints on it."

"When did Ryan tell you about this so-called fishing trip?" Hitchcock asked.

"Not so-called. It's been in the works for weeks. I told you, he and Josh do this about every two months." I pulled out my cell phone. "I'll call Ryan and you can ask him yourself."

But Ryan didn't answer. I called Josh next. Again, no success. Then I remembered they were out on Lake Michigan. "Hold on. They're somewhere on the lake by now. They won't have cell reception until they dock somewhere."

"When are they planning to dock? And where?" Hitchcock asked.

"I have no idea. When they go on these trips, they follow the fish and whatever mood they're in. They could be anywhere on Lake Michigan. Or even farther afield." I twisted the diamond engagement ring on my finger. "In May they went on a fishing trip that took them through the straits of Mackinac and into Lake Huron."

"Do they find a harbor every night, or drop anchor in the lake?" Trejo asked.

"Both. Josh owns a Crownline cruiser, which sleeps two. Sometimes they spend the night on the lake." My hands trembled. I clasped them in my lap to prevent the police officers from seeing how anxious I was. "You can't suspect Ryan of killing Porter. Does he seem crazy enough to murder a man over a tug-of-war game? Because there's no other motive."

"No other motive that you're aware of," Trejo broke in.

"Well, no. But it would have to be extremely serious for him to want to kill someone. And Ryan isn't a murderer. He's easygoing and calm and—"

"He flew into a rage yesterday and had to be pulled off the victim before he strangled him." Hitchcock looked as unhappy as I felt.

"I know Ryan lost his temper at the tug-of-war. He regrets it. But it's tied to this stupid rivalry between the two families. Nothing serious enough to kill someone over. And speaking of motive, I can think of other people with a good reason to want Porter out of the picture."

"Such as?" Trejo asked.

"His wife, for one. Sloane stands to inherit Blueberry Hill. It makes no sense to turn all this attention on Ryan when she's a much better suspect. What does Sloane have to say about all this?"

"Mrs. Gale has been under a doctor's care since last night," Janelle informed me. "When she learned about the tampered-with insulin, she became hysterical and had to be sedated."

"Maybe she's afraid she's been caught," I replied. "Or is overwhelmed with guilt."

"Or maybe she's innocent and can't believe someone murdered her husband," Trejo said.

"Cara O'Neill had no great love for her brother." I felt guilty offering up Cara as a suspect, but better her than my fiancé. "She was cut out of their father's will and resented Porter for it. I don't think she ever forgave her father or Porter. The same with Porter's stepmother, Jacqueline. For all you know, there's a disgruntled Blueberry Hill employee who wanted to see Porter dead. Or a business competitor. Maybe a jealous woman from his past."

Hitchcock held up his hand to stop me from continuing. "Rest assured every person who had access to the cooler containing the vial is a suspect. Unfortunately, the cooler with the insulin vials sometimes sat at the Gale table unattended. We're in the process of tracking down everyone who visited the tent during that time. It may be a lengthy process."

"Meanwhile, we need to look at possible motive. Porter was a wealthy, powerful man. Such men usually have enemies. Which of those people were at Trappers Corner yesterday?" Janelle twirled her sunglasses. She probably couldn't wait to put them back on.

I couldn't shake the memory of Ryan attacking Porter. For a few minutes, he had seemed consumed by rage. But a murderous rage? Impossible. Not Ryan.

"The murderer knew Porter was a diabetic, and

that he used syringes rather than a NovoPen," Hitchcock said. "This individual probably possesses more than a cursory knowledge of diabetes. Many diabetics only need injections once or twice a day. But Porter's condition was severe enough to require six daily injections. An estimate of his injection schedule no doubt factored in."

"How did Ryan react when he learned Porter had died?" Trejo asked.

"What do you mean? He was shocked, of course." I hoped I sounded convincing.

"They weren't friends," Trejo said. "On the contrary, they actively disliked each other."

"True. And Ryan didn't cry about Porter's death. But it wasn't something he wanted to happen." Except Ryan had laughed when he told me Porter was dead. The sound of his laughter had chilled me to the bone. But it didn't prove Ryan killed Porter— only that he could be more ruthless than I imagined.

"One of the EMS drivers told the police that your fiancé appeared amused by the death." Hitchcock sighed. "Marlee, I know this is difficult for you. You're engaged to Ryan. But he attacked Porter earlier that day. He sat near the cooler that contained the murder weapon. And he seemed happy when he learned of the death."

I shook my head. "Ryan did not kill Porter."

"You need to inform us the minute you hear from him," Hitchcock said.

Even though my legs felt shaky from this interview, I shot to my feet. "Ryan is not a murderer. And he doesn't know anything about diabetes or potassium chloride or insulin. How would he even get an insulin vial to tamper with?"

Trejo looked surprised. "Are you telling us you don't know?"

"Know what?"

"About Ryan's mother." Hitchcock gave me a pitying look. "She's diabetic."

Chapter Seven

I didn't remember leaving the police station. Or how I got to my SUV and on the open road. But my subconscious had a destination. The green pastures, barns, and silos rushing past my windows told me I was miles away from town and headed for Humane Hearts, the animal shelter run by my aunt. At least I had the presence of mind to call Gillian and let her know I'd be back at the store as soon as I took care of an errand. I didn't want her to think I'd been detained indefinitely by the police. Or arrested. Although the thought Ryan might be arrested made me break out in a sweat.

Grateful the temperature had dropped, I hung my arm out the window. The breeze blew against my cheeks like a balm. As did the sight of grazing dairy cows and rolling fields of corn, soybean, and alfalfa. Just a few short miles from the sand dunes of Lake Michigan, the soil turned rich, helping Oriole County rank as one of the top three farming economies in the state.

Five generations of Jacobs have grown berries in Oriole County, starting with my great-great-grandparents. Our orchard connection stretched back to the Netherlands, where the family cultivated pears; at least one distant cousin there still did. I'd grown up on my grandparents' berry farm, where Aunt Vicki now lived and ran her shelter.

While I had loved berry picking with my little pail, wading in the pond, and helping my grandmother tend her chickens, my parents found farm life far less entrancing. Since we lived with my grandparents, Mom and Dad pitched in when they could, but they disliked it. And they spent their working lives elsewhere; Mom taught at a local college and Dad ran a conference center in nearby Holland. After I turned eighteen and left to attend New York University, my parents relocated to Chicago, where they finally found their niche: Mom as a professor at Northwestern, and Dad as the manager of a boutique hotel on State Street.

Long before we left, however, life had become uncertain. By the time I turned seven, both grandparents had died. This left my father and his sister Vicki to take over the business, which they did with disastrous results. Six years later, Dad and Aunt Vicki lost a hundred acres of orchards to the bank. At least they managed to hold on to the family's "Painted Lady" on Lake Michigan, along with the orchard farmhouse and its last remaining twenty acres.

As the only Jacob son, his parents left the orchards to my father; Aunt Vicki inherited the Queen Anne house on the lake. This outcome pleased no one. My dad didn't have a bucolic bone in his body. And my aunt had no use for a beach house. Although she hadn't opened an animal shelter yet, she took care of an ever-increasing menagerie of cats, dogs, rabbits, and the occasional ferret. More important, she had two sons, but no daughter.

The lake house had been handed down to a female Jacob since Philip Jacob built it for his wife Lotte in 1895. Because I was the next female Jacob descendant, my aunt believed the house should be passed on to me, although given my young age it was placed in my parents' name.

So brother and sister swapped properties, a deal they never regretted. As much as I enjoyed my childhood on the farm, I'd been thrilled to move into the pretty blue house overlooking the lake. A house Ryan now insisted I sell. He assumed he'd eventually get his way, as he did with so much else. Only in this case, his charm and stubbornness were not going to work. I glanced at the diamond solitaire on my finger. Why was Ryan at the center of so many of my present worries? I hoped to enjoy my engagement. Instead I felt conflicted and under siege. And the last thing I expected was Ryan to be a murder suspect.

When I braked at a four-way stop, my eyes were drawn to two sweeping black marks in the road. I'd made those marks during the Blackberry Road Rally while trying to outrace a homicidal maniac. To say it had been an eventful summer would be an understatement.

A few minutes later, I caught sight of the roadside sign announcing HUMANE HEARTS. Turning up the driveway to my aunt's house, I waved at a large

man in khaki shorts—bare to the waist—riding a
lawn mower. He tipped his baseball cap at me before
swerving his mower around a bed of lavender. Joe
Coyle ran a successful landscaping company. Since
he was also Aunt Vicki's current boyfriend, Joe took
it upon himself to tend my aunt's acreage.

Next, I passed the little green cottage that served
as the rescue organization's administrative office.
Amy, the executive secretary, stood on the porch
with a family who must have just adopted two pup-
pies. The excited children took turns holding the
pups while Amy handed the parents the requisite
Humane Hearts Adoption Kit: samples of recommended dog food, names of referred vets, squeaky
toys, and a metal water bowl with the shelter's name
on it.

To avoid running over a flock of wild turkey on
the front lawn, it took longer than expected to make
my way up the winding drive. In the seventeen years
since Aunt Vicki had owned the property, she had
transformed it from a bankrupt farm into a state-
of-the-art animal shelter, with annex buildings, dog
runs, kennels, an aviary, a barn, even a spanking-
new stable currently housing three rescue horses, a
donkey, and two llamas. The entire property stood
as testament not only to Vicki's fierce determination to save animals in jeopardy, but also to the
devotion of Humane Heart's many volunteers and
generous donors.

When I came to a stop in front of the yellow
farmhouse, I could almost see my younger pigtailed
self on the bottom porch step, eating fresh-picked
blueberries from a pail. It seemed a lifetime ago.
But also as recent as last month. I heard barking

and spied two volunteers walking dogs in the field by the barn.

"What brings you here in the middle of a workday, Marlee?" My aunt stood on the porch, a wide grin on her tanned face. Seeing her reminded me of my dad: both were blond, blue-eyed extroverts. Circled about her were three Doberman pinschers named Buffy, Willow, and Xander. Aunt Vicki was a diehard fan of *Buffy the Vampire Slayer.*

Fighting back a stress headache, I got out of the SUV and went to meet her as she literally leaped off the steps. A full-figured woman, Aunt Vicki nonetheless moved with the agility of a champion gymnast. With a few dozen rescue dogs always kenneled on the property, she and her volunteers spent most of their day exercising the animals. It kept them as strong and muscled as Aunt Vicki's Doberman pinschers, which guarded the shelter more effectively than the Secret Service.

The three Dobermans ran up to me, and I crouched down to give them a little attention. My aunt had rescued them from a drug dealer who kept the dogs chained day and night to protect his contraband. After his arrest, the malnourished dogs were slated to be put down until Aunt Vicki read about them in the paper. She fell in love with them—and they with her—making the Dobermans a part of Vicki Jacob's permanent animal family.

"My turn now," she said, holding her arms wide.

I meant to only give her a quick hug, but when she put her arms around me, I burst into tears.

"What's this?" She patted my back as if I were a colicky baby. "What's wrong, sweetheart? You can tell your Aunt Vicki."

After a few minutes, I stopped crying. Feeling drained, I wiped my cheeks. "You must think I'm crazy."

"I don't think you're crazy. I think you're upset." Taking me by the arm, she led me onto the wide wooden porch. "Let's sit down on the swing and talk about this."

After we settled back on the swing, she put an arm around my shoulder and pulled me close. "What's wrong?"

With their heads cocked to one side, the Dobermans sat in front of us as I told my aunt about Ryan's dislike of Porter Gale, the tug-of-war brawl, the police interest in his possible involvement, and his access to insulin. Because I was in a confessional mood, I also described my fluctuating feelings about our upcoming marriage. After I finished, I was met with silence and the panting of three Dobermans.

"What do you think?" I asked. "Should I contact a lawyer in case Ryan is arrested?"

"Don't be silly. They won't arrest Ryan."

"How can you be so certain?"

"Because Ryan didn't kill Porter Gale."

"I know that, but the police regard him as a suspect."

"They need a motive, Marlee. Porter cheating at tug-of-war is a laughable motive, and they know it. It wouldn't hold up in court. Or in the court of public opinion, either." She took my chin in her hand and made me look directly at her. "I have a feeling it's not only the police who think he's a suspect. Be honest. Do you believe Ryan could have killed Porter?"

"Of course not." I hesitated. "At least not in cold blood. It did scare me when he flew into a rage yesterday. For a moment, I actually thought Ryan might end up choking Porter to death. I don't believe he was aware of what he was doing. That's how angry he was. As soon as he calmed down, the two men made up. And Ryan had no reason to murder him later that night. But because of that stupid fight at the tug-of-war, the police suspect him. And they know he could have laid his hands on an insulin vial. By the way, that's the first time I heard anything about his mother being a diabetic. Don't you think that's strange?"

"It depends. How often would something like that come up in conversation? It's not like he has the disease."

"I wonder if Ryan would tell me even if that were the case. He kept his drug use as a teen hidden from me. Along with his time in rehab. I had to find that out from Piper." The recent Strawberry Moon Bash murder case uncovered more than a killer; I'd learned shocking secrets about several Oriole Point residents. One of those secrets had involved Ryan.

"Ryan might want to forget his past, Marlee. Don't be too hard on him."

"The problem is that people aren't hard enough on Ryan. He's good-looking and charming. And he knows it. That cuts him a lot of slack where the women in his life are concerned. He's also his parents' favorite. Even his brothers admit it."

She chuckled. "So speaks a pampered only child."

"Yes, I'm my parents' favorite. By default. And this isn't the first time Ryan's kept something from me. What else about his life am I unaware of?"

"He's a man, sweetie. Lower your expectations."

"If I have to lower them that much, I don't know why I'm getting married."

She stroked my cheek. "Because you love him?"

"I do." The admission gave me little comfort, however. "But how blind should love be? I've asked Ryan to be honest with me. Except I keep learning there's something else I don't know about him. Or don't understand. We've been engaged for eight months. You'd think we'd know everything about each other by now."

"You should know a fair amount. Especially since you both grew up in Oriole Point."

"He's four years older than me. By the time I got to high school, he had graduated. And I didn't pay much attention to Ryan back then. He lived in the country and I lived in town. Then I left for New York and by the time I came back, ten years had passed. We were almost strangers to each other."

"I assumed the two of you got to know each other during one of your visits back home."

I shook my head. "He's never been part of my group of friends. When I first moved back, I saw him at the farmers markets, where he was friendly and flirtatious. He had a reputation as a charmer, so I didn't think it meant anything. And I was busy getting The Berry Basket up and running. I had no time for romance. Then he began to visit my shop, and the flirting got more intense. All that charm finally worked. Once we started to date, he got serious about our relationship quickly. I think he decided to marry me on our first date."

"He probably had his eye on you for some time. Why wouldn't he? You're a catch."

"I wish I'd been living here during his first marriage. I'd love to know what kind of person his ex-wife was."

Aunt Vicki thought a moment. "I have a vague memory of a redhead with a lot of cleavage. Nothing like you. And I mean that in a good way."

"People told me she was quite the looker. I must seem like the ordinary girl next door."

"Don't start feeling sorry for yourself, Marlee. I won't put up with that. Not when you're such a beauty. Stop making that face. It's true. My goodness, you remind me of Sandra Bullock in *Miss Congeniality*, but *after* she had her beauty makeover in the movie."

Despite my headache, I laughed. "I'm flattered you think so."

"I know so. You also remind me of Kate Middleton. The two of you have the most beautiful hair I've ever seen." She gave an admiring look at my long dark hair, which I had worn loose around my shoulders today. "You look more like Kate than her own sister, Pippa."

My aunt and I were longtime royal watchers, and our admiration for Prince William's wife knew no bounds. While I didn't believe that I was remotely as pretty as the Duchess of Cambridge, it pleased me that Aunt Vicki thought so.

"Now that we've decided who my celebrity doppelgängers are, let's get back to my fiancé. Who may end up being arrested for a murder he didn't commit."

"He won't be arrested," she said. "Although if you keep saying such things, you might make people suspicious about him."

"Ryan's not a killer. I've met a few, so I should know. But his animosity toward Porter seems unwarranted. I've dated Ryan since last summer and never heard him say a word about Porter Gale. Not one word. Where did this hatred of Porter come from?"

"There was a business rivalry between the Gales and the Zellars before you were born."

"No, this thing between Ryan and Porter seemed personal. And Porter kept needling Ryan yesterday. I got the feeling something else was wrong between them." I lowered my voice, as though the police might eavesdrop. "Ryan was happy to learn Porter had died. You should have seen his face. A normal person would have been shocked or subdued. The death was so unexpected." I felt like crying again. "But Ryan laughed. Who acts like that?"

I could see this troubled her. "Someone who's emotionally immature?"

"Or a sociopath. Am I marrying a sociopath?" I shut my eyes. "It can't be true. I feel like my world is about to implode."

"You're too stressed out. And I know the perfect remedy for that." My aunt stood up.

"If you're going to offer me something alcoholic to drink, no thanks. I have no appetite, either."

"I have something much better than food or drink." She took my hand and pulled me up to stand beside her. "Dogs."

I stood in the middle of a field to watch a family of bufflehead ducks glide on the pond. Aunt Vicki was right. A little quality time with canines did wonders for the mind and soul. She and I had spent the last twenty minutes walking two recent rescues: a one-eyed beagle and a timorous sheltie. And we'd done so without a word of conversation. I felt calmer now and ready to figure out what the next step should be.

I tugged gently at the leash to distract the beagle from chewing something inedible. "Thanks. This has helped. I forgot how much I liked exercising your dogs. As soon as tourist season is over, I promise to get out here more often."

She smiled. "One day I might even get you to adopt one of them."

After the dogs completed their business, we resumed our walk. "I work too many hours to have a dog. I bring Minnie to the store now, but I couldn't keep a dog at the shop."

"While I admire your work ethic, you'll need to slow down a bit once you have children."

"Ryan and I want children. But I'm not ready for that yet. I'm still trying to overcome my nerves about getting married."

"To be honest, I don't blame you. The statistics aren't encouraging. I've got two bad marriages behind me and have no intention of trying for a third. Joe says he's happy to hear that, but I think he's a little disappointed."

"I like Joe. Maybe you should reconsider. Third time's the charm, as they say."

She laughed. "Says the girl who hasn't even walked down the aisle once."

"Well, I don't know a lot of happily married couples."

"You know more than you realize, starting with your parents. And 'happily married' doesn't mean there are never problems. Serious ones. But a good marriage is worth saving."

"Then why did you get divorced twice?" I asked her.

Her expression turned sad. "Because neither of them was a good marriage."

We walked for a few minutes, watching the dogs sniff everything in sight. "I don't think I'm afraid of marriage," I said finally. "I think I'm afraid of marrying Ryan. What if I'm not the right person for him? The relationship takes so much work. I feel like I'm always making an effort. It's why I haven't shopped for a wedding gown yet."

"Your mom and I have been concerned about that."

"As soon as we got engaged, everyone insisted we choose the florists, invitations, bridesmaids, ushers, honeymoon locations. It didn't leave much time to think about the actual relationship." I frowned. "And Ryan's driving me crazy about the lake house. He insists I sell it as soon as possible."

She grabbed my arm. "Sell the lake house? What are you talking about? I know he wants you to move out to the orchard, but I didn't think he expected you to sell the house. You can't do that. That is Great-great-grandma Lotte's house and it is to be passed down to a Jacob female. I gave it to you because I never had daughters."

"I have no intention of selling the house. And I'm not moving out to Zellar Orchards, either. I've told this to Ryan a thousand times, but he doesn't believe me. That's part of the problem. He's always gotten what he wanted, and without a lot of effort."

"Marlee, I don't care how much effort he puts into this, he is *not* doing what he wants with Lotte's house," Aunt Vicki snapped. "The nerve of that man! Perhaps you're right. Ryan Zellar may not be the right man for you to marry."

I burst into laughter.

She turned an offended face in my direction. "What's so funny?"

"I tell you the police suspect Ryan may have murdered someone, and you advise me to not be so hard on him. I tell you he wants to sell the lake house, and you want me to kick him to the curb."

"And so you should." She sniffed. "Sell the lake house! Who does he think he is?"

"He thinks he's my future husband and entitled to half of everything I own."

"Ryan Zellar is not entitled to Lotte Jacob's home. You do know how much that house is worth, don't you?"

"A three-story Queen Anne Victorian overlooking Lake Michigan with a private beach? A lot. That's another reason Ryan wants me to sell the house. He thinks the property taxes are too high."

"Of course they're high," she told me. "The house and waterfront property are worth over a million dollars."

I stopped and faced her. "It can't be worth that much. Six hundred thousand at most."

She gave me an exasperated look. "The house alone is worth more than half a million. Add on a beach with two hundred feet of lake frontage and the price doubles. That is a legacy house. And not only because Jacobs have lived there for over a century. Should circumstances ever grow dire, it can serve as the family's safety net. I passed it on to your stewardship."

"Please know I take that seriously. Sooner or later it will sink into Ryan's thick head that I am not going to sell it. Of course, he thinks I'm crazy for loving the house the way I do. If he had his way, he'd tear it down and put up something modern. Thinks we'd get a better price if a brand-new house came with that private beach."

"Tear the house down? It's on the Historic Register!" She grew even more agitated.

I put my hands on her shoulders. "Aunt Vicki, I swear on the soul of every dead Jacob that I will never sell the lake house or tear it down. I give you my word."

"I trust you, sweetheart. I always have. But now I don't trust Ryan."

"Don't worry. He can't sell it without my permission."

She didn't look convinced. "Now I'm glad you never got around to putting the house in your own name. Tell him the truth. That when I first transferred the property, you were only thirteen so your parents' names were put on the title. And they refuse to sell. It may stop him from pestering you."

"I'm afraid that's no longer true. When I visited Mom and Dad in Chicago last month, we went to the lawyers and had my name put on the title. Since I'm the one paying the taxes, insurance, and utilities, we thought it was time that the house be legally mine."

"And so you should." She patted my arm. "I'm being foolish."

"Please relax. I'll make Ryan see reason. Besides, he doesn't need the money. Zellar Orchards is quite successful. And two years ago, Ryan's dad decided to give his sons their inheritance. He wanted the pleasure of watching his children enjoy it while he was still alive. The orchard acreage was divided among all five sons and put into their own names. Ryan's father also gave them an equal share of money: one hundred fifty thousand dollars each."

This seemed to disturb her even more. "If Ryan has all those acres *and* a hundred and fifty thousand dollars, why is he pressuring you to sell your house?"

I regretted telling any of this to her. Ryan was my problem to deal with, not Aunt Vicki's. "He has plans to buy additional acres in the county so Zellars can expand. He also wants to produce and sell hard cider. Ryan worships his dad, and I think he wants to make the Zellar empire even more secure for his own children."

"Ryan might find a way to sell the house, no matter what you say."

"He can't. The property is in my name."

"You always joke about how charming he is, how he always gets his own way in the end. Maybe he will again. Maybe we've all been wrong about Ryan." She looked positively stricken. "And maybe the police are right. What if he did kill Porter Gale?"

Chapter Eight

I left Humane Hearts more worried than when I arrived. Fearful that Ryan would be dragged into a murder investigation, I didn't expect my aunt to plant more doubts. My normal sense of certainty had been off-kilter for a while: a combination of bridal jitters and too much proximity to dead bodies. Porter's murder now made my life even more complicated and unclear.

Some part of me hoped Ryan stayed away long enough for the killer to be caught. After all, this past June the police arrested the wrong person for Cole Bowman's murder. Since our police force had little experience with violent crime prior to this summer, they could make the same mistake again. Only this time, with Ryan.

After leaving Aunt Vicki, I spent the rest of the day and night buried in work. When my shift at the shop ended, I dropped Minnie off at home before going to the fairground to operate my vendor booth. I tried to contact Ryan yet again—with no results. Although I felt exhausted and emotionally drained when I finally returned home, I called Tess. I needed the support of my best friend to help get me to sleep.

We ended up talking for two hours. When we finally hung up, I lay awake for several hours more. What sleep I did manage to get was filled with images of carnival rides, dogs, and men competing at tug-of-war.

Another long day at the store and fairground lay ahead. To prepare myself, I ate a big bowl of homemade raspberry yogurt, then set off for a session of beach yoga. As often as I could, I left my own stretch of private beach to walk barefoot along the lake until I reached Oriole Beach, which was open to the public. There Rowena Bouchet, owner of Karuna Yoga, held a thirty-minute yoga session five days a week at eight a.m. Classes continued to be held on the beach until the first snow, at which time we all reconvened at Rowena's studio in town.

Always in need of a good stretch and a chance to meditate, I tried to attend her beach yoga class before going in to work. Something about staring out at the lake while in Warrior Pose lulled me into a Zen state. I arrived at Rowena's usual spot on the beach, noting a fair number of tourists had joined the daily yoga crowd. I had no sooner rolled out my yoga mat than Rowena called for Child's Pose. I tried to clear my mind of anything but her soothing voice and the lapping of the waves along the shore. By the time we moved into Downward-Facing Dog, I already felt more centered. But the determination to clear my thoughts wavered during Plank Pose as I wondered who hated Porter Gale enough to want to kill him.

How could I once more be connected to murder? Bad enough I'd been dragged into murder cases earlier this summer, but I left New York City two years ago for the same reason. After graduating from NYU, I interned at Dean & DeLuca and discovered I had an affinity for selling and marketing food. This led to a job at the Manhattan headquarters of the Gourmet Living Network, where I helped produce three popular cooking shows.

Sugar & Spice, the most successful of the three, starred husband-and-wife celebrity chefs Evangeline and John Chaplin. As the executive producer of what became the hottest cooking show on TV, I believed we were on the way to food superstardom. And we were, until Evangeline discovered John having an affair with a much younger woman working on the show. Evangeline wasted no time handling the situation. She baked a cake laced with arsenic for her cheating husband and served it to him on their wedding anniversary. The subsequent murder trial lasted almost a year; it ended with Evangeline in prison and me deciding I'd had enough of the big city, television, and celebrity chefs. I returned to Oriole Point, grateful to be home.

I never regretted my decision, especially after I opened The Berry Basket, which allowed me to combine a lifelong love of berries with my marketing skills. Aided by growing online sales, the business was in the black and I had dreams of one day opening more Berry Basket stores in Michigan. Once Ryan and I began dating, even my checkered romantic life looked to be on the upswing. Surrounded by friends, with a thriving business and a wedding on the horizon, I should be euphoric. But there were speed bumps even in a place as beautiful and friendly as Oriole Point. Porter Gale's murder qualified as a speed bump. Maybe even a roadblock.

Following Rowena's instruction on how to get into Wide Leg Forward Bend, I faced the lake. A cloudless sky had turned Lake Michigan a cerulean blue. Even at this early hour, boats were out on the water and visitors had begun to claim their corner of the beach. By noon, a sea of beach umbrellas, sunbathers, small cabanas, and Frisbee players would blanket every square inch of sand. When I bent forward, I glanced to my left. A dozen brightly colored sun umbrellas already fluttered in the gentle breeze, their owners lying on towels or settled back in beach chairs as they read a book or their tablets. Three shouting children ran past me with buckets and shovels to begin the endless fun of building sandcastles.

With only two more weeks until the end of summer, tourists wanted to squeeze every minute soaking up the sun, windsurfing, and swimming in the lake. Another gorgeous day, too: sunny and warm, but not blistering hot. *Concentrate,* I told myself as I relaxed into the forward stretch. While holding the pose, I closed my eyes, but opened them at the noisy arrival of what had to be a group of teenage girls, heralded by high-pitched, breathless voices and laughter.

As Rowena led us into Triangle Pose I craned my neck to see who these new arrivals were. With my head turned one way and my body the other, this wasn't easy. About thirty feet away, I spied four girls laying out their towels and blankets. One of

them was Courtney O'Neill. Joking with her friends
while she applied sunscreen, Courtney looked as if
she didn't have a care in the world. Except her
uncle had been murdered two days ago.

I wondered if Cara's children shared her own
resentment toward Porter. Maybe the hard feelings
caused by Eric Gale's will had led to a serious
breach in the family. If so, why did Wyatt sit at the
Gale picnic table at Trappers Corner? He must
have been on friendly terms with Porter.

Or perhaps it was Porter's wife he wanted to be
friendly with. I recalled how avidly Wyatt had
watched Sloane. Then there was the neck nuzzling
I'd glimpsed right before the tug-of-war. Sloane had
shoved him away. And who could blame her? Wyatt
possessed all the appeal of Richard III, minus the
hunchback.

As for Courtney, I had no idea what her relationship had been with Porter. I reminded myself that
she was only fourteen. Little more than a child.
Death was almost an abstract term for someone that
young. Still, seeing her at the beach surprised me.

With half an ear on Rowena's instruction, I moved
into the next pose while keeping my gaze on Courtney. Pain suddenly shot through me as a charley
horse seized my left leg.

"Ow-ow-ow-ow!" Contorted in the wrong position,
I lost my balance and fell over. I grabbed my left calf
and tried to stop it from completely cramping.

Rowena quickly made her way to my side. Kneeling down, she told me to breathe deep and count
to ten. If I didn't relax, my muscles wouldn't, either.
Easier said than done. Embarrassed because I dis-
rupted the yoga session, I told her I'd be fine and

to please continue. After she went back to leading the class, I took deep breaths while massaging my calf. Slowly, the cramp began to subside. Since I couldn't manage another yoga pose, I rolled up my mat and limped far enough away from the group in order not to distract them further. It was a fifteen-minute walk to my house, and I wasn't ready for a hike yet.

I sat down close to the water. Pulling up the leg of my gray yoga pants, I began to massage the sore muscle. A young couple ran past me into the lake, sending water splashing my way. I peeked over my shoulder. Although I didn't see Courtney now, her three friends were busy texting on their phones. In June, Oriole Point completed work on a nearby cell tower, finally allowing Internet service on the beach. It was welcomed with more enthusiasm than anything that had happened to our town in my lifetime.

"Is your leg okay, Marlee?"

I looked up to see Courtney standing over me. "What? Oh, yeah. It was just a charley horse."

She sat cross-legged beside me. "I figured you pulled a muscle or something. I saw you grab your leg when you were doing yoga." With her gaze on the half dozen people splashing in the lake, she began to swirl her hands in the warm sand. "I always did think yoga was weird. You won't catch me doing it. Give me horseback riding any day."

"It helps if you own a horse." The O'Neills owned three, and Courtney was often seen riding one of them along the country roads.

"True." Her wide smile revealed the braces on her teeth.

"I'm surprised to see you and your friends here

so early. The sun isn't high enough to get much of a tan right now."

"It's the only time all of us could get to the beach today. Jordan and Jane have to help out their dad at the dune buggy rides. He wants them there by eleven." The popular dune buggy rides were owned by the Larson family, of which the twin Larson girls, Jordan and Jane, were a part. "Alice babysits on Wednesday afternoons. And I have to be back home by noon."

"I understand. I have the shop, you have chores at the farm." Because I sold O'Neill homemade blueberry jams and butter, I visited their farm once a month. Whenever I did, Courtney always seemed to be cleaning berries or updating the O'Neill Blueberry Farm website. Farming life meant everyone past the age of kindergarten pitched in.

"It's not that." She brushed sand off her two-piece bathing suit. "My mom doesn't think I should be seen having too much fun right now. You know, because of Uncle Porter."

"I'm sorry about your uncle. Your family must be shocked."

"Yeah. Pretty shocked. Bad enough Uncle Porter just up and died. The police told us that someone may have killed him. Only they must be lying. What do you think?" Courtney gave me a penetrating look. She didn't resemble her mother at all. Both Wyatt and Courtney had inherited the physical traits of the O'Neills: pale, freckled skin, large protruding eyes, thick coppery hair. Her mane was so untamable, Courtney normally wore it tied back. Today that mass of curly hair cascaded past her shoulders. She reminded me of the Celtic princess Merida in *Brave.*

"I'm afraid it does look like someone tampered with his insulin."

She didn't seem convinced. "My mom says the police have been wrong before."

I couldn't argue with that.

"Besides, who would want to kill Uncle Porter?" she continued. "He treated everyone who worked for him really well. And Sloane and him seemed happy. Whenever the family got together during holidays and birthdays this past year, there was a whole lot of PDA going on." She rolled her eyes, remembering those public displays of affection. "It was disgusting. Mom always threatened to throw cold water on them."

"What did you think of Porter and Sloane as a couple?"

She shrugged. "I think Uncle Porter thought his wife was hot."

"And Sloane?"

Courtney picked up a fistful of sand, then let it trickle through her fingers. "She probably enjoyed all the money Uncle Porter had. But I bet she thought he was hot, too. Uncle Porter wasn't bad looking for someone his age. Why wouldn't Sloane like him? And Jacqueline has no reason to get rid of Uncle Porter. This murder thing is crazy."

Unfortunately, I could think of reasons her own mother might want Porter dead. Revenge for being disinherited, for one. And who knew what Porter had specified in his will? Maybe he didn't leave everything to a young wife he'd been married to only thirteen months. Maybe provisions had been made for his sister Cara. And Cara might know it.

"Anyway, Mom is upset," she went on. "I think she's feeling guilty. Her and Uncle Porter didn't get along all that great, with Grandpa Gale leaving everything to his son and nothing to her. I don't blame Mom for holding a grudge. But it's Grandpa who screwed everything up. I never liked Grandpa Gale. He never smiled. And he had such a loud voice, it hurt my ears."

Despite Courtney's breezy dismissal, I did believe someone wanted Porter Gale dead. And that person was not only at the fairground that day, but in close proximity to the cooler holding the insulin. "Is your brother upset about your uncle?"

"Who knows with Wyatt? He acts like he's too cool for school. Although he was actually too stupid for school. Him and those losers he hangs with. He's probably upset. I mean, he hung around Uncle Porter more than the rest of us did. But maybe he was only doing that to see if he could beg money off our uncle." Courtney leaned closer. "Or maybe he went to Blueberry Hill because of Sloane. Everyone in the family knows Wyatt has a thing for her. And how sick is that? I mean, she's his aunt! And even if she wasn't, Sloane is way out of Wyatt's league." She snorted. "Any girl with half a brain is out of his league."

It looked like Courtney and Wyatt were carrying on the family tradition of sibling animosity. Or maybe this was normal sibling rivalry.

"Hey, you've got a berry tattoo." Courtney pointed

at the four blackberries tattooed on my right ankle. "Pretty. Blackberries?"

"Yes. A memento of my two years at the Blackberry Art School. My friend Tess Nakamura has one as well. Along with the girls we shared a summer cabin with back then."

"I want to have a horse tattooed on my arm, but I'm not allowed. And I blame Wyatt. Back in high school, he got this ginormous tattoo of a skull on his back. My parents had a fit. Now I'm not allowed to get any ink until I'm old enough for college."

"Seems reasonable." I smiled at her. "And you may change your mind by then."

"Nope. In fact, I'd like three horse tattoos."

"Don't tell your parents. It will only stress them out."

"We're all stressed right now. That's why I'm at the beach. Mom and Dad thought I should get away from the house. They're discussing funeral arrangements, and it's depressing."

"When is the funeral?"

"Friday. Mom's handling everything because Sloane is zoned out right now on meds. Of course it won't be a proper funeral."

"Why not?"

She threw me a disgusted look. For the first time she brought to mind her mother. "The police haven't released the body yet because they need to run more stupid tests. It doesn't really matter. Uncle Porter wanted to be cremated. But there's a memorial service at our church. I'm sure all the fruit-growing families will be there. Do you think you'll come?"

"Certainly. I want to pay my respects."

"I wonder if the Zellars will show up. That was an awful big fight at the tug-of-war."

"Trust me. Someone from the Zellar family will be there. Probably not Ryan, though."

She laughed. "Don't be silly. I never thought Ryan would come. My uncle and Ryan didn't exactly love each other."

"That's an understatement," I muttered.

"I don't think your boyfriend understood Uncle Porter very well. Uncle Porter loved to tease people. When he found their weak spot, he went after it. If you laughed it off or ignored him, he left you alone . . . eventually. From what I could see, Ryan didn't."

"Nope."

Courtney sighed, stretching out her legs so her toes reached the wet sand near the water. "Uncle Porter did the same thing with my brother."

"What did he tease Wyatt about?"

"Sloane. Uncle Porter told Wyatt that he needed to get a lot richer and better looking if he wanted a girl as sexy as his wife."

"Lovely," I murmured. Those holiday get-togethers must have been awkward.

"But he teased him about money, too. Uncle Porter knew Wyatt would grovel in front of him if it meant he'd throw cash his way. Don't know who Wyatt's going to bother for money now. Maybe Aunt Sloane, although she's too young for us to call her 'aunt.'"

"I guess Sloane will be running things at Blueberry Hill now."

The girl looked as if I had suggested her favorite horse should take over the business. "I can't see

Sloane handling such a big operation. I don't think she'd want to anyway. Maybe another grower will buy the business from her. Uncle Porter said the Zellars wouldn't rest until they owned Blueberry Hill. Except he swore he'd never sell a single acre to them, especially Ryan. Now that Uncle Porter's gone, Sloane might sell it."

"If she does sell, I doubt it would be to Zellars. I've never heard any of them say a thing about wanting to buy Blueberry Hill."

"All I know is Uncle Porter thought it was funny that Zellar Orchards was still afloat, particularly after your fiancé came to him for money. He claimed Ryan had no business sense. Or any sense at all." She blushed. "Sorry. It was Uncle Porter who said that, not me. But it was rude to repeat it to you."

"Hold on. Ryan went to your uncle to borrow money?"

"Yeah. But I think he went to Grandpa Gale first."

"That can't be true."

The adolescent made an exaggerated face. "Hey, I'm only repeating what my uncle told us. The first time he mentioned Ryan asking for money was during the funeral for Grandpa Gale. So it was right before Thanksgiving last year. He said Ryan borrowed money from Grandpa a month or two before. And during my birthday dinner in May, he told us Ryan had just come to him to ask for more money."

"Let me get this straight. Ryan borrowed money from your uncle *and* your grandfather?"

"Forget I said anything. None of this matters. Uncle Porter is dead, and I shouldn't pass on things that might be embarrassing for other people. My mom would ground me for a year."

"Courtney, I need to know exactly what he said about Ryan. This is important."

"Uncle Porter told us Ryan came to him because he needed money. And that Ryan had borrowed money from the Gales more than once. I don't know any more than that, Marlee. I swear." Courtney reached over to pat my hand. "Don't look so worried. Even if your boyfriend owed money to Uncle Porter, I'm sure Sloane won't care about him paying it back. Not with all the money she'll inherit. Everything will be fine."

I disagreed. Last year, Ryan apparently went to Eric Gale for a loan. Then he borrowed more money from Porter this past spring. Why? Ryan had no reason to borrow money from Porter Gale. Not only did he hate Porter, but Ryan and the Zellars were financially sound.

Staring out at the lake, I tried to absorb this latest revelation. At least I had learned one thing. The bad blood between Ryan and Porter involved money, not tug-of-war contests or old orchard feuds. And as every police detective knew, the two prime motives for murder were love—and money.

Chapter Nine

Some people try to forget their troubles with margaritas or Krispy Kremes. I chose to bounce.

I'd forgotten how much fun it was to bounce on things. No wonder kids jumped on beds, trampolines, and inflatable houses. How lucky for me that I had my own Blueberry Blow Out Bounce House. Since the fairground had just opened for the day, only three children bounced with me, but we were having a loud and enjoyable time. Not only was jumping good for the hamstrings, it worked as a much-needed tension reliever.

After my conversation with Courtney, I hurried home, showered, and drove to the fairground. I'd scheduled myself to work at the Blow Out until four o'clock, when I would go on to work at the store until closing. After my hour taking tickets at the bounce house, I would man the Berry Basket vendor booth. I hoped to avoid the sight of the Blueberry Hill Death Drop, but I couldn't help but hear the screams of people plummeting from the ride's tower. Nor could I avoid thinking about what

Courtney told me. Why would Ryan need money? And why would he turn to Porter Gale for financial help? It made no sense.

I stopped trying to text or call Ryan. He should be returning to Oriole Point today or tomorrow. And what would I tell him when I saw him again? Call the police because they want to question you about Porter's death? Which meant I'd have to inform him that Porter had been murdered. I prayed he would be suitably shocked. If he wasn't, I didn't know what I'd do. Thinking about that rattled me, and I bounced off one of the walls, narrowly missing a little girl who sang "Let It Go" from *Frozen* at the top of her lungs as she jumped.

I bounced my way to the exit. Being upset about Porter's death and Ryan's possible involvement did not justify trampling a child in a bounce house. And I was wiped out. Bouncing for the better part of an hour will do that to you. As I stepped out of the inflatable house, two more children waited to enter. Behind them stood Piper Lyall-Pierce.

"Marlee, how did you take tickets if you were jumping around in there?" she asked.

"I'm capable of jumping *and* taking tickets. Don't forget I have a college degree."

"The bounce house has a sign out front restricting entrance to anyone over ten. If I ran the Blow Out this year, I'd make certain everyone adhered to the midway rules. No exceptions." She frowned. "You should see yourself. Perspiring, red-faced. With that ponytail, you don't even look old enough to order alcohol, let alone run a booth and a ride here."

"Thanks." I tightened the rubber band around my

offending ponytail, then slipped into my sandals. However I knew Piper did not mean it as a compliment. But I didn't have the money for her designer clothes or the personal glam squad who spent each morning readying her hair and face like she was Mariah Carey. Her two-person team had worked their magic again. Piper's ash-blond hair had been styled into her trademark chin-length bob that not even a tornado could dislodge. Her impeccable makeup reminded me of publicity photos of Old Hollywood movie stars—the classy ones like Gene Tierney and Olivia de Havilland. And her butter-yellow top and white culottes decorated with splashes of navy came from a runway collection, not Kohl's.

I cocked my head at her outfit. "Stella McCartney?"

"Don't be absurd. Carolina Herrera, Resort 2016. After a decade in New York City, I thought you knew your designers better than that." She shook her head at my white jeans and blue BERRY BASKET T-shirt. "Running that berry store has made you lose all sense of style."

"Sorry. All my money now goes into buying raspberry tea and blueberry vinegar." With a smile, I greeted the carnival worker assigned to the Bounce House. An amiable guy in his early fifties, Rex was my favorite of the three carnies who took turns overseeing this attraction.

Piper noticed him, too. "Good. You can leave now that someone's here to take tickets. I want you to stop by the Blueberry Fun House that Lionel and I have sponsored."

"I'd like to, but I need to set up my vendor booth."

"That can wait." Taking me by the elbow, she

steered me along the midway. "Lionel and I shut the fun house down last night. One of the mechanical figures malfunctioned. I sent a carny to find the person who repairs the rides, but no one ever showed up. Inexcusable! The festival planning committee should have hired independent contractors."

"They did. Jenco Amusements Midwest owns the rides, the games, the concession stands. Most of the people who work here—the carnies—are part of the Jenco package. When they break all this down at the end of the festival, everything will be trucked to Ohio for a Labor Day event. That includes the carnival workers." I pointed at the painted blueberry signs. "But the signage and artwork belong to the Blow Out committee. We can reuse them next year."

"How do you know all this?"

"The man who relieved me at the bounce house told me. He's traveled with Jenco for over twenty years. The season is only eight months long, and he finds other work in the off-season. Or goes on unemployment."

"Haven't you gotten cozy with the carnies. What next? Should Ryan be worried you'll run off with the guy who sells the deep-fried candy bars?"

"Don't be such a snob. Not everyone was born with an entire set of silver spoons in their mouth."

"How droll. I don't care how one earns their living, but I expect them to be reasonably competent. I haven't found that to be the case with the carnies I'm working with."

"No doubt there are a few bad apples in the

carnival barrel. On the first day of the Blow Out, I stopped two carnies from harassing Jacqueline Gale. They chased her through the crowd, whistling and calling her 'honey.'"

"Why would they harass Jacqueline? She's on the plain side, and over forty besides."

"I don't know if you're being sexist, ageist, or rude. First, Jacqueline is a nice-looking woman. Second, the two guys chasing after her had all the sex appeal of roadkill."

"Point taken." Piper pulled me closer to her. "I haven't had a chance to talk to you since Porter died on his Death Drop."

"That was a horrible shock."

"Was it? Porter spent his entire adult life eating and drinking like a frat boy. I heard he was drunk when he went on the ride. Then there was that pie he ate for the contest. A lunatic way for a diabetic to behave."

"I agree."

"Now Lionel has learned the police suspect the death was not due to natural causes. If that's true, the papers in Holland and Grand Rapids haven't seen fit to mention it yet. Lionel doesn't know more than that. And I've been too busy here to ask my own questions. After all, someone has to see to it the Blueberry Blow Out volunteers don't make too many mistakes."

"I spoke with the police yesterday morning." We halted by the cotton candy booth while I told Piper about the contents of the tampered-with insulin vial. The police had not instructed me to keep our conversation secret. And with Suzanne Cabot front and center as police receptionist, she'd get the news out there even if she were gagged. But I saw no reason to mention Ryan had access to insulin. Or that he owed Porter money.

After I confirmed another murder might have taken place in Oriole Point, Piper appeared vindicated, not troubled. "And everyone thought the misspelled T-shirts I ordered last year spelled disaster. Hah! Let's see the planning committee spin this."

"Piper, a man is dead."

"People die all the time. I can't cry over all of them. And I won't pretend Porter's death matters to me. The only Gale I knew well was Heather."

"Porter and Cara's mother?"

Piper nodded. "She joined the book club I started years ago, right after I saw how successful Oprah's was. Poor Heather. A sweet woman, far too good natured for Eric Gale."

"I heard she died of cancer."

"Lung cancer. Heather was a heavy smoker. I finally had to ban her from borrowing my books because they came back reeking of cigarette smoke. She didn't even quit smoking until a year before her death, although she'd already been sick for a good three years."

"And the present Mrs. Eric Gale was her nurse."

"I don't think Jacqueline is an RN. An LPN, maybe. When Heather grew worse, Eric Gale contacted a home health care agency in Grand Rapids. They recommended Jacqueline. I think her name was Jacqueline Turner then. She took care of Heather for five months, right up until hospice took over. Heather died two weeks later. I remember the funeral—standing room only. Everyone loved Heather."

"And Jacqueline became the second Mrs. Gale soon after?"

Piper lifted an eyebrow at me. "Yes. A mere three months later. Heather's friends didn't take kindly to that. But Eric never cared how things looked. Did you ever meet him?"

I shook my head.

"He was a man who let money and success coarsen him, and he was already quite coarse. Heather allowed him to walk all over her. And Jacqueline seems just as mousy. Probably one of the reasons why he married her. Not that he had much time to enjoy his bride."

"How long were they married before he died?"

"Let's see. They got married April of last year. He died right before Thanksgiving."

"Do you think Jacqueline had anything to do with Porter's death? It seems suspicious that three members of the Gale family have died in the past two years. And all since Jacqueline arrived at Blueberry Hill."

Piper didn't often belly-laugh, but she did then. When she was done, she put her hand on my shoulder. "Marlee, you may not know how to dress well, but you do amuse me. My dear, two of those Gales were critically ill. The doctors diagnosed Heather with terminal lung cancer long before Jacqueline arrived to help care for her. I know her oncologist, and two of the hospice workers are still part of my book club. If there had been anything suspicious about Heather's death, we would all have known about it."

"Maybe the first Mrs. Gale died a natural death," I persisted. "But what about Porter's dad? Eric Gale died only six months after marrying the younger woman who had nursed his dying wife. Don't you think that's odd?"

"What I think odd is that you care about any of this." Still chuckling, Piper once more took my arm and led me toward her fun house. "Eric Gale died of liver failure due to complications from his diabetes. That's the main reason he married Jacqueline so soon after his first wife died. He didn't have a lot of time left. To be blunt, he wanted a live-in nurse far more than he wanted another wife. And a wife was cheaper."

"Why did she marry him? It had to be for the money. After all, Jacqueline was more than twenty years younger than Eric Gale."

"The marriage probably guaranteed her a measure of financial security. But Eric never made any secret of the fact that Blueberry Hill would be passed down to his blowhard son." Piper looked a bit guilty. "I probably shouldn't speak about the dead like that. Only I was never a fan of either Eric or Porter. Some people do not know how to handle the responsibilities of wealth and privilege."

"Even if the deaths of his parents were natural, someone did murder Porter."

"I'd cross Jacqueline off the suspect list. Unless Porter's will has a startling bequest to his stepmother, I don't see how she profits by his death at all."

I sighed. "Probably not."

"You seem disappointed. Do you have some grudge against Jacqueline? If not, I don't know why you're bent on turning her into a murderess."

"She's the common denominator in the three Gale deaths." I had no intention of revealing that Ryan was under suspicion by the police. Before this murder case proceeded, I hoped to find someone with a better motive for the deed than the man I had promised to marry.

"Only one of the Gale deaths is suspicious. And I won't waste time worrying about it. Not when I have enough to worry about with this fun house." She pointed at the structure in front of us, its walls plastered with blueberries. A dark blue picket fence festooned with giant foam berries encircled it. "When the lights shine on it after dark, the effect is sinister."

"I never thought of blueberries as sinister, but it is eye-catching."

"Once you see what Lionel and I have come up with inside, you'll change your mind about how sinister blueberries can be. It cost us a pretty penny to alter the interior. There was nothing blueberry themed about the regular carnival fun house, so we did a thorough overhaul. I'm most proud of the Blueberry Burial Ground."

"Burial ground? This I have to see."

Before we could step inside, her husband Lionel walked out the front entrance of the fun house, which bore a sign saying TEMPORARILY SHUT FOR REPAIRS. A tall, broad-shouldered man with a voice as gloriously deep as James Earl Jones, Lionel Pierce possessed superb people skills, which helped him be elected our mayor. Even more noteworthy was his ability to gently keep Piper in check whenever she threatened to grow too overbearing. Most of Oriole Point thought the difficult-to-please Piper would never marry. But within months of meeting each other, the doyenne of Oriole Point and the retired African American executive became husband and wife. I found the match delightful, even if at times they behaved in too patrician a manner.

"Piper, we need to call our own repairmen," Lionel said after giving me a brief nod. "None of the carnival repair crew has shown up yet. We can't allow our fun house to be closed for another night. Half the proceeds go to charity."

"How difficult can it be to keep an animatronic figure operating?" Piper said.

"Two. Another one has broken down." He grimaced. "Ellen's not working correctly."

"You've named the mechanical figures in the fun house?" I asked.

Piper ignored me. "I'm suing that fool who sold us the animatronics."

"Let me call in a favor from an engineer I know. I promise we'll have things up and running again by dinner." With a wave, he marched off into the growing crowd on the midway.

Piper watched him with affection and approval. "This will be taken care of sooner than that. When Lionel goes into executive mode, he can move mountains. Meanwhile, I'll take you through the fun house. If you see anything that needs tweaking, let me know. We can add more."

"No need to go crazy, Piper." I followed her

inside. "This isn't the Haunted Mansion at Disney World."

But I spoke too soon. No sooner had the fun house door shut behind me than a five-foot-tall orange and black bird greeted me, its enormous beak gaping open.

"Whoa." I jumped back. "What's this?"

"A Baltimore oriole. Bigger than life-size, of course."

I eyed its large, shiny black claws. "It looks like a pterodactyl."

"Obviously, I had to pump it up. As lovely as orioles are, there's nothing scary about them." She patted the bird's feathers. "But this one is. Wait till you see the others."

I followed her down a corridor lined with distorting mirrors. Between each mirror stood another version of a dangerous—possibly psychotic—oriole. I hoped my baker Theo didn't venture inside. He adored birds, and seeing his favorite creatures turned into avian monsters might make him upset. Or simply confused.

Things didn't get better in the next room, filled with murderous-looking orioles perched on leafless black trees. At least these were closer to their actual size. All the birds had outstretched wings and wide-open beaks, preparing to pluck someone's eyes out probably. To add to the avian menace, a recording of bird caws sounded from an unseen speaker. More startling was the man in nineteenth-century costume lying facedown on the ground.

"Is he supposed to be dead?" I asked in a hushed voice.

She tapped a small white sign. "This lets visitors

know he is my ancestor Benjamin Lyall. We had to
include him in the fun house. After all, he founded
Oriole Point."

I looked down at the dummy. "Was that right
before he was pecked to death?"

"The dummy is asleep, not dead. You know
perfectly well Benjamin camped along the Oriole
River in 1830. When he awoke the next morning,
he saw flocks of orioles eating the berries of a mul-
berry tree. That's when he decided to found a town
right where he had camped and to name it Oriole
Point."

"This looks like a crime scene."

"I should hope so. That's the fun part."

"All I see are bare trees and demented birds. I
know you're proud of your family, but this *is* called
the Blueberry Fun House. You need to throw a few
blueberries in here. Even if you tell people they're
poisoned."

"Of course I have blueberries." Piper beckoned
for me to follow her.

Because of the shadowy light, I stepped carefully
to avoid the low-hanging branches. My ponytail got
tangled in one of them and I pried it free. Visitors
could easily trip in here. Or be impaled. As my hair
got caught again, something smacked me in the
face.

In front of me swayed an oriole, which hung
upside down from a branch. "Is this a strange oriole
bat?"

Piper stopped the bird from swinging. Because
its fake claws were fastened to the branch, she at-
tempted to right it, with no success. "It broke down.
We have to fix this bird because it's the only anima-

tronic figure in here. It says 'Nevermore' and flaps its wings."

"You're stealing lines from a raven?"

"Only from the best." She wagged her finger at me. "And I can't believe you haven't taught your garrulous parrot to say 'Nevermore.' Perfect for Halloween."

"So is this fun house."

"And we're just getting started."

But after exiting the room, only a long shadowy corridor—one without distorting mirrors—awaited us. "Now what?" I asked.

Strobe lights flashed on, sending pulsating beams everywhere. A second later, I felt a blast of air from the floor. Followed by another, and another.

Piper turned to me with a wide grin, made unnerving by the strobe lights. "Compressed air jets in the floor. Anyone wearing a skirt or dress will be embarrassed."

Squinting from the strobe lights, I felt my ponytail whip about from the air jets. "I'm still waiting for those blueberries." The words had no sooner left my lips when balls dropped from the ceiling. I ducked as they were buffeted about my head.

"Ping-Pong balls painted the color of blueberries," Piper explained. "Because they're attached to strings, you can't step on them. A startling effect, don't you think?"

Even more startling was the sight of her sleek blond bob completely un-mussed by the constant jets of air. Piper's glam squad must mix Gorilla Glue with her hair spray. I breathed a sigh of relief when we left behind the Ping-Pong balls and air jets via a door leading to a narrow hallway. I heard a rattling sound. Remembering the ping-pong balls and upside-down bird, I covered my head with my hands. Piper chuckled.

A panel in the wall opened, and a life-size figure rolled out. Like the dummy of Benjamin Lyall in the first room, this, too, wore nineteenth-century garb. But the figure was female and severe looking: white hair pulled back in a topknot, its doll eyes dark and accusing.

The figure lifted her right hand. "Beware the blueberry bog," a robotic voice said.

Although impressed with the fun house efforts of Piper and Lionel, I was disappointed she couldn't get the most basic things about berries straight. "Blueberries grow on bushes," I reminded Piper, "not in bogs."

"They do here."

I waited for something to happen. The ground to turn into a bog, maybe.

Piper sighed. "Lionel was right. Ellen is not working properly." She rolled the figure back into the hidden wall panel she had emerged from. "My ancestor Ellen Lyall deserves better than to be honored with a malfunctioning robot."

I peered at a white sign beside the hidden panel. It read ELLEN LYALL, WIFE OF ORIOLE POINT FOUNDER BENJAMIN LYALL, AND FIRST MATRIARCH OF THE COMMUNITY.

Oriole Point's original power couple reminded me of Sloane and Porter Gale. "Piper, do you think it's possible Sloane could have killed her husband?"

"Why not? Young, pretty wife. Lots of money to

be gained." She threw me a jaundiced look. "If Porter Gale was murdered, I'm sure the police are looking into her background even as we speak. I think she's from Delaware."

"I heard he met her in Baltimore."

"I don't care if she hails from Mars. Don't spoil my fun house talking about the Gales."

Eager to finish the tour, I marched down the short hallway that led to the next room. I paused at the doorway. The shadowy room appeared empty. And the lighting did not extend to a dark, suspicious-looking floor.

"The blueberry bog?" I tried to make out the shapes below me.

"Step inside," Piper said from behind me.

Taking a deep breath, I entered the room—and fell into a sea of plastic balls.

"It's a blueberry ball pit," Piper crowed.

Falling at least fifteen inches to land in a ball pit had not been pleasant. I struggled to find my footing in the pit, batting large balls out of the way. "I can't wait to see you in this pit!"

"If you had looked a little closer, you would have seen the narrow walkway by the wall. When the fun house is in full operation, we have it better lit so no one can miss it." Piper minced her way along the aforementioned catwalk while I floundered through the balls to the other side. "But most people will want to play in the ball pit."

"Except you." I batted another ball aside. "And me."

A short ladder at the other end of the ball pit allowed me to climb out. "I've had enough fun. How do I get out of here?" I grumbled as I entered yet another corridor. At the end of this one, a closed door awaited. A sign with the words BLUEBERRY BRIDGE shone above it.

I threw a warning look over my shoulder. "If I end up falling again, I'll beat you over the head with one of those stuffed birds."

Piper pushed past me. "Don't be such a stick-in-the-mud. No more surprise falls. To prove it, I'll go first."

The automatic door slid open at her approach. I hurried after her. The last thing I wanted was to be left alone in this loony bin. As the sign promised, a long swinging bridge spanned the room. At least everything was brightly lit, with no sinister birds or balls in sight. Instead, green trees and blueberry bushes decorated the walls. And lined up along one wall were at least a dozen mannequins. All of them wore costumes from different time periods, from the Colonial era to the early twentieth century.

"Welcome as we bridge the years from 1760 to the present," a taped voice announced from a speaker. "By following the lives and exploits of Oriole Point's celebrated Lyall family, we can trace the evolution of our great nation."

Piper squeezed my hand. "I wanted to include my Lyall ancestors in seventeenth-century Cornwall, but Lionel said we should keep it strictly American. Besides, we only had room in here for so many mannequins."

"I don't see what a bridge has to do with your family aggrandizement."

"Don't be sarcastic. People enjoy walking across a swinging bridge. And the intro mentions how the room will 'bridge the years.' Rather clever, I think."

The bridge swayed as I took my first steps on it, but it seemed sturdy. And the roped sides of the bridge were tall enough to prevent someone from toppling over. Below I saw only the dark shiny surface of the floor reflecting tiny purple and blue spotlights on the ceiling. Although the bridge swung with every movement, the motion was no more than a gentle rocking.

I stopped before each figure, trying without success to read the tiny font on the accompanying signs. At least the dummies were close enough so anyone on the bridge could stretch out an arm and touch them.

"They're all mannequins," Piper said. "Lionel and I didn't have enough time to get more animatronic figures created. Also, the expense was rather alarming."

"Who's this?" I pointed at a female figure who wore a blond wig of corkscrew curls and a homespun gray gown covered by a white apron. In her hands she held a metal basin.

"Prudence Edith Lyall. When her husband Josiah went off to fight in the Civil War, she joined the war effort by helping to nurse the wounded in several Union camps."

I moved on to the bewhiskered mannequin beside her, outfitted in suspenders, boots, and a hunting jacket. He cradled a shotgun in his crossed arms. "And this one?"

"Artemus Lancaster Lyall. The figure beside him is his sister, Cornelia Martha Lyall. From 1875 to the turn of the century, the pair was known as the best hunters in Oriole County."

This explained why the Lyall sister also wore boots and a hunting jacket, along with a calf-length brown corduroy skirt. Instead of a shotgun, Cornelia wielded a large hatchet.

"What did Cornelia hunt with a hatchet? Are you sure she isn't a Lyall ancestor who went all Lizzie Borden and hacked someone to death?"

"Cornelia and her brother both hunted with guns. But I only had one rifle to use in the display. That's why I gave Cornelia the hatchet. Although if you read her bio, you'll learn she did use a hatchet as a weapon in 1882."

I chuckled. "Did she run around the farm chopping off the heads of chickens?"

"Don't you know anything about the history of our town? In 1882, three rabid wolverines terrorized Oriole Point. Artemus and Cornelia hunted them down and killed them. Family legend claims she killed the last wolverine with a hatchet when it attacked her as she chopped down bushes." Piper held up her hand. "Before you ask, it wasn't a berry bush."

"I thought wolverines haven't been seen in Michigan since the 1700s. Where did this trio of killer wolverines come from?"

"How do I know? Maybe Canada. Anyway, Cornelia killed a wolverine with a hatchet, and Artemus shot two with a Henry repeating rifle. Those very ones, by the way. They're part of the family antique collection."

"Wait a second. This is real?" I leaned closer to the mannequin brandishing the hatchet. When I reached to pluck the hatchet from the mannequin's hand, Piper stopped me.

"Don't touch it. We have the objects affixed to the figures so they don't fall off. But it wouldn't take much to dislodge them."

"Exactly. Anyone on this bridge could steal the rifle or this." I frowned at the shiny, lethal-looking hatchet. "What if some nutjob comes in here and decides to go postal?"

"Don't be ridiculous. More likely a teenager would grab it as a joke."

"That's just as bad. Piper, replace the iron hatchet with one made out of plastic. You can't leave a hatchet within arm's reach in an amusement park attraction. That's like leaving butcher knives lying around."

She looked surprised. "How did you know there are butcher knives in the Blueberry Burial Ground?"

"I didn't." I followed her across the bridge. "And I should confiscate the knives."

"You'll never reach them." Wearing a smug smile, Piper ushered me into a spooky chamber filled with tombstones and skeletons hung from the ceiling. A wind machine kept the skeletons swinging, their bony toes brushing the heads of any visitor over five feet five. The skeletons did hold butcher knives, but they were just out of reach. I feared Piper was as well, at least where this fun house was concerned. Although a closer look revealed it would be easy to pull a skeleton down and snatch its knife.

"Okay, why is this a blueberry burial ground?" I

read the names on the tombstones. They appeared to be Lyall ancestors. "Did they all die of blueberry-related botulism?"

"No, but that isn't a bad idea. I simply thought a graveyard was a perfect way to end the fun house ride. And visitors get to learn a little of my family history."

"A little? By the time people leave here, they'll know more about the Lyalls than the Kennedy family." With the exit door in sight, I quickened my pace.

"I certainly hope so. The Lyalls have been much more decorous."

At the end of the room stood a raised grave—the tombstone above it larger than the others. As soon as I moved directly in front, the tombstone flew open like a door. A deafening growl filled the air before a furry animal lunged right for me.

With a scream, I fell backward onto the floor. A large badger-like creature stared down at me. It was a stuffed animal, the growl recorded on some damn tape machine.

"That's one of the rabid wolverines!" Piper said, choking with laughter.

I looked over my shoulder at her. "You're lucky I don't have a hatchet on me, Piper. Otherwise the next Blueberry Burial Ground tombstone would have your name on it."

Chapter Ten

After the rabid wolverine attack, I retreated for what I hoped would be a few relaxing hours at my Berry Basket fairground booth. But every local seemed to make their way to me at some point during the day, all of them eager to talk about Porter Gale's unexpected death. The fact that it occurred on his own Blueberry Hill Death Drop made the subject especially poignant. And irresistible.

The police hadn't yet released information regarding the tampered-with insulin. Today's conversations revealed the general consensus that Porter died of some combination of diabetes, bad diet, and the stress of a death tower ride. Although several people did mention rumors claiming he had been murdered. The gossip meter would go through the roof once it became official. I also learned the Blueberry Hill Death Drop had grown even more popular since Monday night. I found this ghoulish, but not surprising. What did surprise me was the sight of Wyatt Gale operating the Ferris wheel that afternoon.

More than one local who visited my booth remarked that the nephew of Porter Gale should have been at home with his grieving family, not at the carnival. I didn't mention his younger sister began her day sunbathing on the beach. Except for their mother, I doubted any of the O'Neills grieved at all. Although, as Courtney hinted, Cara might be more guilt stricken than sorrowful. Unresolved family feuds left emotional wreckage behind. So did murder.

At least Sloane had behaved as any woman would upon learning her husband had been murdered: sedated and under a doctor's care. Unless she only pretended to grieve. My cynicism made me feel like a dreadful person. What if she was innocent of her husband's death? Sloane was only twenty-four. And Porter died right in front of her. As Chief Hitchcock reminded me, shock and grief were natural reactions to something as unnatural as murder. But I'd been involved with three murder cases, beginning with the Chaplins. It had left its mark. I found it harder to trust people now, no matter how innocent they might appear.

If Sloane Gale inherited the bulk of the Blueberry Hill estate, she had a strong motive for murdering her husband. Film noir and detective novels were filled with "black widows"; so was real life. Natasha, another sexy young widow in Oriole Point, had also been under suspicion in the murder of her rich husband. Because she was a friend of mine, I never believed Natasha to be guilty. But I understood why many people in town did. I also would have sympathized with her had she actually killed him.

A former Russian beauty queen, Natasha Rostova married a local real estate tycoon twice her age and lived to regret it. A number of people in Oriole Point had reason to murder Cole Bowman, her abusive and malicious husband. One of them did. And I played no small role in catching the killer. The end result was justice served, the guilty punished, and Natasha left a relieved and wealthy widow. I wondered how similar her story was to Sloane's. Who really knew what went on behind the closed doors of a marriage? Or was that my misgivings about marriage speaking?

As though I had summoned her with my thoughts, Natasha emerged from the midway crowd like a Victoria's Secret model slumming at the fairground. With a curvaceous figure often enhanced by short skirts and clingy dresses, and a wavy mass of almond-brown hair, Natasha Bowman turned heads just as much as she provoked gossip. A pity more people hadn't taken the time to get to know her as I had. They would have learned how warm, funny, and generous she was. And more than a little indiscreet.

Catching sight of me, Natasha waved with one hand, while she tugged at the arm of the older gentleman beside her. Naturally, she was with Wendall Bowman, the uncle of her dead husband. The twenty-eight-year-old former Miss Russia and the seventy-year-old retired inventor had been inseparable since Cole's murder, and no one knew if their relationship should be viewed as romantic or avuncular. Wendall, known to everyone as Old Man

Bowman, had helped rescue her from his abusive nephew. Was this gratitude on Natasha's part . . . or something more? I wasn't sure I wanted to find out, but Andrew and Dean spent hours discussing the subject.

"First time I've seen either of you at the Blow Out this week," I said when the pair reached my booth.

Natasha bent down to give me air kisses. "I mean to come, but there is much to do. We drive to Chicago yesterday to handle more business. Uncle Wendall makes us leave too early. I do not know why. It is an hour earlier in Chicago. So I am tired before we get there, and then I must be busy with lawyers and people who sell buildings. They explain what I should do with all the properties I now own."

Along with dozens of acres in the surrounding county, Cole's death left Natasha the owner of a number of commercial buildings on Lyall Street, including the one that housed my shop. I couldn't have asked for a better landlady. Especially after dealing with her late husband, who made Scrooge appear warmhearted.

"And there are tax things. What do I know about taxes? In Russia, we do not fill out tax return. Government takes it out of paycheck. I know government is not honest, but at least we do not worry about tax papers and file forms."

"If you need help, I have an accountant you can call," I said.

"Don't bother, I've got three. And they're all afraid of me." Old Man Bowman grinned. "So are my lawyers."

Natasha shook her head. "It makes me crazy, all this lawyer talk, when all I want is to build my spa.

And sell my house. And find new place to live. I am lucky Wendall is at the meetings with me. He has been rich a long time. They cannot fool him."

"Damn right they can't." Old Man Bowman winked at me. "I had a few of 'em try to cheat me after my invention brought in big money. Put them in their place, I did. I sure as hell won't let them pull any funny business with Natasha. Trust me, I know my way around those snakes in Armani suits."

I marveled he knew what an Armani suit was. I eyed his cargo shorts, loose cotton shirt, and Birkenstock sandals. This was Old Man Bowman's daily uniform until winter arrived, at which time he donned a pair of socks and a jacket. As an added touch, his long white hair hung down his back in a skinny twisted ponytail. He made a striking contrast to Natasha, currently decked out in a turquoise summer minidress, five-inch espadrilles, and a Chanel straw handbag that jerked about on her arm.

I looked at the handbag more closely. "Is Dasha in there?"

The head of a Yorkshire terrier popped up and gave a tiny yip.

"Of course I bring Dasha." Natasha raised the purse so she and her Yorkshire touched noses. "I cannot leave my baby at home. She will miss her mama."

"She takes the little thing everywhere. Even to the lawyers." Old Man Bowman rolled his eyes. "Back in my day, dogs stayed at home unless you needed them for hunting. Although with the kind of hunting I do now, I wouldn't risk bringing a dog. Too dangerous."

Old Man Bowman had spent the last thirty years

of his life trying to capture Bigfoot. Once every season, he went up north on another Bigfoot hunting trip loaded with traps, cameras, and guns—but apparently not dogs.

"It looks like things are dangerous around here as well," I said. "I'm assuming you've heard about Porter Gale."

"The Blueberry Hill man? *Da,* he is man who dies on the tower ride." She crossed herself. "Is bad luck to give something the name of 'death.' The spirits do not like it. They think you make fun of them."

"Natasha's right," Old Man Bowman said. "Don't tempt fate."

"I don't think angry spirits had anything to do with Porter's death. But someone must have been angry at him."

He narrowed his eyes at me. "You saying we had another killing in Oriole Point?"

In another day or two, news of Porter's murder would break. Maybe sooner, given that Lionel and Piper already heard rumors. I saw no reason to keep it a secret from Natasha and Old Man Bowman; they mainly socialized with me and each other. "Let's say his death is suspicious."

"Blueberry Hill is famous. That mean this Porter man is rich. Is why he is killed. People are jealous of rich people. And now I am rich, maybe I must be afraid." Natasha cuddled Dasha even closer, as if her terrier might in danger, too.

"I bought Natasha a gun," Old Man Bowman told me. "Nice little .38 special, perfect for a lady's hand. Soon as we got it registered, I took her to the gun range. Now we go every week. She's a natural. Can shoot your eye out at twenty yards."

"Is true," Natasha said with pride. "I am what they call a 'shark shooter.'"

"She means 'sharpshooter,'" he said in a stage whisper.

"I figured." I wasn't sure how comfortable I felt about Natasha shooting people's eyes out, but at least she'd be able to defend herself if another abusive man entered her life again. Although Old Man Bowman would probably deal with him first. I beckoned him closer. "You've known the Gale family for decades. If Porter was murdered, who's the likeliest suspect?"

He shrugged. "Might be a rival fruit grower. Porter didn't wear his success well. Treated his workers like gold, but he loved to brag and embarrass the other growers. Made fun of them in public all the time. Led to a lot of bad feelings. And he did it long before his daddy died."

I remembered the tug-of-war brawl, the air filled with tension even before the contest began. "The police will look into his dealings with all the growers, don't you think?"

"The grower with the biggest grudge against him would be his own sister Cara," he said. "No love lost there. Brother and sister been sniping at each other for twenty years. I was at the Sandy Shoals Saloon the day Eric Gale's will was read. Cara came in with her husband Brody, both of them angrier than Bigfoot protecting his feeding ground. I don't blame them, neither. Eric didn't leave a dime to Cara, not even any trusts for her kids. No call for someone to do that to their own flesh and blood."

"Cara told me her father always favored Porter. But if she was enraged about being left out of the will, why wait nearly a year to kill her brother?"

He gave me a knowing look. "There's an old saying, 'Revenge is a dish best eaten cold.'"

"Maybe." I glanced down the line of vendor booths to where O'Neill Blueberries had set up shop. For the past few hours, their booth had been run by Jessica O'Neill, Brody's cousin. But in the past hour, her place had been taken by Wyatt. Tipped back in his chair, he'd been texting on his phone every time I looked over.

I gestured in Wyatt's direction. "Clearly, the family isn't shaken up by Porter's death. Wyatt spent the day running the Ferris wheel. Now he's selling blueberry butter at their booth."

"I respect that. Don't pretend to feel something you don't. And everyone in the county knew Porter and his sister could barely stand each other."

Natasha sighed. "I do not know about this brother and sister. But I do know I want to have fun at the Blow Out. There is much we have to see. We rode carousel. And roller coaster, but Dasha not like. I went in Fun House, which was not fun at all."

Recalling my own time in the Blueberry Bog, I agreed. At least Piper and Lionel must have gotten their repairs done; otherwise, the attraction would still have been closed.

"But Uncle Wendall promises to take me on something called Tilt-A-Whirl."

"And the bumper cars," he added. "I'll give little Dasha credit. She likes the rides as much as Natasha does."

"Of course. She is my brave baby." Natasha kissed

her again. "Oh, and I want to win one of those big stuffed animals at the shooting range."

"One of the carnies told me the gunsights are crooked," I told Old Man Bowman. "Adjust your aim accordingly before shooting."

He laughed. "She's the one who'll be shooting, not me."

Natasha looked insulted. "Yes. I am the shark shooter, not Wendall."

"Sorry. I forgot."

"And tell the man you're going to marry to be a little friendlier," Old Man Bowman said.

"What did Ryan do?" I asked.

"Acted like he didn't know who I was. Here we were honking the horn and waving 'hi' to him, and he turned his back on us like we was both strangers."

Natasha nodded. "Is true."

While Ryan didn't care for either Natasha or Old Man Bowman, I never imagined he'd be rude to them. "When did this happen?"

"Early yesterday morning at the gas station. I'd just got back in the car when Ryan drove up. He went to the pump at the other end."

"I thought you both drove to Chicago yesterday morning."

"*Da*. And early." Natasha sighed. "I am tired as baby."

"We stopped at a gas station in Indiana," Old Man Bowman said. "Near the exit for Valparaiso."

"It couldn't have been Ryan," I explained. "He's on a fishing trip with his buddy Josh. And he would have been headed north toward Muskegon. Not south."

"I'm telling you what I saw. Your boyfriend was at a gas station in Indiana yesterday morning around seven thirty." He screwed up his face as if thinking. "We was maybe forty minutes or so from Chicago then. I stopped because Natasha wanted coffee, but I decided to buy some beef jerky for myself as a snack."

"I'm sorry. Whoever you saw, it wasn't Ryan. He would have barely arrived at Josh's house in Muskegon by then."

"There was a man with Ryan," Natasha said. "Maybe it was this Josh."

I didn't know whether to be irritated that they persisted with this, or alarmed. "I doubt it."

"Does his college buddy have pitch-black hair that he wears in a buzz cut?" Old Man Bowman shot me a shrewd look. "And a birthmark on his left cheek? This was a big guy. As tall as Ryan, but about eighty pounds heavier."

"He had very big nose," Natasha said. "Like *murav'yed*. What you call 'anteater.'"

I needed a stunned moment before I could answer. "That sounds like Josh."

Bowman nodded. "Then it was Ryan and his buddy. And they were in Indiana. Maybe they planned to rent a boat and go fishing somewhere south."

"Josh has his own boat. He keeps his cruiser docked in Muskegon Harbor." What was going on? Why did Ryan lie about going to Muskegon to fish with Josh? And what were they doing in Indiana? Were the two men headed to Chicago or farther south? If so, for what purpose?

"Well, I don't care where they was headed," he

grumbled. "It's only decent for a man to return another man's friendly greeting."

Natasha must have realized this news had upset me because she tapped the old man on the shoulder. "Leave Marlee alone. It is not her fault Ryan does not say hello. Maybe Ryan does not realize it is us." She gave a careless lift to one shoulder. "Or he does not like us. That is why he turns away. What does it matter? I am finally at Blow Out and I want to win a stuffed animal. And maybe we can eat one of those ears of elephants. Now Marlee must sell her berry things. We have bothered her enough." She bent down and gave me a quick hug.

With a resigned grunt, Old Man Bowman let Natasha lead him away. I envied them. They had nothing to think about tonight but carnival rides and sugary treats. While the only thing I would be able to think about was that Ryan had lied to me . . . again.

Chapter Eleven

When some people become angry, it's best to leave them alone until their anger has cooled down. I'm not one of those people. The longer I thought about things, the more worked up I got. After my conversation with Natasha and Old Man Bowman, I spent my remaining three hours at the fairground growing more irritated by the minute.

If Ryan and Josh decided to change their plans, why keep it a secret? Unfortunately, I couldn't reach him, although I tried a half dozen times. Since there was no cell reception out on the lake, I understood when Ryan told me he kept his phone turned off while on Josh's boat. On occasion, he sent a brief affectionate text, but not often. It didn't bother me. I wasn't the clingy sort. And I had enough to do at The Berry Basket.

I didn't mind if Ryan enjoyed spending a little time away from work—and me. As someone who had been single for thirty years, I enjoyed my alone time. Why wouldn't he enjoy fishing with his best buddy? It never occurred to me that he might be doing something else. Was another woman the reason for these trips? I doubted it. Natasha and Old Man Bowman had seen him with Josh, which meant half of what Ryan told me was true. But why were he and Josh in a gas station outside Valparaiso, Indiana, instead of a hundred and fifty miles north in Muskegon?

Maybe they changed plans and decided to go to Chicago. Or perhaps they met up with someone in Indiana. But I was awake yesterday morning when Ryan left at six thirty. He explained how he needed to get on the road ASAP because Josh wanted to be on the lake before eight. Except he and Josh were in Indiana. No matter how I tried to spin it, Ryan was keeping something from me.

By the time I brought the vendor booth boxes back to my downtown store, Gillian had closed The Berry Basket. I was glad. No one could see me stomp about the store as I held an imaginary—and accusatory—conversation with Ryan. While I ranted aloud, I threw in too many arm gestures, knocking over a neatly stacked pile of kitchen towels decorated with raspberries. Refolding them helped calm me down.

"Get a grip on yourself," I said aloud while smoothing the last of the folded towels. "Might as well save this energy for when Ryan returns." If he kept to his usual fishing trip schedule, it could be as early as tonight. Certainly, he'd be back no later than tomorrow.

Drained by the long day at the fairground, I wanted to eat dinner and enjoy a little chat with Minnie. Because I'd been at the Blow Out all day, Minnie had stayed home. She must be dying for company, or at least a willing listener. But I couldn't go home until I'd entered the daily receipt totals on the computer.

To keep me going, I ate one of the pastries that hadn't sold out today: a mini blueberry cheesecake. Perched at my computer on the store counter, I counted the cash and change in the register drawer. Next, I opened the small metal cashbox I used at the fairground and tallied its contents. I'd just entered the last of these figures in my computer when one of my large hoop earrings fell off. Since both ears were sore, I pulled the other off as well. Even my jewelry wanted to call it a day. Before I could, someone knocked on my shop door.

It was after nine thirty and growing dark. But lots of tourists still walked past my window. Maybe one of them saw my lights on and hoped I might reopen for a quick peek. I'd done it before. After-hours visitors often resulted in sales. I closed up the cashbox on the counter, laying my earrings on top of it. But when I hurried to the door and opened it, Wyatt O'Neill stood outside. He held a cardboard box labeled BERRY BASKET.

"You left this under your booth at the fairground," he said. "One of the other vendors spotted it. I had to drive my buddy Seth home. He lives only three blocks from here. Thought I might as well drop it off."

"Thank you so much. I can't believe I didn't see it. That's the box holding my berry syrups." I reached for the box.

"Nah. It's heavy. I'll take it in for you."

I held open the door to let him enter the shop. "Put it on the counter. Thank you again. We've all been putting in extra hours because of the Blow Out, and I think it's starting to show."

"Tell me about it. Bad enough I work at the farm, now I'm pulling shifts at the fairground." Wyatt placed the box on the counter. "I don't mind running the Ferris wheel. But I'm bored stiff at the O'Neill booth. I'm not doing that again, no matter what my parents say."

"How are your parents?"

"Upset."

"I'm sorry about your uncle."

"Yeah." He slouched against the counter. "I guess these things happen."

According to what Courtney said at the beach this morning, the police had informed the O'Neill family that Porter had died under suspicious circumstances. Wyatt had to know this, yet he seemed to be taking a casual attitude about it. It could be a pose. Even though he was twenty, Wyatt affected the indifference of a teenager. The gangly young man looked like one, too: thick mop of shoulder-length hair, ripped jeans, Yeezy Boost sneakers, silver piercings in his ears and nose.

"I heard Sloane isn't doing well."

Wyatt's indifferent mask dropped to reveal a concerned expression. "I feel bad for Sloane. She's really upset. But I think she's more in shock than anything else. The doctors gave her something to sleep. We all went to the house right after Uncle Porter died, and she was hysterical. Screaming, sobbing, knocking things over." He shot me a questioning look. "Is that how people act when someone dies? None of us even cried when Grandpa Gale died."

I walked over to my computer and shut it down.

"I think it depends on how well loved a person is. Obviously, your aunt loved Porter."

He grimaced. "I don't think of Sloane as my aunt. She's only twenty-four. I'm almost as old as she is. I bet she hasn't had a lot of people close to her die. Probably why she fell apart like she did. Let's be honest. It isn't like she was married to my uncle all that long."

"They'd been together over a year. And they must have loved each other."

"Maybe. It looked like it was all about sex with those two. Not that I blame Uncle Porter. Sloane's beautiful. But he didn't appreciate her."

"Why do you say that?"

"I saw with my own eyes every time I went to Blueberry Hill. Uncle Porter left her alone too much while he handled the business. She had nothing to do but swim, work out in the basement gym, and watch TV. All by herself, too. If Sloane was mine, I'd be with her twenty-four-seven."

This confirmed not only what Courtney told me, but what I'd witnessed myself. Wyatt had a serious crush on Sloane. Although *crush* sounded like a juvenile term when talking about two people in their twenties.

"Now she's really going to be alone," he continued. "Sloane's not close to her own family. She has an older sister somewhere that she likes, but I don't think they see each other all that much. And her friends live back east. So Sloane is on her own. I feel terrible for her."

"You seem to know a lot about Sloane."

"I visited Blueberry Hill as much as I could. And I made time to talk to her. She liked talking to me, too. Otherwise it would have been just her all by herself on that huge property."

"Jacqueline lives on Blueberry Hill, too. Their houses can't be more than a couple minutes' walk from each other. Didn't the two of them spend time together?"

"Not much. Sloane and Jacqueline get along okay, but they have nothing in common. C'mon, Sloane's young enough to be her daughter. And did you ever spend time with Jacqueline? She's the single most boring person I ever met. I don't know why Grandpa Gale married her. She's not even pretty."

"There's nothing wrong with the way Jacqueline looks," I said. "Not every woman cares about makeup and fashion."

"It's too bad she never let Sloane give her a makeover. Sloane's been dying to fix her up. If anyone can make Jacqueline look decent, it's Sloane." His gaze fell on the empty plate on the counter; I'd eaten my mini cheesecake, leaving only crumbs. "Do you have anything left to eat? A muffin? Cupcakes?"

"There are a dozen blueberry mini cheesecakes left in the refrigerator. You can have all of them. Theo will be making a fresh batch tomorrow morning." Hurrying into the shop kitchen, I grabbed a plate, fork, and the pastry tray in the fridge holding the remaining cheesecakes. After putting three of them on the plate, I boxed up the remaining cakes for Wyatt to take home. As I tied string around the pastry box, I smelled a sweet fragrance coming from the store. I frowned. I knew Wyatt was a stoner, but he had no right to light up a joint in my store.

Marching back into the shop, I found Wyatt smoking pot. "You need to put that out. Pot is illegal, and the last thing I need is for a tourist or the local police to suspect I'm letting people get high in here."

"The store's closed. No one will see." He took another toke.

"I'm not kidding, Wyatt."

He pinched the end of his joint. "I didn't know you were such an old lady."

"And I didn't know you were such an idiot as to smoke grass in downtown Oriole Point." I pointed at four tourists who had stopped to admire my window display. "If the door had been open, they would have smelled your joint."

I placed the pastries on the counter, reminding myself to not be hard on him. After all, his uncle had been murdered two days ago. "Here you are. I boxed up nine mini cakes for you to take back to your family. And I put three on a plate for you. Why don't you sit at one of the bistro tables? If you're thirsty, I have berry iced teas in the cooler. Bottled water, too."

"Water." He sat down at the table. "I hate tea."

Once I gave him the water, Wyatt turned his attention to the mini cheesecakes. "These are good." Ignoring the fork I'd given him, Wyatt chose to eat the cheesecakes with his hands.

"I'll pass on your compliments to Theo." I sat across from him. "I spoke to Courtney at the beach today. She said the police informed your family they have reason to believe Porter did not die a natural death."

Wyatt unscrewed the water bottle and took a

long swig. "Yeah. Looks like someone had a big-ass grudge against him. My mom and sister don't believe it. They think Uncle Porter died because he didn't take care of himself. You know, the diabetes thing."

"Oh, no." I looked at the cheesecakes in alarm. "I'm sorry. I shouldn't have given you any pastry. Your mom told me that you're diabetic, too."

He moved the plate closer to him. "I can eat this. I'm only a little bit diabetic."

That sounded like being a little bit pregnant.

"Mom had better stop telling everyone I'm diabetic," he went on. "People will think I'm sick or something. Uncle Porter had a bad case of diabetes. Not me. I only need to check my insulin once in a while. But Uncle Porter had to shoot up a bunch of times a day."

"Did the police tell you how they think your uncle was killed?"

He finished off the second mini cheesecake in a few bites, increasing my guilt. "Yeah. Something about his insulin being switched to potassium chloride. They explained it's a metal salt. Got no odor, no color. The police said it had been dissolved in water." Wyatt picked up the third cheesecake. "Easy to get hold of. Hell, most farms use it in their fertilizer. Mom said people take potassium chloride for some diseases. So I don't understand how it killed Uncle Porter."

I had conducted my own research on the Internet, where I learned potassium chloride was available as a prescription medication to treat insufficient potassium levels in patients suffering from an electrolyte imbalance. Common side effects involved gastric upset. But diabetics such as Porter Gale who suffered from kidney problems already had high levels of potassium. By injecting himself with potassium chloride, Porter had effectively overdosed on the drug. Within minutes, it had produced severe heart arrhythmia and sudden cardiac death.

I explained this to Wyatt, who seemed more interested in the cheesecake than the particulars of his uncle's death. "The police will be looking for anyone who had a reason to want your uncle out of the way," I said. "The person at the top of the suspect list is often the spouse. Especially if the dead husband or wife had a lot of money."

"Are you trying to say Sloane killed my uncle?" He smirked. "Get out of here. Sloane's the best. She couldn't hurt anyone."

"I'm not saying she did. But the police are certain to investigate her, particularly if she inherits Blueberry Hill."

"They'll be wasting their time. Whoever did it knew a lot about drugs. Maybe it was Jacqueline. She's a nurse. You know she still works one day a week at some free clinic in Grand Rapids. I bet Jacqueline could get her hands on anything she wanted there."

"Or the murderer simply researched a good drug to kill a diabetic with."

"Yeah, but Jacqueline's the only person in the family who knows about medicine and diabetes."

"Actually, your entire family has a working knowledge of it. After all, your grandfather suffered from the disease. Along with you and your uncle. Besides, why would Jacqueline kill Porter? Do you think she's angry because your grandfather left everything to Porter and nothing to her?"

"Jacqueline wasn't cut out of my grandfather's will. She's allowed to live in the big house for as long as she wants. Well, she'll have to leave if she gets remarried. And she inherited sixty thousand dollars. Grandpa Gale wrote in the will that she would get ten thousand dollars for every month they had been married. Too bad she wasn't a better nurse. She might have kept him alive longer. More money for her." He wiped his mouth with the back of his hand. "I guess she deserved it. Being married to an old sick guy can't have been fun."

"I didn't know Jacqueline had inherited the Blueberry Hill house. I thought Porter was just being kind."

"Kind to Jacqueline? He thought she was a drag. And he didn't like her marrying his dad so soon after his mother died. But the will said she can't be kicked out of the house. Although Uncle Porter always hated the place. That's why he built that cool modern house when he got married to his first wife. Besides, Uncle Porter walked away with everything else." His face darkened. "Pissed the hell out of my mom. Me too. My grandfather totally shut me and my sister out of his will. We're half Gales. We deserve half of that Blueberry Hill money."

"I saw you sitting with your uncle at Trappers Corner on Monday night. You two looked like you got along."

"Sure. Why not? I mean, I am his nephew." He paused. "*Was* his nephew. I didn't see any reason to act all resentful around him, like my mom did. And I barely get by on my O'Neill paychecks. Why would

I be stupid enough to get on the bad side of my rich uncle?"

"Then he helped you out when you needed money?"

Having eaten three mini cheesecakes, Wyatt turned his full attention on me. "Sometimes. We were family. And I worked at Blueberry Hill once in a while. But I had to keep that secret from my mom."

"Did your uncle pay you for working there?"

"Damn right he did. Twice what my parents pay me. I think he only did it because he hoped my mom would find out. The two of them always tried to score points off each other. Drove my mother crazy that Uncle Porter always won."

I gave him a sobering look. "Not always."

"Yeah, I guess she did win." He ran a hand through his tangled hair. "Uncle Porter's dead."

"And someone killed him."

"Shows there are a lot of nutjobs in this world."

It didn't seem to occur to him that one of those nutjobs might be in his own family. "Why do you think he was murdered?"

"How the hell do I know? He was successful. I'm sure the other fruit growers wanted him gone. Maybe one of them had the balls to do it. A berry grower with berry balls." He chuckled.

"Wyatt, you don't seem that upset by all this."

"What do you want me to do? Get hysterical like Sloane?"

"No. But Porter was your uncle. The two of you looked friendly the other day at the Blow Out. It would be only natural to feel sad or shocked. A little upset, maybe."

He stood up, scraping the chair back. "I am upset. That's why I needed to smoke a little weed. But you had to start acting like a stupid narc."

"Your uncle was murdered. That's a terrible thing. You're allowed to show emotion."

"Back off, Marlee. This is none of your business." He snatched up the white box of mini cheesecakes. "But don't be surprised if your boyfriend is acting happier than usual. Instead of hinting around that Sloane offed my uncle, you should be looking at Ryan. 'Cause he took more money from Uncle Porter than I ever did."

"Yes, I heard about that. I wonder if you know why Ryan asked your uncle for money."

"I don't poke my nose into other people's business," he said with a sneer. "You should do the same. And why don't you ask Ryan about this? Unless you're afraid of the answer." Wyatt yanked open the shop door. "But thanks for the cake, Marlee. And I won't tell my mom how you fed me sugar even though you know I'm diabetic."

With his mocking laugh still ringing in my ears, I locked the door after he left. Every time I had an encounter with Wyatt, I remembered why I didn't like him. I should have thanked him for returning the box to me and gave him the cheesecakes in return without any conversation.

I shut off the lights in the store, except for the one above the front counter. But when I reached for the cashbox I'd used at the fairground, I stopped. Before I let Wyatt in, I had placed my earrings on top of the box. Now they lay on the counter beside it.

With a sinking heart, I turned on my computer and opened the file where I had recorded today's receipts. Lifting the lid of the metal box, I quickly recounted the money, then compared it to what I had recorded no more than twenty minutes earlier. The total was two hundred dollars short.

While I had been in the back room to get cheesecake for Wyatt, he did more than light up a joint. He stole my money.

Chapter Twelve

By the time Tess entered the Sourdough Café, I was well into my second vanilla latte. She didn't need my big wave to spot me; I'd snagged one of a handful of tables that only seated two. The rest of the café tables and booths were large enough to hold eight diners.

Slinging her purse over the back of the chair, Tess sat across from me, a bit out of breath. "I didn't expect an invite to an impromptu breakfast at Sourdough. And on a Thursday, too."

Because of our work schedules during high season, we usually only ate here for an early Sunday breakfast in the summertime. "There was an incident last night at the store."

She shot me a nervous look. "Does it involve a dead body?"

"No. Only some petty larceny. But there is a connection of sorts to a dead—"

"I assume neither of you need a menu," Drea, my favorite waitress at the café, interrupted me. "You've both eaten here more times than our cook."

Tess and I smiled up at the young woman. "My usual," I told her. "A California scramble, rye toast, no potatoes."

"Baked blueberry French toast for me," Tess said. "And a cup of Earl Grey."

"Wait a second. That sounds good. I'll have the blueberry French toast, too."

After Drea left, Tess yawned. "I forgot to set the alarm on my phone last night and overslept. If you hadn't called, both David and I would still be snoring." She spread a napkin on her lap. "Shouldn't you be at yoga right now?"

"Not feeling in much of a namaste mood today."

"Tell me about this petty larceny. Did someone break into The Berry Basket last night?"

"Nope." I sipped my latte. "I had an after-hours visitor: Wyatt O'Neill."

"I'm not a Wyatt fan. And I wouldn't have let him in after closing. Or any of his friends."

"Have you had a bad experience with Wyatt?"

"Tell me about your incident first."

"I'd finished tallying the day's receipts and entered the numbers in the computer, when Wyatt showed up at my door. He had a legitimate reason for being there. I'd left a box of syrups behind at my vendor booth, and he was nice enough to return them to me."

She appeared skeptical. "Seems uncharacteristic, but go on."

"I let him in, of course. He mentioned he was hungry, so I went in the back to get some pastry from the kitchen. I was gone only three or four minutes." I didn't bother to mention he'd lit up a joint during the interval. "He ate, we talked about his uncle, then he left. That's when I noticed the earrings I'd left on top of the metal cashbox had been moved." I paused as Drea set down a mug of tea before Tess.

"Let me guess." Tess spooned honey into her tea. "Wyatt stole money from the box."

"Two hundred dollars."

"Did you call the police?"

"No. His uncle was murdered this week. The family has enough to deal with without me bringing charges of theft against their son. But I thought you should know."

"Why?" After blowing on her tea, Tess took a tentative sip.

"Wyatt has shown that he's a thief. A brazen one, too. You and David need to be on your guard if he ever turns up at Oriole Glass."

"Too late. We're familiar with the light fingers of Wyatt O'Neill." She sighed. "If I'd known he was still doing this kind of stuff, I would have warned *you*."

"Did he steal from your store? When?"

"Four years ago, before you moved back to Oriole Point. It was during the Holiday Open House at Christmastime. David and I held a glassblowing demonstration in the shop. Business is always great for our demos, and we had a big crowd. Wyatt and three of his friends were there that night. I remember because they kept calling out stupid things for us to make, like reindeer tails. Everything went well until after we'd finished blowing our last glass figurine."

"What happened?"

"A woman discovered her wallet was missing.

Since she purchased an item from us right before the demo began, she had her wallet when she entered our store. Someone snatched it during the glassblowing. Her handbag didn't have a zippered top, which made it easy for the thief."

"You suspected Wyatt?"

Tess nodded. "He stood behind the woman during the demo. And a customer actually saw him take the wallet—an elderly lady too afraid to speak up while Wyatt and his buddies were in the store. Once they left, she told David and me what she witnessed. David doesn't get angry often, but when he does, you better steer clear. He ran out of the store and came back holding Wyatt by the scruff of his neck." She grinned at the memory. "David made Wyatt apologize and give the wallet back to the woman. When we asked if she wanted to press charges, she said no. I didn't blame her. She was about to leave for Florida to spend the holidays with her family."

"Then Wyatt got off with a slap on the wrist," I noted glumly.

"Not quite. My blue-eyed Dutchman has a strong sense of justice. David called Wyatt's parents and told them what happened. They were furious at what their son had done and swore they would deal with him accordingly. To be honest, we thought it was a phase Wyatt was going through. He was only sixteen. For all we knew, this was the first time he had pulled something like that." Tess looked disgusted. "Given that he stole from you last night, it appears he's still a dishonest little creep."

Almost finished with my latte, I hoped I had

enough self-restraint not to order a third. "I'm surprised you never told me about any of this."

Tess shrugged. "Didn't see any reason to. Like I said, you were living in New York at the time. And we banned Wyatt from Oriole Glass. He hasn't set foot in our store since that night."

"Here we are." Drea set down the colorful Fiesta plates holding our breakfasts. "Let me know if you need anything else."

"This will be fine. Thanks." My mouth watered at the sight of the golden-brown, baked French toast, deliciously gooey with blueberries and syrup. I savored my first bite before saying, "This tastes like Emeril's French toast. I bet the café is using his recipe."

"You and your celebrity chefs." Tess smiled. "For all you know, Emeril got it from some cook in a small-town diner." She enjoyed a big forkful. "As long as it tastes this good, I don't care who came up with it."

"Back to Wyatt, I wonder how many other businesses in town he's tried to rip off."

"We talked to several shop owners afterward," Tess said. "Told them to keep an eye on Wyatt if he ever came into their stores. But we didn't want to make a big public announcement about it. David and I figured Wyatt's family would take care of the problem."

"It doesn't look like the O'Neills are good at handling family problems. Neither are the Gales. Now I learn one of them is a thief. Makes me wonder what else those two families are capable of."

"Do you think an O'Neill or a Gale had something to do with Porter's death?" she asked.

"Who else?"

"I agree. There's a lot of Blueberry Hill money up for grabs. And we know Wyatt can't be trusted."

"Sloane has become a rich young widow." I lifted an eyebrow at her. "Let's not forget two Gale men have died since Nurse Jackie arrived."

"There's also Porter's sister," Tess reminded me. "You mentioned how bitter Cara seemed at the Blow Out. She may have killed her brother out of sheer resentment and hatred."

"As we discussed the other night, there is another suspect: Ryan. The police want to speak to him as soon as he returns."

"Only because of that fight at the tug-of-war. They have no other reason to suspect him."

For a moment, I considered telling Tess about Ryan owing Porter Gale money. But I only had Courtney's and Wyatt's word on that. Courtney was a kid, while Wyatt was a thief. I thought it wiser to hold off spreading rumors about Ryan's debts to Porter until I had confirmation from a more reliable source.

"I hope Wyatt doesn't steal from another shop owner. If so, I'll feel guilty for not calling the police last night."

"Since he stole from you only a few hours ago, I'll bet he steals on a regular basis."

"We can't let this continue, Tess, especially if he's ripping off tourists, too." I drank the rest of my latte. "I'll ask around town and see if he's stolen from any other store owners."

"If he has?"

"Then I'm going to the O'Neill farm to confront him *and* his parents. His life of crime is about to come to an end." I slammed my empty mug down on the table. "And to think I gave him a dozen free mini cheesecakes!"

Whether due to the gorgeous beach weather or the Blueberry Blow Out activities at the fairground, store traffic was light that morning. I'd brought Minnie to work, but with few customers to talk to, she spent most of the time grooming her feathers or napping on her perch. Dean and I busied ourselves with tasks we normally did only when complete boredom set in: rearranging the shelves beneath the counter and cleaning the computer keyboard.

"Where are all the tourists?" Dean asked for the fourth time as he stacked the berry teas in alphabetical order. "I wish I'd volunteered to work at the fairground today instead of Gillian. Although I guzzle too much blueberry lemonade when I'm there. It gives me gas."

"Probably because you're drinking it too fast." I pulled out the Windex bottle to spray the computer screen. "I bet everyone's at the beach. Summer's officially over in two weeks. The tourists want one last chance to swim in the lake. Plus, I think some big country and western singer performs at the fairground later today."

"The Blow Out is also hosting the competition for 'Best Tasting Blueberry' this morning. That's a big draw. All the commercial growers will be there, along with amateur and hobbyist gardeners."

"I hope a hobbyist wins," I said. "We don't need more tension between the growers."

"Speaking of the fruit growers, don't you think

it's weird the O'Neills are participating in all the Blow Out activities? Even if Cara wasn't crazy about her brother, it doesn't look right to have the family at the fair like nothing's happened. Wyatt ran the Ferris wheel for hours yesterday."

"How well do you know Wyatt?"

"Not well. Because I'm six years older than he is, we never had much to do with each other." He took a closer look at the tea tins and switched a few around. "Gillian and he are close in age. You should ask her about Wyatt."

"I did. Gillian only knows him by reputation, which as we all know isn't a sterling one. Like you, she went to Oriole Point public schools. Wyatt attended Christian schools in Two Rivers." I frowned. "An education that seems to have been wasted on him."

"I know he's a party animal, same as half the young guys around here," Dean said. "And I've heard from friends in Two Rivers that he sold prescription meds to students when he was in high school. My best friend's brother bought pills from Wyatt every time an exam was coming up."

This was disquieting news. "What did he sell?"

"Adderall. Weed, too, but that's pretty easy to find. There are rumors he sells 'Molly' once in a while. According to my sources, Wyatt's still selling to the high schoolers. I never had any interest in getting high myself. My drugs of choice are caffeine and gossip."

Learning Wyatt pushed drugs to teenagers troubled me even more than the thefts. "Have you heard anything about Wyatt stealing from the stores downtown?"

Rather than being surprised by my question, Dean's expression turned thoughtful. "Funny you say that. A few years back, my mom said the owner of Brouwer Jewelry filed charges against Wyatt for shoplifting. Don't know what happened after that, though."

Unfortunately, I wouldn't be able to find out anything from Sylvia Brouwer. She closed her jewelry store two years ago and retired to Georgia to be near her grandchildren.

"Why do you ask?"

I quickly told Dean what had occurred last night. When I was finished, he said, "Knowing you, I'm sure you aren't mistaken about how much money was in the cashbox."

Dean knew me well indeed. I counted the end-of-day receipts twice every night. "Nope. I counted it before leaving the fairground and wrote down the total. When I got back to the store, I counted it again. I still have both slips of paper with the same amounts on it. After Wyatt left, the cashbox was two hundred dollars lighter."

"What are you going to do?"

I finished cleaning the computer screen. "Go next door to talk with Denise. Maybe she's had a similar experience with Wyatt. I learned Wyatt stole a wallet four years ago in Tess's studio. Now I find out that he's shoplifted from a local jewelry store. He could be stealing from shop owners and tourists all the time."

"I wouldn't be surprised if he's using Adderall, as well as selling it. That screws up your thinking. And he might have flipped out over his uncle's death and went back to stealing. Grief can make you do crazy things."

I threw him a sardonic look. "Right. Because that's what people do when a relative dies: go out and steal something. No. He's been dishonest for years. I should do something about it."

"Until they figure out who killed Porter, I'd stay away from the O'Neills and the Gales."

"Wait a second. How do you know Porter was murdered?"

He laughed. "Not only does my mom handle every call that comes into the police station, she has a genius for eavesdropping. She's been telling me and Andrew all week that Porter's death was suspicious. I mean, c'mon. What thirtysomething guy just up and dies on an amusement park ride? The O'Neills have more important things to deal with right now than you getting robbed. It's a bummer that Wyatt ripped you off for two hundred dollars, but now isn't the best time to do anything about it."

I disagreed. It might be the perfect time, especially with Ryan soon to return. Once he did, the police were sure to question him about Porter's death, and I already feared he ranked near the top of their suspect list. Yes, I wanted Wyatt's thieving to stop. However, if Wyatt had been dishonest about stealing money and jewelry, he might also be lying about his uncle's death.

When I walked into the Tonguish Spirit Gallery, I found Denise relaxing in her favorite Bentwood rocker by the back wall, immersed in a book. Surrounded by rough-hewn wooden bookshelves and a cushioned armchair, she called this her reading nook. I had tried to replicate such a cozy corner in my own shop, but my merchandise and the building layout didn't allow it.

At the sound of the chimes tinkling over the door, Denise looked up. "Marlee, how nice to see you." She closed her book and laid it on the shelf beside her rocker. "You're the first person to cross my threshold in over an hour. It's one of those days. Come and sit down."

"Dean and I have cleaned everything in the shop. In another hour, we'll be washing windows." With a contented smile, I sank into the armchair beside her. I loved the chair's plush, coppery-brown cushions. More than once, I'd considered buying it, even though the chair's moose and fall leaf pattern didn't match the décor in my house.

"How about some tea? I have a hot plate in the back and a kettle."

"No thanks. I only wanted to chat. Didn't mean to interrupt your reading."

"Rereading, actually. I've decided to dip into the Jane Austen novels again. It's been years."

I laughed. "My English professor mom would be so proud of you."

"Just don't tell her that I prefer French literature, aside from Jane, of course." She began to rock back and forth. "I discovered Balzac and Flaubert in college and never looked back."

Closing my eyes, I took a deep breath. Denise burned incense or scented candles in the shop; today I smelled wood smoke, which meant she was burning a candle called Rustic Cottage. Like my beach yoga class, the gallery made me feel calmer, more centered. I attributed it to the CDs of Native American flute music playing softly in the background and the aromas of her carefully selected candles. I also enjoyed the textiles, pottery, paintings, and jewelry artfully placed around the store. Because Tess knew how much I loved the gallery, she often bought my birthday and Christmas gifts here. Last year, she spent an outrageous sum of money on an exquisite Star Quilt, which I slept under every night. I owed Tess one great birthday gift this autumn.

Thinking about the quilt on my bed prompted me to look at the adjacent wall, where dream catchers of all sizes were on display. "I need one of those. How do they work exactly?"

"The Ojibwe believe the dream catchers' netted hoops were magical webs protecting people while they slept, especially children. The night air was thought to be filled with dreams, and the dream catcher attracted them. Bad dreams could not get through the 'web,' but good dreams passed through to enter the sleeping person below." Denise gave me a concerned look. "If you need a dream catcher, your sleep must be troubled."

"Not my sleep. My waking hours." I trusted Denise. While not a close friend like Tess and Natasha, she and I had shared a few dinners. We also loved superhero movies and went to see them together, regardless of what the latest reviews said. I valued her opinion and her counsel.

I took a deep breath. "The news hasn't officially come out, but the police suspect foul play in Porter Gale's death."

"I've already heard. Suzanne Cabot popped in

yesterday. Although I suspect she had less of a need to replenish her supply of lavender and sage candles than to let me know the latest gossip from the police station."

"How does she keep her job as their receptionist? Talk about loose lips."

"Maybe she knows so much about everyone who works there that they're afraid to let her go."

We laughed.

"Thanks to Suzanne, a lot of the shopkeepers are aware the police view Porter's death as suspicious," she continued. "Cindy at the cheese shop stopped by earlier to talk about it."

"The question is who wanted Porter dead. Given the success of Blueberry Hill, family members seem the most likely to benefit. Therefore the most likely to want him out of the picture."

"Blueberry Hill is a huge commercial enterprise. Anyone involved in the fruit-growing business here may have had a reason."

"True. But I only know the family members, and what I do know of them makes me uneasy." Leaning forward, I told her about Wyatt's theft the night before, Tess's experience, and Dean's assertion that Wyatt had been charged with shoplifting.

Denise rubbed at her temples when I finished, as if I'd given her a headache.

"I only wish I'd known Wyatt made a habit of stealing," I said. "I would have called the police after he left. Now I'm afraid if I don't say anything, he'll continue to steal. That hurts local businesses and puts the tourists at risk. If I can find another shopkeeper he's stolen from recently, the two of us can talk to Wyatt and his family. I hope to convince his parents that Wyatt has a problem that needs to be addressed."

"You want to know if I am one of those shopkeepers." She didn't state this as a question.

"Are you?"

"Wyatt came into the gallery last month during Fourth of July week. I had a store packed with people, and only noticed Wyatt because he has such bushy red hair. He also acted odd. Jumpy. Laughing to himself."

"Did he seem high?"

"I couldn't say. But he acted strange. When you've worked in retail long enough, you develop a sixth sense about customers. As busy as we were, I kept one eye on Wyatt."

"What did you see?"

She pointed at the glass jewelry case in the center of the store. "A customer asked to see a silver and turquoise bracelet from the case. She decided not to buy it, but left the bracelet on the counter after trying it on. Wyatt snatched it up when he thought no one was looking and stuck it in his jeans pocket. I grabbed him right before he got to the door."

"What did he do?"

"He became angry that I'd stopped him. When I pulled the bracelet out of his back pocket, he turned as red as his hair. Wyatt immediately claimed he'd meant to purchase the bracelet, but wasn't done shopping yet." She smirked. "He had literally opened the door to leave when I caught him. I should have waited until he reached the sidewalk because he started to make a scene. I was jammed with customers, and I'd gotten my bracelet back. It didn't seem worth the trouble to call the police, especially if he stuck to his story about planning to buy the bracelet. But he did try to steal it. An expensive piece of jewelry, too, by a Zuni artisan from New Mexico. Five hundred and fifty dollars."

I whistled.

"I'd show it to you, but I sold it last week."

"Dean told me that Wyatt sells Adderall to the high school kids. Apparently he's been doing it for years, since back when he was in high school himself."

"Doesn't surprise me. My cousin works at a treatment center in Lansing. Adderall abuse among teens has been on the rise for a decade. Prescription opioid abuse is also a serious problem."

"This is all so unpleasant. I hate to think those problems also affect our little village, but of course they do. If only there was something I could do." I thought a moment. "If Wyatt is selling pills to teens, why does he need to steal from the stores?"

"According to my cousin, that's not uncommon. If his drug supply runs low, he's not making as much money from dealing; therefore, he steals in order to get money to buy more drugs. A vicious cycle, especially if he's a user himself."

"I hope Wyatt doesn't involve his sister in any of this. Courtney is such a sweet girl."

"Courtney's a good kid," Denise agreed. "And such a horse lover. She comes here every month to see if I have any new jewelry with horse motifs. Her mom bought her a horse-themed charm bracelet for her birthday this past spring."

"Do you think Cara O'Neill and her husband know what's going on with their son?"

Denise stopped rocking and steepled her hands. "The only way to discover the truth is to confront them. You wanted a shopkeeper to help confirm that Wyatt is a thief? Well, here I am."

"You'll come with me to the O'Neill farm?"

"The sooner, the better. If his parents don't know about his stealing and drug dealing, it's high time they did. Before he—or an innocent like his sister—gets hurt."

"How about this afternoon?"

"I can't leave until three. That's when Keira comes in for her shift."

I shot a grateful smile at the feathered dream catchers on the wall. While I didn't need them to catch any bad dreams, I sent a silent prayer, asking them to help us catch a foolish young man before his life of crime became too dangerous. I couldn't help but wonder if we weren't about to catch a killer as well.

Chapter Thirteen

Bright blue balloons floated above either side of the open front gate when Denise and I arrived at O'Neill Blueberry Farm. Puzzled, I continued up the driveway past a retaining pond and a long, white building that held the farm's commercial space. A parking lot accommodated U-Pick visitors. At least a dozen U-Pickers, plastic buckets in hand, walked along the rows of mown grass between the blueberry bushes. In the distance I spied a mechanized blueberry harvester and several farm workers. One of the figures had shaggy red hair. At least I knew Wyatt was on the property.

"What's with the balloons?" I parked in front of the tri-level house that served as the O'Neill family home. A shiny black Lincoln that I didn't recognize was parked there as well.

Denise opened the door of the SUV. "Maybe it's in honor of the Blueberry Blow Out. Balloons are a festive touch, if a little inappropriate this week."

"Could be a way of honoring Porter. He *was* the Blueberry King around here." I hesitated before walking toward the house. "I saw Wyatt in the field with the harvesting crew. Maybe we should walk out there and talk to him first."

Before we could discuss it, the screen door flew open and Courtney burst out of the house. Running to greet us, I was surprised when she flung her arms around me, then Denise. She took a step back, her freckled face beaming. "Isn't it wonderful?"

Denise and I shrugged at each other. "We don't know what you're talking about," I said.

"We won! O'Neill Farm won Best Tasting Blueberry of the Year at the Blow Out this morning!" She clapped her hands. "O'Neill's has never won before. It's always Blueberry Hill or the Janssens or Zellars. But this year, the vote was unanimous. O'Neill Blueberry Farms grows the best-tasting fruit! We bought balloons at the fair to decorate the farm. And Dad is ordering signs saying 'O'Neill Blueberries Voted Tastiest Blueberry In Oriole County.' I already announced it on the website and our Facebook page and Twitter." She stopped to catch her breath. "I thought you were here to congratulate us."

Denise smiled at her. "No, but congratulations, Courtney. Your family should be proud."

"Absolutely," I said. "This is great publicity for the farm."

"If you didn't know about the award, why are you here? Have you sold out of our jams and butters already, Marlee? We haven't had a chance to make a fresh batch, not with everything going on. And this morning was crazy busy."

"No. Denise and I came to speak to your parents."

On one hand, I felt bad about bothering the O'Neills with news of their son's activities. However, Porter had died a few days ago and none of the O'Neills seemed upset over it. Indeed, they had now moved into celebratory mode. Besides, clearing the air about Wyatt was best done before too much time elapsed following his latest theft.

Her happy expression grew cautious. "Is something wrong?"

Denise cleared her throat. "Marlee and I learned about a problem concerning your family. We thought it best to speak with them directly."

"It's about Wyatt," I said.

She looked disgusted now. "Is he stealing again?"

Taken aback, I asked, "How do you know about any of this?"

"He's been caught before, starting back in middle school. And some jewelry store owner in town reported him to the police. He had to do community service: four weeks picking up trash along the freeway. Too bad he wasn't shipped off to *juvie*. It would have served him right."

"That may be a little harsh," Denise said with a small smile.

"Not really. Wyatt steals from everyone. He lies. He sells drugs."

"Hold on." I held up my hand. "You know your brother sells drugs?"

"He's been doing that since the doctors put him on Adderall in eighth grade. Before that he took Ritalin, only he was too young to figure out how to sell it back then. He's supposed to have ADHD. I think he just likes to act like an idiot. He gets a lot of attention that way."

Denise and I exchanged troubled glances.

"Do your parents know he's selling drugs?" I asked.

"Oh, sure. Like I said, he's been caught a few times. The principal suspended him when he was in eleventh grade. My parents grounded him for the rest of the year when that happened, but it didn't change anything. It doesn't help that Mom treats him like he's still in kindergarten. Like nothing is ever his fault because he has ADHD. It drives me and my dad crazy." She crossed her arms. "What did he do this time? Did he steal something from your shops?"

I told her about his theft last night, along with his attempt to steal a bracelet from Denise's gallery. "We were afraid your parents didn't know he was still stealing."

"They probably don't. The last theft we heard about was last year. Wyatt stole a case of beer out of a liquor store in Berrien County. Mom paid off the store owner to keep it quiet, but my dad got really steamed. I don't think he'll let her bail out Wyatt again. If both of you tell them he hasn't changed his ways, my moron brother might not get off scot-free this time." She sighed. "I'm only sorry you came on a day when we've had such good news."

"I'm sorry. But Wyatt's problems seem even more important than winning Best Tasting Blueberry," I said. "And we're worried he may be stealing from the tourists."

"Oh, it's not only that. The family lawyers showed up this past hour." Her freckled face creased in yet another wide grin. "Uncle Porter's will has been read. And guess what? It leaves half of Blueberry Hill to my mom! Half of all the money, the business, and the property. Isn't that incredible?"

I found this incredible indeed, although it made sense. "What about Sloane?"

"She gets the other half. After all, she's the wife. But the rest belongs to my mom. Actually, she deserves all of it, but half is better than nothing."

Denise's obvious confusion mirrored my own. "I didn't think Porter and your mother got along," she said.

"They didn't. But blood is thicker than water, Mom says. Too bad for Sloane. If Uncle Porter had lived longer, she might have gotten everything."

"Why would it have made any difference?" I asked.

"Uncle Porter wrote in the will that if he and Sloane had children at the time of his death, his widow—and the mother of his children—would inherit everything. Sloane must be totally bummed she never got pregnant. Blueberry Hill would be all hers now if she had."

"Wow," I said.

"I know. I couldn't believe it when the lawyers read the will to us. This means me and Wyatt will inherit Blueberry Hill one day. Although I'll need to find a way to stop my brother from screwing things up. I'll have to take over things when I'm older."

Another generation of sibling rivalry over Blueberry Hill appeared well under way. "Do you know how much longer the lawyers will be here?"

She shrugged.

"Maybe we should do as you suggested, Marlee," Denise said. "Let's talk to Wyatt first. Once the lawyers have left, we can have this conversation with Wyatt and his parents."

"Please let your parents know we're here," I told Courtney. "And give them a heads-up about what we've come to discuss."

"Sure thing. I can't wait to see what Dad does to Wyatt when he learns he's still stealing." She pointed at the grassy path that wound past several low-lying sheds. "If you go along there, you'll bypass the U-Pickers."

"Thanks." I waved at Courtney as she ran back to the house, her mass of coppery hair flying behind her.

"What do you think of all that?" Denise raised a curious eyebrow in my direction.

"I think Cara should be grateful Sloane never got pregnant. Only I wonder if she had an inkling of what was in the will. Maybe Porter said something to his sister. Or to Wyatt." I followed the path along the sheds. "Do you think Sloane knew about the details of the will?"

"Unlikely. If she had, she would have gotten pregnant as soon as possible."

I recalled my conversation with Cara the first day of the Blueberry Blow Out. "Cara told me that Sloane and Porter had been trying to have a child for months. Sloane was apparently upset about it."

"Any woman who wanted to be a mother would be upset."

"It could prove Sloane wanted a baby because she knew the terms of the will." My frustration increased. "Or maybe she didn't marry Porter only for his money. From all accounts, she's taking his death hard. Sloane could be the innocent party in all this. I'm not so sure about Cara and Wyatt."

"A dark cloud surrounds every murder. It ends up affecting far more than the killer and the victim." Denise sighed. "And it is possible no one in the family had anything to do with Porter's death. The murder could have been committed by a business rival. You shouldn't automatically assume a relative killed him."

"I'm trying not to assume anything." I stopped, my attention drawn to the white plastic bags stacked along the wall of a nearby shed. I knelt down to examine them.

"Why the interest in the bags?"

"You might be interested as well." I traced my finger along the bag's green lettering. "They're filled with potassium chloride."

Luckily, the whirr of the motorized harvester drowned out my conversation with Denise as we approached the crew picking blueberries. "Bags of potassium chloride on the property doesn't mean anyone here killed Porter," Denise said. "It's not an uncommon substance. My great-aunt had a potassium deficiency and used it in cooking instead of table salt. I even tasted it once." She made a face. "I found it too bitter."

"Wyatt told me yesterday that it's used in fertilizer."

"This is a blueberry farm. Makes sense the O'Neills keep a supply on hand."

"I don't dispute that. But I'm not forgetting Cara and Wyatt had access to insulin vials, potassium chloride, and Porter Gale. Along with a motive to want him dead."

"*Only* if they knew about the will," Denise said with emphasis. "I prefer to think someone outside the family did it."

Because Ryan may have wanted Porter dead as well, I disagreed. But I wasn't going to drag my fiancé into the conversation. And we had now drawn the attention of the seven-man harvesting crew, who threw curious glances our way as we got closer.

"I thought the berries were picked by hand," Denise said.

"Many smaller blueberry farms handpick their berry crop," I explained, "but the acreage of the O'Neill farm requires a mechanized harvesting machine." While some farms owned several harvesters, I knew the O'Neills rented a single harvester each August.

Denise pointed at the driver visible atop the eleven-foot-tall machine. "How does he keep the bushes perfectly in line with the harvester?"

"The driver sits high enough to see exactly where he needs to go, and the blueberry bushes are planted on slightly raised mounds. Also, normal speed for a harvester is no more than one mile per hour, which makes it easy to keep the vehicle on track, even after dark. On big farms like Blueberry Hill, the harvesters come equipped with lights to enable them to harvest at night."

We watched as the open center of the tall harvester drove over the bushes. Within the harvester, rotating rods methodically stripped the blueberries from the bushes.

"Why does it look like some berries aren't getting picked up?" Denise asked.

"No matter how much the base of a plant is wired or trellised, some fruit will be lost. You lose less berries when you handpick with rakes, but the cost in labor and time is high. A big farm has to use a motorized harvester, which can pick ten thousand pounds of berries in one day. Even with a driver and crew, it's intensive work."

At the moment, that didn't seem to be the case for Wyatt and a young man in torn jeans and red T-shirt. Both of them stood talking on the rear deck of the harvester as the rest of the crew placed plastic containers known as "lugs" beneath chutes in order to catch the blueberries. This process occurred on either side of the harvester as a worker handed off filled lugs to other crew members, who sorted through the berries, tossing away unripened fruit and leaves.

While the rest of the crew sorted berries and restacked lugs, Wyatt and the guy in the red T-shirt jumped off the deck. Once on the ground they huddled close, and I saw Wyatt pull something out of his jeans pocket and hand it to the other man. He, in turn, handed something over to Wyatt.

I looked at Denise. "I hope we didn't see a drug transaction."

She frowned. "I know the kid in the red shirt. His name is Lucas. He works part-time doing landscape work for the village with his dad. You've probably seen him. He handles the driving mower like it's an Indy 500 car. This past spring, he got so reckless that he cut down the giant forsythia by the post office."

"If he's buying drugs from Wyatt, it may explain why he's so careless on the job."

"He's looking a little unsteady right now," she remarked as Lucas took a step back and stumbled. Wyatt grabbed him by the sleeve to keep him from toppling over. "And Wyatt doesn't seem in a good mood."

"Is he ever? Besides, we can't wait on Wyatt's moods. We need to get all of us together with his parents and resolve this. I also want my two hundred dollars back."

"Good luck with that."

"Oh, I expect him to deny, deny, deny. But at least we'll let him and his family know that he's not fooling us."

Since Wyatt and Lucas stood in the cleared row between blueberry bushes that Denise and I walked along, they couldn't avoid seeing us headed straight for them. After giving his unsteady friend another shake, Wyatt marched over to meet us, his bare torso gleaming with sweat. I suspected it was less from exertion than the hot August sun overhead. As a true ginger with pale skin, he risked a severe sunburn by not wearing a shirt when working outdoors in summer. Then again, Wyatt O'Neill had never proven himself to be a practical young man.

"What are you doing here?" he barked. "U-Pick's on the other side of the farm."

"We're not here for U-Pick. Denise and I need to talk to you. And your parents."

He wiped his sweaty palms against his faded, berry-stained jeans. "I don't know what you have to say to me or my parents. And I don't care. But you have no business being in the field while we're harvesting."

"It's the fastest way to speak to you," I said. "Courtney is letting your parents know we're here."

"Why the hell are you here?"

"Because you stole two hundred dollars from me last night."

Panic flickered in his gaze for a second, before being replaced by scorn. "You're crazy. I never took a dime from you."

"I'm not here to argue the point. I want my money back, Wyatt. And you need to admit to your parents that you stole it. I also want you to receive some counseling."

His laugh had a raw, mean tone to it. "Like I care about what you want."

"You already have a reputation as a thief," I informed him. "You did community service after stealing from Brouwer Jewelry. And I know your mom paid off a liquor store in Berrien County last year after you stole from them. So don't pretend you're some innocent."

This sobered him. "Are you running around town asking questions about me?"

"All I had to do was mention your name and some story about your dishonest behavior came up." I shot him a hard look. "Like the time you stole a wallet from a lady's purse during Holiday Open House at Oriole Glass."

He smirked. "Of course you'd believe the geisha glassblower."

My temper flared. "One more nasty word out of your mouth, and I'll make sure everyone in town knows you're a lying, drug-dealing thief."

Wyatt leaned toward me. "Be careful, Marlee. I could make your life much more unpleasant than you realize."

"Oh, really? And how do you think you're—"

Denise stepped between us. "Wyatt, it's no use denying you stole from Marlee last night. Or that you tried to steal an expensive bracelet from my gallery last month."

He shook his head. "You're as wacko as she is," he told her. "I never took a thing from your stupid gallery. But I do remember you accused me of something I didn't do. You're lucky I didn't go to the police to report how you harassed me."

"Enough with the pretense. You had the bracelet stuffed in your pocket."

"Try and prove it," he said, and sneered. "Only you can't. Take my advice. Don't go on the warpath with me because you'll lose, Pocahontas."

Denise flinched at his open contempt of her.

"Shut up, Wyatt," I said. "You're caught and you know it."

She put a hand on my arm. "This is pointless, Marlee. He's a liar and a thief."

"He sounds like a racist, too. But why should that surprise us? He's dumber than a brick."

Wyatt swore at me as Denise sighed. "He'll never admit to anything," she said. "Let's go back and talk to Cara and Brody. And maybe we should call the police as well."

"Tell the cops. You think they're gonna arrest me for having a bracelet in my pocket a month ago? Get real. You didn't even report it, Denise. Besides, I never actually walked out of the store with it." He turned to me. "And how will you prove I took anything from your cashbox on the counter?"

"I never mentioned the money went missing from the cashbox," I said with disgust. "It could have gone missing from my register drawer. Of course, only the thief would know that."

"Like I told the Indian princess"—he gestured at Denise—"prove it."

"I'm done here." Turning on her heel, Denise stalked off.

"You're such a pathetic loser, Wyatt," I said.

He chuckled. "You may as well join her. But if you go to the cops, I'll tell them I was in your store last night because you forgot an entire box of Berry Basket stuff at the fairground. Now why should the cops trust the word of a woman who leaves behind merchandise belonging to her store?"

"I'll take my chances. After all, I'm not the one who's been charged with theft before."

The two of us stared at each other for a tense moment as the sound of the approaching harvester grew louder. "You can't prove anything," he said finally. "Neither can your friends."

"Maybe not. But your parents need to be made aware of all this."

"Leave my family alone, Marlee. We got enough to deal with."

"Yes, I heard. Courtney told us about the will."

He lifted his chin in defiance. "It's about time my family gets what they deserve."

"It looks like Porter thought Sloane deserved half of Blueberry Hill as well. Are you upset about that?"

"Why would I be upset? Sloane was my uncle's

wife. It would have been fine with me if he'd left her everything."

"You *are* fond of Sloane."

"What of it? And you have no right to be here. You and your Indian scout buddy."

I shook my head at him. "Denise is right. It's a waste of time talking to you."

He laughed. "You're the one wasting your time with that boyfriend of yours."

"What does that mean?"

"There's lots of stuff you don't know about the guy you're going to marry."

"Like what?"

Turning away from me, Wyatt walked toward the harvester stripping blueberries from a nearby row. When he did so, I saw the large skull tattooed on his back that Courtney had told me about. I ran to catch up to him.

"What don't I know about Ryan?" I asked.

He glanced over at me with a wily expression. "That he's an even bigger loser than you accuse me of being."

"If you're referring to the money he borrowed from the Gales, I already know."

"Bet you don't know *why* he borrowed the money."

I grabbed his arm. "Why did Ryan need the money? Tell me!"

"Who's the pathetic one now?" Wyatt shook free of my grasp. "Get lost, Marlee."

Stunned, I watched as Wyatt went to meet Lucas, who seemed more off balance than before. Indeed, the young man walked along the path in so unsteady a manner, his shoulder kept brushing the blueberry bushes. A few yards behind, the harvester slowly made its way toward them. I wasn't certain what was the matter with Wyatt's friend, but he looked to be in no shape to be harvesting berries today. I didn't feel in such great shape, either.

Obviously Wyatt was trying to hurt me any way he could. Only why bring up Ryan at all? I didn't think Ryan had ever exchanged more than five words with Wyatt. He's lying, I told myself. After all, that's what Wyatt does. But as I walked away, I fought back tears. The past few days had shaken my trust in Ryan, starting with his attack of Porter at the tug-of-war. The last thing I needed was someone else insinuating that Ryan might be keeping things from me. Because I could no longer deny that he was.

I quickened my pace, eager to escape the sound of the harvester and Wyatt's mocking presence. When I reached the end of the rows, I glanced over my shoulder in time to see Wyatt pull Lucas away from the bushes about to be harvested. I watched in alarm as Lucas suddenly doubled over.

A moment later, Lucas fell right in the path of the harvester.

Chapter Fourteen

The next few moments turned into a panicked blur of frenzied shouts and blueberries. By the time I raced over, the driver had stopped the harvester. Lucas had landed inside the open center of the machine, which was bordered on either side by metal walls. As I batted away blueberry branches, I noticed a crew member speaking on his cell phone. Help would be on its way shortly.

Three crew members, including Wyatt, reached inside to pull Lucas out. I winced to see the bloody scratches on his face, but I was more concerned that he appeared to be having a seizure. "How bad is he hurt?"

The driver of the harvester, a brawny middle-aged man with a graying beard, grimaced. "I stopped in time. I would have felt it if the harvester had run over him. Aside from the branches scratching him when he fell, I don't think he was injured by the harvester at all."

The crew lay Lucas down on the grassy path. The

scratches along his face and arms appeared minor, but Lucas shook violently.

"Does he suffer from epilepsy?" I asked.

The crew either shrugged or shook their heads. One of them said, "I don't think so. If he does, Lucas never told me about it and we grew up together."

I looked at Wyatt, who seemed frightened. "Wyatt, when Denise and I arrived, Lucas looked unsteady. Did he complain of feeling ill?"

Rather than answer me, Wyatt pulled out his cell phone from his back jeans pocket and swiped at it. I took out my own cell and called Denise to let her know what had happened. With so many of us on our cells, it came as no surprise when EMS soon arrived. Because of the narrow space between the rows of bushes, they left their vehicle at the end of the row and hurried toward us with a wheeled gurney.

"What happened?" one of them asked. His partner knelt beside the jerking body of Lucas and took his vitals.

A chorus of bewildered answers greeted him. None of us really understood what had happened—with the possible exception of Wyatt.

I repeated my observation that Lucas had appeared wobbly on his feet and how he doubled over right before he fell in front of the harvester. "He was with him." I pointed at Wyatt.

Shooting me a hate-filled look, Wyatt told the paramedic, "Lucas said he felt nauseous and hot. I thought it was sunstroke. Or maybe he'd had too much to drink last night. It wouldn't be the first time." He paused. "That's why he and I jumped off the harvester. He looked shaky and I thought I'd better get him on solid ground."

I didn't think now was the time to add that I'd seen some sort of exchange transpire between the two of them. The paramedics conferred briefly. "Blood pressure and heart rate elevated," one of them said to the other. "Signs of dehydration. His temperature is over a hundred and three."

Was Lucas suffering from sunstroke and dehydration, rather than a drug interaction? After all, I only saw the two men exchange something. I never saw Lucas ingest any substance.

"Could be heatstroke," the driver concurred. "I've seen it happen lots of time in the fields under an August sun. The young ones don't realize they're in danger until they get too confused to do anything about it."

"Is he having a seizure?" I worried Lucas might not make it to the hospital in time.

"The tremors are likely due to his high temperature." The EMTs opened up a case and removed ice packs. Next, they positioned a shaking Lucas onto the gurney, laid ice packs on pulse points, then strapped him securely. Feeling as unsteady as Lucas, I went with the others as we followed the EMTs back to the ambulance and watched as they loaded him into the vehicle.

While they were doing this, a sheriff's car pulled up. When Deputy Atticus Holt emerged from the driver's side, I gave an audible sigh of relief. His eyes widened when he saw me. No doubt he was thinking, Why is Marlee Jacob once more in the middle of trouble? I was simply glad to see a friendly face, especially one belonging to such a capable law enforcement officer.

"If anyone has contact information for his family, please give it to us," the driver of the ambulance requested. "And what is the young man's name?"

"Lucas Hendriksen." Wyatt held out his phone so they could copy the numbers. Holt briefly spoke with the EMTs before they finished loading Lucas in the vehicle and sped away.

As the wail of the siren filled the air, the ambulance disappeared from view. Holt turned to us. "I'm Captain Holt, head of Investigative Services at the sheriff's department. We got a call about someone being injured by a harvester machine. What happened? How did Mr. Hendriksen fall in front of the harvester?"

I let the crew and driver tell their versions of events. As they each described Lucas's earlier erratic behavior, I began to think heatstroke might be the likely culprit. After all, the day was sunny and in the eighties. And the harvesting team had probably been in the field for hours.

After the work crew answered Holt's questions, the driver looked at Wyatt. "How about if we finish up this last row and then I'll give everyone a break?"

Wyatt nodded, and the driver and harvesting crew made their way back to the harvester. I'd forgotten that the driver and crew worked for the O'Neill family. This gave Wyatt the final say as to what they should do next.

Holt smiled at me. "Surprised to see you, Marlee. Although since this is a blueberry farm, I assume you're here on business."

"Not really." I looked over at Wyatt.

Holt instantly grew suspicious. "Is there a problem?"

"Yeah, there's a problem and I might as well be the first to say something because she"—Wyatt gestured in my direction—"is determined to make my life miserable."

"Don't be so dramatic. We came here to speak with your parents, not the police."

"Yeah, right," he said with a scowl. "More lies."

Holt held up his hand. "What is going on?"

"She thinks I stole from her store last night," he said. "And here I was being nice by bringing her a box she'd left behind at the fair. Which shows you how on the ball she is. She leaves the room for one minute—"

"Longer than that," I told Holt. "I went into the kitchen to get mini cheesecakes for him. I wrapped a few for him to take home to his family, so I was back there several minutes. During that time, he went into the cashbox on the counter and stole two hundred dollars."

"Don't forget she left a big box of store items back at the fair. Do you really think she remembers how much money was in the cashbox? Give me a break."

"Why didn't you report this as soon as it happened?" Holt asked me.

"I didn't want to cause more trouble for the O'Neill family. His uncle died a few days ago. I also thought it might be a onetime thing. That he took advantage of my being careless enough to leave the cashbox out, which I deeply regret. Only I've learned Wyatt has been stealing for some time: from Tess at Oriole Glass, Denise at Tonguish Spirit Gallery—"

"They can't prove a thing," Wyatt interrupted with disgust.

"And he was charged with stealing from Brouwer Jewelers. His sister Courtney said he did community service for that one."

Holt threw Wyatt a jaundiced look. "Mr. O'Neill, how old are you?"

"Old enough to know my rights."

"I haven't accused you of a crime," Holt replied.

"Well, they have." Wyatt crossed his arms and threw us a challenging look. "Only Marlee and her friend Pocahontas can't prove anything."

"All I want is my two hundred dollars back," I stated. "And for his parents to put a stop to this behavior in the future."

"Do you wish to press charges?" Holt asked.

A pickup truck beeped at us, coming to a stop a few yards away. Denise and Courtney jumped out of the backseat, followed by Cara and her husband Brody. Everyone looked agitated.

"What's going on here?" Brody possessed the manner and movements of a bantam rooster, accentuated by his thick crop of red hair.

"Denise got a call from Marlee saying there had been an accident. Then Wyatt called to say Lucas collapsed from heatstroke and had to be taken to the hospital." Cara rushed over to her son and felt his forehead. "Are you okay, Wyatt? You're not feeling overheated, too?"

"I'm fine." He pushed her away. "Lucas is the one who's on the way to the hospital, not me."

"He's right," I said. "Denise and I got here in time to see Lucas and Wyatt jump off the harvester. And the young man did seem shaky."

"I keep telling the boys to wear hats and keep themselves hydrated." Brody shook his head. "Looks like I'll have to make it a rule. We sure as hell don't need our harvesting crew collapsing from the heat."

"Dad, the last time a worker got heatstroke was three years ago," Courtney reminded him. "And Lucas knows the signs of dehydration. He must have ignored them."

"We should go to the hospital right now," Cara said. "I'll call Lucas's father and have him meet us there. I hope the boy only got too much sun, but what if it's more serious?"

"Lucas will be fine." Wyatt now looked bored with the whole discussion. "He probably partied too hard last night and wasn't up to a day of harvesting."

Denise stared at him. The disapproval in her eyes would have given me pause had I been Wyatt. "Lucas may have been affected by something else."

"What do you mean?" Holt asked.

"As Marlee said, we arrived just as Wyatt and Lucas jumped off the harvester. And yes, he seemed unsteady. What she didn't mention was that we saw some sort of transaction between the two of them."

"Lying hag." Wyatt spat at her.

"Shut up, Wyatt," his father said in a rumbling voice.

"Wyatt took something out of his jeans pocket and handed it to Lucas," Denise went on, unperturbed by Wyatt's outburst, "who then handed something to Wyatt."

"What did it look like?" Holt took a small note-pad and pen from his shirt pocket.

"Hard to say. But whatever they exchanged was small enough to be placed in their back pockets."

"She's making it all up." Wyatt protested. "They both came here to stir up trouble. Maybe you should ask why they have it in for me."

"What's going on here?" Cara said. "I don't understand."

"Wyatt's stealing again, Mom," Courtney said in a stage whisper.

"What the hell!" Brody turned to his son. "If you've stooped to robbing people once more, I swear on my mother's grave I'll let them throw you in jail this time. See if I don't!"

"Brody, please!" Cara took her irate husband by the arm. "Let's hear what Wyatt has to say. This could all be a misunderstanding."

"None of the others were," Brody replied. "And I don't want to hear one more excuse for his behavior. He's a grown man. High time he started acting like one."

Courtney snorted.

"Should you tell them why we're here, Marlee, or should I?" Denise asked.

"Since I'm the one who came to you about all this, I will." Taking a deep breath, I told the group how Wyatt stole from my store last night, and how I had learned about his other attempts at Denise's gallery and Oriole Glass.

Brody stared at his son with contempt. "You stole

two hundred dollars from Marlee? Just how low are you?"

"Of course you believe these bitches rather than me!" Wyatt shouted back.

"Shut your mouth." Brody jabbed his finger at his son. "You're already in enough trouble."

"It can't be true," Cara protested. "Marlee, you must be mistaken. You probably counted the money wrong."

"Your son stole the money," Denise said. "And he tried to steal an expensive bracelet from my gallery only last month. Who knows how many other people he's been stealing from?"

"Bad enough he steals from the shop owners, but we can't have him robbing tourists," I added. "This has to stop."

"You're right about that," Wyatt said. "This lying needs to stop. Starting with you two."

"We also shouldn't forget Lucas and why he may have collapsed." Denise ignored Wyatt's latest outburst. "It could have been drug induced. We've heard that Wyatt has been selling prescription drugs to high schoolers for several years."

I had to hand it to Denise. When she was determined to see justice done, nothing stood in her way. Courtney looked as impressed as I was.

Wyatt swore at Denise, while Cara appeared close to tears. "That all happened a long time ago, back when he was a teenager," she explained. "He didn't think anything was wrong with selling it. After all, the doctor prescribed the Adderall for him. I'm sure he didn't know it was illegal to sell the pills to the other kids. And he was just a kid himself."

"Stop, Cara." Brody shook his head. "Our son is not a kid any longer. We've looked the other way too many times." He stepped closer to Wyatt, who jostled from foot to foot, as if searching for a chance to escape. "Are you still selling drugs? I want the truth."

Wyatt jutted his chin out. "No. I'm not selling drugs."

"Mr. O'Neill, I need you to turn out the pockets of your jeans," Holt said in a crisp tone.

"I think you need a warrant for that."

"I know that I don't." Holt stared back at him.

"Fine." With a long-suffering expression, Wyatt turned out his pockets, which proved to be empty except for the right back pocket. That held a thick wad of folded twenty-dollar bills.

"Is this payment for any drugs you sold to Lucas this afternoon?" Holt asked.

"No." Wyatt looked like he was about to say more, but decided silence was the wiser choice.

Cara turned to Holt. "Officer, I admit my son may have done some foolish things when he was younger—"

"He broke the law," Brody reminded her.

"Yes, but he learned his lesson. I assure you that he no longer sells drugs nor does he steal." Cara shot me a beseeching look. "Marlee, I'm sorry that you think Wyatt stole from you, but I know he didn't. He's changed. He's grown up."

I'd never seen a person so desperate to ignore the truth. My heart ached for her. "I'm sorry, too. But he took the money. You need to admit that because you're right. Wyatt *is* grown up. And he may start committing even worse crimes."

"Shut up!" Wyatt snarled at me.

"Would either of you like to press charges against Mr. O'Neill?" Holt asked.

"Will it do any good?" Denise sighed. "The incident in my store occurred a month ago, and I should have reported it back then. Marlee might have a better case."

Cara grabbed my wrist. "Marlee, please let us handle it within the family. This has been a terrible week, and I don't know how much more stress I can take."

I looked over at Brody, who I suspected was the only one able to put the fear of God into his son. "Brody, I'm not here to cause trouble. But Wyatt's stealing has to stop. And he needs counseling."

"Screw you," Wyatt said.

"Shut your mouth, Wyatt. Or I'll shut it for you." Brody turned to me. "I'm docking two hundred dollars from Wyatt's next paycheck so the family can pay you back for his latest theft."

Wyatt swore under his breath.

"I apologize to both you and Denise for my son's behavior," he went on. "And if he refuses to go to a counselor, he will have to pack his bags the next day and leave this property, never to return."

Cara gasped.

"I mean it, Cara," he said in a grim voice. "I'm done."

"Calm down," Wyatt muttered. "Everyone is making a big deal out of nothing."

"Theft is a big deal," Holt said. "You're lucky

Ms. Jacob and Ms. Redfern aren't pressing charges. As for your transaction with Lucas Hendriksen, if illegal substances are found on his person while at the hospital, that, too, will be viewed as a big deal." He paused. "And a crime."

Chapter Fifteen

"I'm such a blueberry fiend. They're my favorite fruit." I looked down at the fresh berries cradled in my palm. "But after this blueberry season, I may switch my allegiance to raspberries. Too many bad memories." I tossed the berries into my mouth.

Denise smiled. "If you eliminate berries that are tied to bad memories, you may run out of varieties soon. Don't forget what happened during the recent strawberry and blackberry seasons."

"You're right. Not even murder should knock blueberries off my number one slot."

"Strawberries for me." Denise held up her strawberry milkshake. "My grandmother made *wojapi* all summer, using whatever berry was in season. I loved her strawberry *wojapi* best."

"That's a Native American sauce, isn't it?"

She nodded. "Tasted wonderful with a slice of fry bread. But I'm fond of blueberries, too." Denise finished off her milkshake. "When will your sheriff friend arrive?"

"He said he'd be here soon. I certainly hope so. This day seems fifty hours long."

Denise and I had already closed our shops and now sat at one of the bistro tables near the Berry Basket ice cream counter. Business dramatically picked up after dinner, which meant neither of us had the opportunity to dwell on what had happened at the O'Neill farm. With the CLOSED sign posted on our doors and our employees sent home, Denise and I couldn't wait to do likewise. But Kit Holt called to say he had information that we might be interested in about what had occurred at the farm.

However, it wasn't interest that Denise and I felt about the O'Neills: it was concern. Yes, Wyatt was a dishonest, unlikable young man, probably doomed to messing up his life every step of the way. Yet his parents loved him and suffered over his insolence, his reckless behavior, his lies. I didn't have to be a parent to sympathize and pity them. I hoped for everyone's sake that Brody could get his thoughtless son on the right track. Only I feared Wyatt possessed neither the will nor the intelligence to do so. A sad business all the way around.

"I wonder if Deputy Holt has learned what happened to Lucas." Denise gave a last noisy slurp with her straw to finish off the shake.

"I'm sure he has. I met him last month when he was working on the murder connected to the Blackberry Art School. He's a good guy."

"Attractive too. Curly-brown hair, big brown eyes. A little on the husky side."

"It's muscle, not fat. Kit works out at the gym four days a week."

Denise lifted an eyebrow. "You're on a first-name basis *and* you know his workout schedule. I thought the two of you kept throwing glances at each other when we were on the farm." She laughed. "Don't look so guilty, Marlee. You're engaged, not dead. You're allowed to find other men attractive."

"It's more than that. Kit's kind and smart and funny. And he listens to me. I wonder what would have happened if I'd met him before Ryan and I began dating."

"Are you having second thoughts about marrying Ryan?"

"Third thoughts, too. I'm worried I can't trust him."

She laid her hand over mine. "Without trust, any love between you will die. That much I do know."

"What's your opinion of Ryan?"

"I don't know him well enough to judge. He seems easygoing. Cute, sexy. Responsible and hardworking from all accounts. Am I wrong?"

"No. Except I've learned he's also like an iceberg—most of him lies hidden beneath the surface."

Denise frowned. "I don't like the sound of that."

A rap on the glass door made us jump. I got up to let Kit Holt in.

"Thanks for waiting until I could get here," he said. "But I wanted to let you know what happened at the hospital. First, Lucas Hendriksen is fine."

"Thank God," I murmured.

"Because you'd seen an exchange between the two men, we searched Lucas's clothing and found a plastic bag containing pills."

"What kind of pills?" I asked.

"The long version is 3,4-methylenedioxy-N-methylamphetamine. The drug is also known as crystal MDMA, Ecstasy, Molly."

"Isn't Ecstasy a club drug?" Denise looked worried.

"Yes. The drug induces euphoria. Only Lucas didn't experience much euphoria today. The doctors found traces of MDMA in his system. When he recovered, he admitted that he took a pill earlier. One of the drug's side effects is overheating, which was exacerbated by him working in the sun. Other side effects include chills, fast heartbeat, high blood pressure. It explains his erratic behavior."

"Did he admit Wyatt sold him the pills?"

"I'm afraid not, Marlee. Lucas said he bought them from some guy in Grand Rapids. And that the money he gave Wyatt today was to pay him back for concert tickets."

Denise wore a frustrated expression. "What happens next?"

"We charged Lucas with possession of a Schedule One drug. Maximum penalty is ten years in prison or fifteen thousand dollars in fines."

"Oh, no," I said. "That's too severe."

"Lucas is still a minor. He doesn't turn eighteen until next month. A minor charged with possession on a first offense is likely to get no more than probation."

"What about Wyatt?" Denise asked. "Obviously, Lucas lied to protect him."

"We got a warrant to search the O'Neill premises. Turned up nothing," Kit said. "Wyatt must have cleaned the place out. He knew we'd find the pills on Lucas and that his family house would be the next place to look. Unfortunately, neither of you was close enough to Wyatt and Lucas to actually see what Wyatt gave him."

"It had to have been the plastic bag of pills," I said.

"Not necessarily. Lucas also had an e-cigarette in his pockets and a bag of butterscotch hard candies. He claims Wyatt handed over the candy, not the pills."

"Of all the ridiculous things to say!" Denise grabbed her purse from the table. "As if a young man with a reputation for peddling drugs to teens is giving them candy instead. So Wyatt has evaded justice once again. This is disgraceful."

Kit had his mouth open to speak, but Denise had already stormed out. "Too bad she left," he said. "I wasn't done."

With a heavy heart, I cleared off the bistro table. "Denise has a strong sense of justice. I also suspect she knew someone with drug problems in the past. Probably a young person. I don't blame her for being upset. Wyatt seems to be skating around every roadblock, whether it concerns his thefts or his drug dealing. It's not right."

"The sheriff's department has a strong sense of justice, too," Kit said with a small smile. "And I think we'll be able to get Lucas to change his story about Wyatt."

"How?"

"I spoke with his dad at the hospital. His name is Frank Hendriksen; he owns a company that mows lawns and shovels snow. When he learned Lucas could have been seriously injured because he'd popped some pills, he got even angrier than Brody O'Neill. Blames all this on Wyatt. Says he's been selling drugs to his kid since he was in tenth grade. The only way to prove it is for Lucas to change his story." Holt followed me into the store kitchen where I put Denise's glass in the dishwasher. "He gave me his assurance that once Lucas has completely recovered, he'd make certain his son told the truth to the authorities. I believe him."

"Then Wyatt may finally have to face the consequences."

"If he's charged with possession and sale of a drug, they'll be serious consequences. Michigan has tough drug laws."

"Kit, I know you're not assigned to the Porter Gale case, but I'm sure Greg has spoken to you about it."

He stared back at me with a quizzical expression.

"I don't expect any inside information," I continued, "but I already know Porter died under suspicious circumstances."

"An official statement will be released tomorrow. Everyone is about to know that his death is being treated as a homicide."

"Exactly. A homicide where potassium chloride may have been the weapon. Denise and I saw bags of potassium chloride by the sheds on the O'Neill farm today."

He remained impassive. "It wouldn't surprise me if every fruit grower in the county kept the substance on their property."

"But not every fruit grower stands to benefit if Porter Gale dies. His will was read today. The Blueberry Hill fortune has been split evenly between

Cara O'Neill and Sloane. Someone in those two families could be the killer. And Wyatt already has a criminal record."

"Marlee, please let the police handle the case. You've made an enemy of Wyatt, and I know the type. He thinks he's smarter than he is, but he's vindictive. Lucas seems frightened of him. Maybe with good reason. You're already on Wyatt's radar, which means he may want to strike back. Don't get any more involved."

"I can't help but feel involved. After all, Greg and Chief Hitchcock want to speak to Ryan as soon as he gets back from his fishing trip. And it isn't to ask him about how much perch he caught. He's a suspect."

"The Gale homicide is not my case. But I will say that if your fiancé doesn't return to Oriole Point soon, a warrant may be issued for his arrest."

"Why? What have you learned?" I braced myself to hear the worst.

"Too bad you didn't hold off on taking that vacation to Illinois. I'd feel better if you were out of town right now. You're too close to all the players in this case." He leaned over the washboard near the sink. "How was the trip, by the way?"

"Wonderful. I always enjoy visiting my parents in Chicago. And going to Champaign to meet Theo's family was the right thing for both of us, especially after everything that happened last month. We needed to unwind." I gave him an inquisitive look. "If you're so interested in how my trip went, I'm surprised it's taken two weeks to ask me about it."

"I knew you'd have a lot to catch up with after being gone. And I'm working on a tricky case."

He hesitated. "I also thought it best to stay away for a while."

"Your brother-in-law told me. I got the impression Greg advised you to keep your distance from me. Which I find a little hurtful. I thought we were friends, Kit."

"We are, and I value that friendship. But don't be hard on Greg. In the ten years Greg's been married to my sister, he's become like a brother to me. I went through a bad breakup a couple years ago, and he doesn't want to see me get hurt again. He can't help himself. Being overprotective is in his DNA."

"I understand him watching out for you, but our relationship never turned romantic. Why all the concern?"

Kit sighed. "Because he could see I'd grown fond of you, and not just as a friend. I have, Marlee. No point in denying it. I think I knew I was in trouble from the moment I first saw you at the picnic table on the Sanderling farm, petting that Great Dane lying all over your feet."

When Kit, representing the sheriff's department, arrived that day, Piper's giant puppy and I had just discovered a buried skeleton on the property. From the first I'd found Kit appealing. It appeared the feeling was mutual . . . but I had suspected as much.

"I care for you, Marlee," he went on in a low voice. "Far more than I should, given that you're engaged to someone else. Greg was right to warn me off. The last thing I want is to get between you and Ryan." He shrugged. "But maybe I'm misreading the signs, and I'm the only one of us that feels this way."

The darkening kitchen felt close and intimate, as if the rest of the world lay sleeping and only this curly-haired man and I were awake. A wave of emotion swept over me—equal parts guilt and happiness. I shouldn't be having such strong feelings for Kit while engaged to Ryan. Yet learning the attraction between us was mutual gave me a rush of pleasure.

"You're not mistaken. I have romantic feelings toward you as well." My heart quickened at the smile that sprang to his lips. "Only I don't know what to do about it, especially at the moment. This week has left me reeling. I feel like I'm caught in something, Kit. Only I don't know how to get out."

"I understand. You need time to think about what you really want for the future. That's why I've kept my distance."

"It's more than that. I'm afraid Ryan has been lying to me."

"About what?"

"About everything." I choked back a sob. "It makes me afraid for him. And me."

Kit came over and took me by the arms. "Are you afraid he's done something wrong? Illegal? Are you afraid he might hurt you? Be honest with me."

I would have loved nothing more than to lay my head against Kit's chest, but I needed to keep focused. "Ryan could never hurt me, at least not physically. But he's keeping things from me, and I'm worried it might get him into trouble."

"Something to do with Porter Gale's murder?"

"It can't be. Ryan is not a killer."

"Please trust no one until the Porter Gale case has been solved. Except for me." He brushed the hair back from my face. "I want you to trust me."

"I do." I stared up at him. "I trust you, Kit."

I don't know who made the first move, but it was as close to mutual as one could get. As we pressed against each other, I felt his own heart racing to match that of mine. Small wonder. Our kiss seemed endless, ardent, and intoxicating. My cell phone on the nearby counter began to wail its *Mission Impossible* ringtone, but neither of us cared. We let the kiss continue through all five rings, only breaking apart as a familiar chime signaled that someone had left a voice mail.

When we stepped back from each other, his dazed expression mirrored my own.

"Yes," he said in a voice barely above a whisper. "More than friends."

"Definitely." My feelings had seesawed all week. A passionate kiss from Kit Holt had intensified them. But I was no longer confused. If I had such strong feelings for another man, I couldn't marry Ryan. Even if nothing came of my romance with Kit Holt, what just occurred proved I could not walk down the aisle with Ryan Zellar in January. Or ever.

As if echoing my phone, Holt's cell vibrated and he took it out of his shirt pocket.

"Sheriff business?" I asked as he read the text message.

"I'm officially off duty, but I asked one of my officers to text me if further information surfaced about a suspect. It has." After replying with his own text, Holt stuffed the phone back in his pocket. "Sorry, Marlee. I have to go."

"Of course. But let me give you and your officers something to snack on." Grabbing a white pastry box, I filled it with slices of blueberry coffee cake, then tied it up with string. "Theo used an old Betty Crocker recipe he had from his mother. It's a classic. Delicious too."

He took the box from me with a grin. "You had me at coffee cake."

"Wait until the winter. Theo won an award at last year's Winter Carnival for his cranberry nut coffee cake."

"Ah. Then you intend to provide me with coffee cake year-round?"

I gave him a careless shrug. "If you like."

Holt leaned over for another kiss, this one gentle and sweet. "I do like." His expression grew serious. "Be careful, Marlee. If you suspect Ryan is lying about something, I'd feel a lot happier if you kept your distance from him. At least until the Gale case is solved. Maybe you should keep your distance from me as well. You need time to think about everything without any distractions."

"I like distractions. They make life interesting." I also liked the way his eyes crinkled when he smiled, which he did right before hurrying out the door.

"That was unexpected," I said aloud to my empty shop. Unexpected, but welcome. I hadn't felt this giddy and excited about someone of the opposite sex since my adolescent crush on David Boreanaz on the TV show *Angel*. I found Kit even more appealing. And he wasn't a vampire, either. How in the world did I ever imagine I was ready to marry Ryan? Maybe my biological clock had kicked in early. Or I'd simply had too many unsatisfying relationships. Despite my bridal jitters, part of me wanted a lifelong commitment. But Ryan had been the wrong man. I wondered if Kit Holt could be the right one.

I bit back a yawn as I shut off the lights and locked the front door. Walking through the kitchen to reach the rear parking lot, I spied my phone on the counter. Picking it up, I checked to see who had left a voice mail while I was kissing Kit. My buoyant mood burst like a punctured balloon when I saw Ryan had called.

His voice mail announced he was on his way to my house.

I sped through the village streets to reach my home on Lakeshore Drive, breathing a sigh of relief when I saw Ryan's truck was nowhere in sight. At least I had made it here before him. But I didn't know what the advantage in that was, aside from giving me extra time to prepare myself. There was a lot we needed to discuss. I wasn't looking forward to the conversation.

As I took Minnie out of her cage, I reminded myself that we also had to discuss my feelings for Kit Holt. And what it meant for the future Ryan and I had planned. "What do you think, sweetie?" I asked Minnie as I stroked her head. "Is this the time to bring all of this up? Because if I do, I'm pretty sure that's the last either of us will see of Ryan."

Minnie whistled and replied, "Hello. Who's a pretty bird?"

"You are," I reassured her.

I heard the front door swing open. "Hey, babe. It's me."

At the sound of Ryan's voice, Minnie cried, "Daddy's home."

Placing Minnie on my shoulder, I went to greet Ryan. Slinging a duffel bag on the floor, he swept me up in his arms for a kiss, careful not to dislodge Minnie from her perch. I felt my cheeks burn red as I kissed him. Having recently done the same with Kit, this kiss seemed dishonest and wrong. I wasn't cut out for anything but a ruthlessly honest life.

"Are you hungry?" I quickly stepped out of his embrace. "I ate dinner in town, but I've got chicken salad in the fridge."

"Nah, I stopped for dinner on the way back." He grabbed me by the arm to prevent me from walking away. "I've missed my girl."

"I'm surprised you were gone three days. With the Blueberry Blow Out still going on, I expected you back yesterday."

He shrugged. "The fishing was good."

I looked at the duffel bag near the door. "I don't see a cooler with perch for me to clean."

"I let Josh keep all of them."

"You're kidding. You love perch."

"I love you even more. And I didn't want to be bothered with anything but you and me when I got back. I've made plans." He wore a mischievous look.

"Plans for what?"

"Wait till you see." He went over to the duffel bag and pulled out an envelope. "These are airline tickets, hon. In the morning we leave for Vegas."

I couldn't have heard right. "Vegas? Why?"

"Because I can't wait until January." His grin grew wider. "We're getting married tomorrow!"

Chapter Sixteen

Minnie expressed my exact thoughts when she said, "Are you crazy, mate?"

Ryan laughed at her response, but I was not amused. "You can't be serious, Ryan. I'm not running off to Vegas to get married."

"Why not? It makes more sense than waiting until January. Even my dad advised me to elope. He's been through this whole thing with all my brothers. The Zellars are wedding fatigued."

"How nice for the Zellars. But I'm a Jacob. And an only child. Do you really think I would hurt my parents by getting married without them by my side?"

He rolled his eyes. "Okay, okay. I'll go online and see if I can book them tickets, too."

"You're not doing any such thing. Neither my parents nor I are going to Vegas tomorrow for some tacky last-minute wedding. I can't believe you thought I'd be okay with this."

"Excuse me? Tacky?" He shook his head. "I've booked a suite at The Bellagio. And Josh told me about this great wedding chapel called Chapel of the Flowers. His cousin got married there last year. It's first class all the way. Nothing tacky about it."

"Tacky, tacky, tacky," Minnie repeated, no doubt thrilled to imitate a new word.

"Cancel it." I crossed my arms. "We're not going to Vegas. I've had enough of you making decisions without a word to me first. It's rude and selfish."

"You're the selfish one." Ryan stuffed the airline tickets back into his duffel bag. "How about asking what I want once in a while?"

"I don't have to. You tell me all the time. You don't want a big wedding this winter. You don't want to spend time around my friends, except for Tess. You don't want to live in this house after we get married. In fact, you want me to sell my family home as soon as possible."

"Yeah. And have you done it? Of course not. That's because you're the selfish one. Too bad you didn't have brothers and sisters. They might have taught you to compromise."

Minnie whistled. Since she sat on my shoulder, I winced at the piercing sound.

"Are you kidding? You've gotten your way with every female you've ever met. Starting with your mother. And please tell me when you've made a single compromise since we became engaged? Really, give me an example. All I've heard you do is plan every step of our lives."

"I thought we wanted the same things."

"Which proves you don't listen to me."

"Well, I'm listening now. And I don't like what I'm hearing." Ryan kicked his duffel bag. "Here I was all excited about you and me going to Vegas tomorrow so we can officially start our life together. I can't believe I was so stupid."

"Not stupid, Ryan. Oblivious." With a heavy sigh, I walked over to my tartan love seat and sat down. Minnie hopped off my shoulder to perch on the nearby upholstered arm. "And you have more important things to be concerned about than an impromptu trip to Vegas. The police want to speak with you as soon as possible."

"About what?"

"Porter Gale's death. It's being treated as a homicide."

"Homicide? Are you kidding me?"

I told him about the potassium chloride in Porter's insulin shot and the deadly effect it had.

His expression went from frustrated to amused. "Looks like I wasn't the only one who couldn't stand the bastard."

"Ryan, this isn't funny. The police want to see you because you're a suspect."

"That's ridiculous."

"You physically attacked Porter hours before he died. And you made no bones about how much you hated him."

"I'm not the only one." Ryan threw himself down on the glider rocker across from me. "His sister Cara couldn't stand him. Let the police go after her. Or his stepmother, who didn't get much of anything from his dad's will. Maybe Jacqueline is the timid little mouse who finally roared." He grinned.

"You need to take this seriously, Ryan. To the police it looks like you had a vendetta against Porter. The EMS guy at the fairground told them you appeared happy when you learned he was dead."

This sobered him. "Damn."

"Even worse, they know you have access to vials of insulin. And I had no idea your mother was diabetic. When the police told me, it came as a shock. You never mentioned it."

He waved his hand. "Why should I? I don't see how my mother's diabetes has anything to do with you."

This made me even sadder. "I've told you everything about my family, including my dad's heart problems. People about to get married do tell each other about their families."

"Fine. My mother was diagnosed with diabetes when she was fifty-one. Are you happy?"

"Tie me kangaroo down," Minnie sang out.

I counted to ten, trying to keep my composure. "There seem to be other things you haven't told me about."

"Like what?"

"Like why you were seen at a gas station in Valparaiso, Indiana, on Tuesday morning."

I knew Ryan well enough to recognize when he was rattled. "What are you talking about? I was in Muskegon about to go out on Josh's boat."

"Are you sticking with that story?"

Minnie whistled, then added, "Peeky boo, I see you."

His tanned cheeks grew flushed. "It's not a story."

"Natasha and Old Man Bowman visited my booth at the fairground Wednesday evening. They'd taken a day trip to Chicago on Tuesday. He told me that he'd seen you at the gas station around seven thirty that morning. He even said hello to you, but you ignored him."

"You believe that kook? Old Man Bowman is off his rocker, and you know it. The man spends half his time hunting for Bigfoot, the other half doing God knows what with that Russian beauty queen."

"Natasha saw you, too. And she's not crazy."

"Isn't she?"

"Give it up, Ryan. Old Man Bowman also described Josh. And we both know Josh is a distinctive-looking guy. So why were you in Indiana instead of up north?"

Ryan began rocking the glider. "I can't believe I'm being cross-examined like this. You're worse than the police."

"And you're lying to me. I don't know why. Have you lied about all your fishing trips? If so, what have you been doing every other month when I thought you were out on the lake in Josh's boat?"

He remained silent.

"Can you fly?" Minnie murmured.

I took a deep breath. "Fine. Keep lying. Say nothing. Pretend everyone but you is crazy. Only I suggest you come up with a better story when Detective Trejo and Chief Hitchcock question you. Otherwise, you may be arrested."

Ryan brought the rocker to a standstill. "If you must know, Josh and I weren't fishing. We went to Indiana Grand instead."

"Indiana Grand? What's that?"

"Indiana Grand Racing and Casino. It's in Shelbyville, about thirty miles south of Indianapolis."

I wondered if I had misheard him. "You've spent the past three days gambling in Indiana?"

"Yeah. Josh and I need to blow off steam once in a while, and gambling relaxes us."

"Fishing's not relaxing?"

"We do that, too. But some of our trips are spent at the casinos in Indiana."

I was confused. "Why Indiana? There are casinos a lot closer to home here in Michigan."

"Because we'd rather not run into people we know. The point of the trip is to get away and relax. And don't act like we're doing something illegal or shocking. Going to the casinos is fun. It's a welcome break. Josh and I bust our backs most of the year working on our farms. Why shouldn't we spend a few days at the dice tables or playing blackjack? Do you have a problem with that?"

"Where's the owl?" Minnie murmured.

"Ryan, I don't care if you become a blackjack dealer. What I care about is that you've been lying to me for months about these trips. Is this why you turn off your phone when you're gone? Are you afraid I'd hear all the noise and know you weren't out on the lake?"

He avoided my gaze. "I thought it was easier that way. No need to make you and Sara suspicious."

Sara was Josh's wife. "Josh is lying to her, too?"

"You're making too a big deal about this. Look, Sara is tight with the family finances. She doesn't even want Josh to buy a lottery ticket. If she knew he spent a few days at the casinos, she'd make his life miserable. Besides, we only do that half the time. The rest of our trips we do go fishing."

"So you say."

"You think I'm lying?"

I stared back at him. "Can you blame me?"

"You're just spoiling for a fight, aren't you?"

"No. I'm trying to get at the truth!" I looked down

at my hands, trying to compose myself. "Did you owe Porter Gale money?"

"I can speak," Minnie said. Only it was Ryan I wanted to hear from, not her.

Instead he sat rigid and silent. "Where did you hear that?" he said finally.

"Someone in the O'Neill family told me." If I said it was Courtney, Ryan would dismiss anything repeated by a fourteen-year-old girl.

"Was it Cara?" he asked. "I should have known he'd tell his sister."

Then it was true. "Does it matter who said it? Why did you borrow money from Porter? And from Eric Gale as well. Two years ago, your father decided to give his inheritance to you and your brothers. All of you received large amounts of cash and your own acres at Zellar Orchards. Why would you need to borrow money from anyone? Particularly a person you disliked as much as Porter Gale."

"It's complicated. And it doesn't concern you."

"You wanted me to fly to Las Vegas tomorrow and marry you. Would it have concerned me once I was your wife? Or were you going to keep me in the dark?"

"I've been dealing with this on my own, Marlee. The last thing I need is you hassling me about it. And maybe it's time for you to be more honest. You don't want to marry me, do you? You've already tried to postpone the wedding. Why? I treat you like a queen."

I gave him a disbelieving look. "You can't be serious."

"Damn straight, I'm serious. Are you bored with me? Is that it? Or is there someone else? I wouldn't be surprised if your old high school boyfriend Max has won you back. The way he always calls you 'marzipan' and acts so sweet around you."

"I've told you a hundred times, Max and I are just friends."

"Maybe it isn't Max." He narrowed his eyes at me. "It could be the sheriff's deputy you met last month. The one with the curly hair. Are you going to tell me that you and he are just friends, too?"

As if she knew I needed support, Minnie hopped over to me and I placed her back on my shoulder. "No, I won't tell you that. Kit and I have become more than friends."

Wearing a shocked expression, Ryan jumped to his feet. "I knew it! I knew there had to be another man to make you so reluctant to marry me. Only I couldn't believe you'd be this dishonest. How dare you accuse me of lying when you've been cheating with another man all along? And while wearing my engagement ring! You're disgusting." He began to pace.

"No one has been cheating, Ryan. Nothing romantic ever transpired between Kit and me." I hesitated. "Not until tonight when I kissed him."

He whirled about to glare at me. "You kissed him?"

"We kissed each other. Nothing else happened. Before this, we were only friends, but—" I hesitated.

"But?" he spat at me.

"But I liked him. I also suspected his feelings were growing for me. I was right." Minnie made kissing noises in my ear. I stroked her feathers, hoping to quiet her.

"Are you in love with him?"

I shook my head. "Of course not. I don't know him well enough to be in love with him."

"But you don't love me any longer." There was anger—and pain—in his voice.

"I do love you, Ryan. But you loved your first wife and it didn't matter. The marriage fell apart. I've been having second thoughts about us for months. You know that. We're too different to make this work. I can't believe you don't see that as well."

"What I see is a woman who lied to me. Who deceived me with another man."

"That's not true! Until our kiss tonight, Kit and I have been as proper as Amish teenagers. And less than an hour later, I'm telling you all about it. So I refuse to sit here and play the scarlet woman just to make you feel better about your own lies."

"You're comparing a romance with another man with me not telling you about my casino trips!"

"I want a cashew," Minnie piped up.

"Let's get the semantics right. You *lied* about your gambling trips." I stood up. "And you won't tell me why you went to Eric and Porter Gale for money. Do you have a gambling problem? Is that why you borrowed money from them? This past June I learned you had a drug problem when you were a teenager. Is gambling another addiction I don't know about?"

"Don't deflect the conversation away from you and your curly-haired boyfriend. Is he waiting for me to leave? He'll probably move right in, won't he? I'm betting that a man who works for the sheriff's department doesn't pull in a big salary. He'll enjoy living on the beach in this old house you're so attached to." Ryan stomped over to his duffel bag and picked it up.

I followed him. "Speaking of my house, why have you been pushing me to sell it?"

"Are you kidding me? You're going to bring up the house at a moment like this?"

"Kiss for Mommy," Minnie said in my ear.

"To be clear, you brought it up first. Like you've been bringing up the subject of selling it ever since we became engaged. Why was it important for me to sell the house? You'd already claimed your Zellar inheritance. We didn't need the money." I gave him a long look. "Except if you borrowed from the Gales, you did need money."

"You know I don't want to live in the village. My home is at the orchards, where I've always intended to build us a house. We don't need this white elephant you're living in. Although given the color, I should call it a blue elephant." He shook his head at me. "But you won't give it up, will you? Even though you didn't live here for the ten years you worked in New York. I think you're holding on to this house just to spite me."

"What?"

Minnie echoed my own disbelief by adding, "Wassup?"

"You heard me."

"This house belongs to the Jacobs, and it's meant to be passed on to a Jacob when the time comes. I'm sick of your indifference to my family and our traditions when you spend every waking moment with the Zellar clan. There are cults less tight-knit than the Zellars!"

"Leave my family out of this. This rickety old

house is why you're second-guessing our marriage. It's not your deputy boyfriend at all. You want to break up with me because I asked you to do the smart thing and sell it."

I took a step back as something dawned on me. "I was told that you borrowed money from Eric Gale last autumn. Several months later, you proposed to me."

"What are you trying to say?"

"You borrowed more money from Porter this spring," I continued. "For months, you've hounded me to sell the house. Now you want us to get married ASAP. But is it because you can't wait to start our life together? Or because, as my husband, everything I own would become yours? Including this house."

"You think I'm marrying you to get the house?" Ryan asked in a hoarse voice, which meant he was now quite upset. However, so was I.

"I think you need money. Maybe the money you borrowed from the Gales wasn't enough. But if you were looking for another source of money, my beachfront property is a great place to start. I bet you've already looked into the current market price for it, too."

"How low will you stoop to get out of our engagement?" Ryan shook his head at me. "Sure, I've asked a Realtor about it. After all, once we were married, the house would have been half mine. Why shouldn't I learn its value? And it is valuable, Marlee. We could list it tomorrow for one million one hundred and ninety-five thousand dollars! That's a fortune for people like us. And you want to keep it?

You're either stupid or the most obstinate woman I know."

I felt like I'd been punched in the stomach. "You never loved me at all. You only wanted to get your hands on the money if I sold it."

"Do you hear yourself? Making crazy things up because you want to break off the engagement. I never thought you'd sink so low."

"Tacky, tacky, tacky," Minnie repeated.

"And I never thought our relationship would end like this." I pulled off my engagement ring. "Take your ring back. And please go."

With shock in his eyes, Ryan stared at me for a tense moment before snatching the ring from my fingers. A moment later, he was gone.

Tears rolled down my cheeks. "What do you think of all that?" I whispered to the bird nestled on my shoulder.

For the first time since I'd adopted her, Minnie had nothing to say.

Chapter Seventeen

The following morning I arrived at the church for Porter Gale's memorial service in a mood as dark as the navy summer dress I wore. No matter how many chilled spoons I had used to reduce the swelling around my eyes, I suspected everyone could see I'd been crying. Attendees might wonder why I appeared to be grieving so much for Porter. I hoped rumors wouldn't surface of some secret affair I'd had with the dead man. I considered wearing sunglasses, but they didn't seem appropriate inside the church.

Trying to remain unobtrusive, I took a seat in an empty back pew, then busied myself with the hymnal. My sudden interest in church music might prevent anyone from speaking with me. I felt talked out after last night.

As soon as Ryan left, I called Tess, who rushed over like the stalwart best friend she was. The pair of us deconstructed my relationship with Ryan for hours, accompanied by bouts of crying from me and endless sympathy and support from Tess. I also remembered a bottle of wine being consumed at some point—along with an entire box of dark chocolate truffles. At least the wine helped me sleep, but as soon as I woke up I remembered that any future with Ryan was officially over. And that he had probably never loved me.

It left me in the proper mood to attend a memorial service. I was officially in mourning over the sad end to my relationship with Ryan.

Pretending to be interested in the lyrics to the hymn "Let All Mortal Flesh Keep Silence," I ignored the people who streamed into the church for the eleven o'clock service. Every snatch of conversation I overheard seemed devoid of any reference to Porter. Instead, people talked about the Blueberry Blow Out, the perfect summer weather, and the latest debate about a local biking trail that had been proposed. Curious over whether any of Porter's family had arrived, I peeked up from my hymnal in time to see Cara and Brody O'Neill walk down the aisle. Dressed in what I would have dubbed their Sunday best, the couple greeted everyone with a sunny smile. Courtney trailed behind, waving at her friends. Their good cheer didn't surprise me. Porter's death had made them one of the wealthiest families in Oriole County.

I scanned the crowded church, but didn't see Wyatt. Maybe the sheriff's department or Lucas Hendriksen's father had been able to convince the teenager to admit Wyatt sold him drugs yesterday. Wyatt might be in custody. But the rest of the O'Neills appeared in high spirits, so I dismissed that scenario. Wyatt must still be at large.

Speak of the devil, I thought when Wyatt entered

the church with Sloane. With an arm protectively
draped over her shoulders, Wyatt led his young
aunt to the front pew where the rest of the family,
including Jacqueline, sat.

Despite Wyatt's solicitude, Sloane appeared calm
and dry eyed. Indeed, she looked a lot better than
I did. I was glad to see she had recovered from her
collapse following Porter's death. In fact, she seemed
to have reverted to her former vivacious and allur-
ing self, outfitted in a flirty black skirt and sleeveless
white sweater. However, she had pinned her long
blond hair up, which probably signaled the seri-
ousness of the occasion for her. I wasn't passing
judgment. Married only a year, Sloane and Porter
had barely known each other before that. No doubt
the shocking circumstances of his death had been
too much for her. But it looked as if Sloane was already bouncing back. I hoped she had enough
sense to make the unsavory Wyatt keep his distance.

"Could you move over, Marlee?"

I tore my attention from Wyatt and Sloane.
Ryan's mother looked down at me from the aisle,
her normally friendly expression replaced by one
far sterner than I was accustomed to. She gestured
at the empty pew I sat on.

With a sinking heart, I scooted over. "Good morning, Mrs. Zellar."

"I wouldn't call it a good morning for Porter's
family members. Or for my son. Not after what you
did last night." She sat beside me.

An uncomfortable silence followed. "Is Ryan
here?" I asked finally.

"No. He's at the police station. It appears you told

him that Chief Hitchcock wanted to speak with him as soon as he returned."

Although grateful that he went to the police before they came for him, I worried at the outcome of his interview with Hitchcock. "Did Ryan send you to talk to me?"

"Of course not. My son has too much pride. Although you've managed to destroy that. Along with breaking his heart."

I looked around to make certain our conversation remained private. No one sat in the three rows ahead of us, and our own pew was still empty. "Mrs. Zellar, your son has broken my heart as well. He's kept too many things from me. Or maybe he hasn't told you about that."

Her blue-eyed gaze, so like the eyes of her son, bored into me. "If you mean his drug use as a teen, I thought you had moved past that. It happened years before the two of you dated. And Ryan quickly recovered from his youthful indiscretions. I'm shocked to learn you're such an unforgiving person."

I saw little benefit in discussing this with Ryan's mother. It wouldn't change anything. Still, it hurt to have her hold such a low opinion of me. When Ryan and I announced our engagement this past winter, the entire Zellar family had been overjoyed. Although my own family was no longer in the orchard business, I made a living from berries. This marked me as one of them, and not an outsider like Ryan's first wife. But overnight, I had fallen from the Zellars' good graces.

"I also never thought you were a cheater," she went on, disapproval in her voice. "Your parents would be ashamed of you, cheating on my son with another man. With a law enforcement officer, too. Ryan told his father and me all about your sorry affair."

I changed my mind about setting her straight. "Mrs. Zellar, I never cheated on Ryan. Yes, I kissed another man last night—just a kiss—but nothing else happened. And I told Ryan about it as soon as I could. I wanted to be honest and aboveboard with him."

She snorted with derision.

"Which is more than I can say for your son," I went on. "For example, he lied about his fishing trips this past year. Did he tell you that half those trips were spent gambling in Indiana?"

"Impossible. Ryan never gambles. He doesn't even buy lottery tickets."

"He gambles. So does his buddy Josh. And this latest trip was spent at a place called the Indiana Grand Casino in Shelbyville."

She appeared startled. "If he did, it must have been a onetime thing. Maybe Josh came up with the idea." Determined to deny her son had lied, she reminded me of Cara O'Neill. "And what would be so awful if he did spend the trip gambling?"

"Nothing. I wouldn't care if he'd flown off to Monaco to play roulette. I do care that he's lied about these trips for a year." I nervously tapped the hymnal in my lap. "Mrs. Zellar, this isn't the time or place to discuss Ryan or our relationship. I do love your son, but we just couldn't make things work out."

"I doubt you tried very hard, Marlee."

"You're wrong. I wanted to make it work so much

that I ignored the truth. I can't do it any longer. If we got married, it wouldn't be fair to either of us."

"This is sad. I looked forward to you joining our family." She shook her head. "So did Ryan. Now I understand why he's been out of sorts these past few months. I thought he was impatient to get married again and start a family. Ryan has always wanted kids. But he must have guessed you weren't happy and was afraid you'd break things off. And so you have." Grabbing the back of the pew in front of us, she pulled herself to her feet.

"I'm sorry. I wish things had turned out differently."

"My poor boy. He's alone again. No wonder he seems in a desperate state."

"Desperate?" I didn't like the sound of that. "You don't mean suicidal?"

"Don't be silly. Ryan is much too stable. But he is tense. Agitated. I'm sure it's because of the breakup." She shot me an accusing look. "And you."

Even after Ryan's mother walked away, her statement *No wonder he seems in a desperate state* rang in my ears. Ryan's desperation probably had little to do with losing me and everything to do with his need for money. Given the church setting, I decided to pray that Ryan's desperation hadn't led to Porter Gale's death.

After the service ended, I couldn't wait to head for The Berry Basket. Gillian, the Cabot boys, and my customers had never seemed so appealing. No wonder I was a workaholic. But as I mingled with the crowd leaving the church, other people caught sight of me, necessitating lots of brief conversations. Since most of the attendees were either fruit growers or somehow connected with the industry, we were on a first-name basis.

When I finally stepped outside, I gave thanks that no one had noticed I no longer wore a diamond solitaire on my left hand. However, I steeled myself for the reaction of the Cabot boys, who would notice the ring's absence within seconds.

Cara and Brody stood along the brick path that led to the church entrance. With the minister beside them, the trio exchanged greetings with everyone who passed by. Courtney and several youthful friends mingled by the church sign, laughing and looking at their phones. I decided to cut across the lawn to the parking lot. Given what happened yesterday at the O'Neill farm, I thought the family may not want to deal with me again so soon.

"Marlee, please wait."

I turned around, relieved it was Jacqueline Gale who approached, not an O'Neill. "Jacqueline, allow me to offer my condolences."

She reached for my hand and held it tight. "It was kind of you to come. I haven't lived in Oriole Point long enough to appreciate how supportive a small town can be. The church seemed nearly packed, didn't it? A fine testament to Porter and Sloane. And Blueberry Hill."

"The O'Neill family, too, especially Cara."

"Of course. I think there may be even more people here than there were for my late husband's funeral. Sloane must be touched."

I looked over my shoulder to where Sloane and Wyatt stood talking beneath the elm that shaded the church. "She looks rested and calm. I'm glad. We heard she took the news of Porter's death quite hard."

"Sloane's young. The young are resilient, even after such a shock. After a shaky few days, she's seems to be holding up well." Jacqueline glanced at Sloane with a rueful expression. "I'm afraid I didn't bounce back that quickly after Eric's death. The doctor prescribed pills to help get me through it. Although it's been months since he died, I still find myself overwhelmed with grief." She gave me a sad smile. "And loneliness."

"That's to be expected."

"Is it? Some people didn't expect me to grieve at all. I'm aware of the rumors that I only married Eric for his money. But I did care for him. More than I realized."

Since she still held on to my right hand, I gave it a reassuring squeeze. "I wouldn't pay attention to any rumors floating around Oriole Point. Gossip is the lifeblood of residents, along with lawsuits. You aren't officially a citizen until someone threatens you with a lawsuit. The same is true of the gossip. Ignore it." I released her hand and took a step back. "I should go. I scheduled myself to work at the shop and the fairground today."

She lowered her voice. "Are you all right? Forgive me for saying so, but you look tired."

"I am tired. And I don't expect to get much sleep until the Blow Out is over."

"I'm sorry to ask this of you. But could you stop by my house today?"

"Do you want me there for the memorial luncheon? Thank you, but I can't." Before the service ended, Cara had thanked everyone for attending, then invited all of us to the luncheon that would be served on the grounds of Blueberry Hill within the hour. The catered event was certain to be lavish, and I regretted not being able to do so. But my day was packed. I also didn't want to mingle in a crowd that included both Wyatt and Ryan's disgruntled mother.

"This has nothing to do with the luncheon or the memorial service. It does concern you, though. At least by association." She paused. "It's about your fiancé, Ryan."

I opened my mouth to tell her we were no longer engaged, then decided against it. I even placed my hands behind my back so she couldn't glimpse my bare ring finger.

"Okay. If you think it's important."

"I do." Jacqueline looked down at her watch. "Now I need to leave as well. I've left the housekeeper to direct the caterers, but I should be there, too."

"I can make time later this afternoon. Four thirty?"

"Thanks. That will work out fine. Just drive up to the big house." With a gracious smile, Jacqueline set off to where a black SUV and driver waited along the curb.

If Jacqueline had information about Ryan, it might concern the money he had borrowed from her stepson. Since she assumed I was Ryan's future wife, she no doubt looked on me as the best person to speak with about the matter. I preferred she continue to believe that, at least until after our conversation. It could be my only opportunity to learn what he had been hiding from me. Even though I'd broken up with Ryan, I'd do what I could to protect him. At the least, I'd warn Ryan about any trouble lying ahead.

From the depths of my cluttered purse, my phone sang out its *Mission Impossible* theme. By the time I found it, the call had gone to voice mail. With some surprise, I listened to Natasha's heartfelt message as she poured out her sympathy over my breakup. She had run into Tess at Coffee by Crystal, where the two shared several iced teas and the woeful tale of the end of my engagement. Despite my glum mood, I chuckled at Natasha's message, half of which she delivered in Russian. The few English words she did manage expressed her hope that I not stay sad because "Ryan is like *Sibirskaya rys*: pretty, but do not get too close or your heart could get eaten."

I didn't know what a *Sibirskaya rys* was, but it sounded like something to avoid. As I put my phone away, I saw someone else I had hoped to avoid. Too late. Cara strode toward me in her usual energetic pace. Despite the sad occasion and the events at the farm yesterday, she looked even more serene than Sloane.

"Hi, Marlee. I didn't see you in the church. Brody and I were hoping you'd come."

"I sat in the back."

"It's good to see you here. After what happened yesterday at the farm, I worried there might be hard feelings between us. Please know that I don't blame you for accusing Wyatt of stealing money from your store. Given his past, your suspicion is understandable. But I know my son. He didn't do it. Any more than he sold drugs to Lucas. By the way, Lucas is going to be fine. Thank heaven."

"Yes, I heard he had recovered. And let's leave whatever happens next to law enforcement, not us."

When her smile dimmed, I added quickly, "I thought it was a lovely service. And the testimonials from Porter's workers were touching."

"Florence, Ken, and Wally have worked at Blueberry Hill for over twenty years. Porter regarded them as family. Until recently, he treated them better than family, too." She said this last with some bitterness.

"You must have been happy to learn Porter had left half of Blueberry Hill to you."

She nodded. "Thrilled. Vindicated. Relieved. I don't know what I would have done if the entire family business had been handed over to Sloane. Despite all my brother's sadistic taunts, in the end, blood was thicker than water for him. Blueberry Hill also belongs to me and my children now. Although I've spent years doubting it, there is justice in the world."

"Courtney told me about the terms of the will. How does Sloane feel about all this? As his wife, she may have expected to inherit everything."

She sniffed. "Sloane should count herself lucky. She and Porter were only married thirteen months.

And there were no children. I've never been so grateful that the two of them never managed to make me an aunt. I'd be in a much sorrier place if they had."

"Since you both own Blueberry Hill now, you'll be working together closely. I'm sure she has a lot to learn about running such a huge enterprise."

"From what I've seen of Sloane, it would take decades to turn her into a businesswoman. And I have zero interest in teaching her. I hope she allows me to buy her out. Using my share of Blueberry Hill as collateral, I'll be able to make her a handsome offer. I think she's shrewd enough to take it. With luck, she'll be packing her bags before autumn."

"Wyatt will be sad to see her go."

She gave me a weary look. "He makes no attempt to hide his obsession with her. Porter thought it was funny, but I don't. Sloane might set her sights on Wyatt next. After all, Blueberry Hill will belong to him and Courtney one day."

"Do you really think Sloane is that mercenary?"

"I don't know. But I prefer not to take the chance."

Both Cara and I turned to watch Sloane, who still stood beside Wyatt beneath the elm. At that moment, she said something to Wyatt, who appeared concerned. Sloane swayed as if buffeted by a strong wind, then crumpled to the ground.

Cara and I ran over before anyone else had even realized Sloane fainted.

We knelt on the grass beside her, while a pale Wyatt held Sloane in his arms. "What's wrong with Sloane?" he cried out. "Help her, please!"

"She fainted." I looked up at the onlookers who now crowded around. "Give her some air."

A long minute later, Sloane opened her eyes. She appeared confused. "What happened? Did I pass out?"

"Should I call EMS?" Wyatt seemed panicked.

"Please don't," Sloane said as I helped her to sit up. "I just got a little light-headed."

"I bet you didn't eat breakfast," Cara told her. "Porter always said you hated breakfast."

"Or maybe the stress of the memorial service was too much," I said.

"I know why I fainted. It's not stress. Or not eating breakfast." She smiled. "I'm pregnant."

Chapter Eighteen

Sloane's announcement took me by surprise. It had a different effect on Cara.

"Pregnant? Impossible!" Her face twisted with rage. "There's no way you're pregnant."

"But I am." Sloane wore a much calmer expression than I would have anticipated. Particularly since Cara seemed like she wanted to pummel the girl.

"You scheming little liar! This is some game you've cooked up to get Blueberry Hill."

"Mom, stop." Wyatt put up his hand in an effort to keep Cara at bay.

"How big a fool do you think I am?" she hissed at Sloane.

"Why can't she be pregnant?" Wyatt scowled at his mother. "Porter only just died."

"Don't be an idiot. She's not pregnant!" Cara got to her feet, as if she couldn't bear kneeling so close to Sloane on the ground.

"Cara, I've taken several home pregnancy tests," Sloane said with a weary sigh. "If you want further proof, I'll buy more test kits."

"Oh, I'll buy the test kits, young woman, and stand over you while you pee on them!"

"You sound crazy, Mom."

"You're the one who's crazy," she told her son. "Or plain stupid. Don't you see she's pretending to be pregnant because she wants all of Blueberry Hill? How convenient this little announcement is. As soon as my brother dies, she magically discovers she's having his baby. She's a liar and a gold digger! As I always suspected."

Brody joined our group. He looked even more distressed than the minister, who wisely kept his distance. "Keep it down, Cara. Everyone can hear."

"Your husband's right. Having this discussion in public isn't wise." I nodded toward the service attendees who hadn't left yet; everyone's attention was now on us.

"They may as well hear because I intend to prove what a liar she is." Cara shook a finger at Sloane. "Scheme all you want. Play my son for a fool. Pretend you're pregnant. But I will never let you steal Blueberry Hill from my family. Do you hear? I'll see you in the ground first!"

Brody pulled Cara away. Wyatt ran after them. By this time, Courtney had joined her family, all four of them arguing at the top of their lungs on the steps of the church.

Worried Cara might return, I turned to Sloane. "Do you feel strong enough to stand?"

She nodded and I helped her to her feet.

"Could you drive me back to Blueberry Hill?" she asked. "I don't care to be shouted at in public any longer."

"Sure. Would you like to wait here while I get my

car?" I thought she seemed a little shaky; I wasn't sure if that was because of the pregnancy or Cara's accusations.

"I'm pregnant, not ill. And to get away from Porter's sister, I'd crawl to the parking lot."

"No need for that." I took her by the elbow. "I'll get you there. No crawling necessary."

"I hope you're right. I always suspected my sister-in-law would love to see me crawl." She glanced over at where a red-faced Cara shouted at her family. "Now I know she'd love to see me dead, too."

Sloane put her head back and closed her eyes as we drove away from the church. Now that we were alone, I felt a little awkward. Sloane was almost a complete stranger. Living in what seemed near seclusion at Blueberry Hill, she'd taken on the trappings of a princess confined in a tower. Albeit one who made a lot of shopping trips to Grand Rapids and Chicago.

"Do you think Wyatt will be upset when he realizes you left?" I asked.

"Wyatt's feelings aren't high on my list of priorities right now."

"He does seem fond of you."

"Too fond."

I glanced over at her. Opening her eyes, she turned in my direction. I marveled anew at her extravagant use of makeup. Somehow the effect was neither gaudy nor cheap, but it made her look as if she were getting ready to film with the Kardashians.

"Wyatt's in love with me," she said. "At least that's

what he says. He hasn't had a lot of experience, so it's probably infatuation. Trust me, I never encouraged him. Even if I hadn't been married to his uncle, Wyatt's not my type. But from the moment I arrived at Blueberry Hill, he's let everyone know I am definitely *his* type."

"Cara said Wyatt made no secret of his feelings for you. Didn't that bother Porter?"

"Not at all. He thought it was funny how Wyatt acted like a lovestruck fan whenever he was around me. He dropped by the house whenever he thought Porter wouldn't be there. I didn't mind. It gave me someone to talk to when Porter was busy. We often worked out together with my personal trainer. Wyatt was certainly better company than Jacqueline. She's dull enough to put a person into a coma. And Wyatt can be fun."

That seemed difficult to believe. I guess there was no accounting for taste. "I don't know Jacqueline well, but I've spent time around Wyatt. I find him unlikable."

"Oh, he's clueless about everything, including women. And incredibly immature. But Porter had a soft spot for Wyatt. He felt sorry for him. We both did. Do you know Wyatt has ADHD? It led to problems with school and drugs. And everyone can see he's lazy and not the brightest bulb on the porch. Wyatt's father is disappointed with how his only son has turned out. Cara tries to make up for that by treating Wyatt like a toddler. It has the effect of making him act like one. Despite all that, he's not a bad guy. Only I wish—"

"What?" I asked when she didn't continue.

"I wish he would back off and give me some space. These past few days have been awful. I spent the first part of this week sedated."

"I heard. I'm sorry. This must be a nightmare for you."

"You have no idea. But Wyatt believes he has a chance with me now that Porter is gone. He had the nerve to ask me to marry him on the way over here in the car today."

My mouth fell open. "You're kidding?"

"Thank God, his family came in another car. If Cara knew he'd proposed, I'm afraid she'd kill both of us. Wyatt may be defensive and lazy, but Cara is dangerous. Her own brother thought she was unbalanced. According to Porter, she made his life hell from the time he was little. All because she was jealous that their dad preferred Porter to her. Like it was Porter's fault." She sighed. "The Gale family drama never stops, but I do not have the energy to deal with either Wyatt or Cara right now. Especially since I found out I was pregnant."

"Did you really learn about the pregnancy this morning?"

"I found out last week. Porter and I had been trying for months. That's why I kept home pregnancy kits on hand. Every time my period was late, I gave myself the test. That's what I did a week ago Tuesday. And this one showed I was pregnant. Porter and I were so excited. He wanted to announce it right away, but I thought we should wait until I saw a doctor and it was official." She bit back a sob. "Now Porter will never see his child, and he desperately wanted an heir. Someone to carry on the Gale family name."

"You can take some comfort in knowing his child will inherit Blueberry Hill."

"Except Cara will do everything she can to prevent that." Sloane crossed her arms and legs, arranging herself in a defensive position. "You think she'd be decent enough to honor her brother's wishes. If I wasn't pregnant, I would never have contested Porter's will and tried to keep her from inheriting half of the estate."

I thought that might be easier to say when you were the one benefiting from the will. "Did you know about the terms of his will beforehand?"

"Of course. Porter had a new will drawn up this year. If we had no children, Cara and I were to split the estate evenly. I had no objections. After all, Porter was only thirty-four and likely to live a long time, even if he was diabetic. And the odds favored me getting pregnant sooner rather than later. Who knew things would turn out so tragically?" She sniffed.

The murderer certainly knew, I thought.

"And I resent being labeled a gold digger," she continued. "Porter was not the only rich man who ever hit on me. If all I cared about was money, I could have married a man much older and richer than Porter. But Porter and I loved each other. We were two of a kind: passionate, self-confident, determined. A little reckless, too. That's why we got married only eight weeks after we met. We were soul mates."

As I made the turn onto Blue Star Highway, a

Janssen Blueberries truck drove past. It reminded me of what Cara had told me of Porter and Sloane's first meeting. "I heard that you and Porter met at a fruit growers' conference in Baltimore. Is that where you're from?"

"No. I was in Baltimore that summer staying with a friend. Because I liked being close to the D.C. area, I thought about moving there. I took a few temp jobs. Helping out at the conference was one of them." Sloane busied herself re-pinning a few strands of hair that had come undone. She had the kind of silky hair that didn't lend itself to being confined in an updo.

"Where did you live before that?"

"Connecticut, Rhode Island, New Hampshire. I went to three different colleges, but never graduated. I always got bored and wanted to move on."

"Where's your family from?" I sounded nosy, but Sloane seemed a little too evasive.

"New Hampshire, but my mom left when I was ten. She ran off with another man."

"That must have been hard for you to deal with."

"Not as hard as you think. She wasn't much of a mother."

"How about your father?"

"He was better. At least he *tried* to be better. But he never got over my mom leaving. He died of a heart attack five years later."

I felt a wave of sympathy for this young woman, who seemed plagued with tragedy. First, the loss of her parents, and now her husband. "How sad. I hope you have other family members."

"I do." Her voice grew soft. "I have a big sister. She's the best."

"I'm surprised she didn't come to Oriole Point to be with you."

"She wanted to be here, but she and her ex are in the middle of a nasty custody battle over their daughter, and she doesn't dare miss a court date. As soon as I can, I'll fly to see her. I've had enough of the Gales and Blueberry Hill. To be honest, I'd like to sell the company and the orchards. I want to raise my child far away from here."

I didn't think it was my place to say that such a move was the last thing Porter would have wanted for his child. "According to the police, someone murdered your husband, which makes this even worse. Who would kill him? A jealous associate? Someone he fired in the past?"

"I have no idea. It's confusing enough trying to understand the family dynamics. When I moved to Blueberry Hill, Eric Gale was on the decline. It was clear he didn't have a lot of time left. That didn't stop Porter and Cara from arguing whenever they saw each other. Usually, Cara started it. Jacqueline was run ragged looking after Porter's dad, who treated her like a hotel maid. And Wyatt trailed after me. It was exhausting sometimes."

"Sloane, did you know that Ryan borrowed money from Porter?"

"It wasn't a secret. Porter loved to brag about how he had Ryan on the ropes, at least financially. However, Porter was a savvy businessman. I'm sure Ryan isn't the only person who owed money to him."

My spirits sank. Ryan's fight with Porter at the

fairground and his access to insulin already made him a suspect. If the police got hold of his financial dealings with the victim, it would make him the prime suspect. "Anyone who owed money to your husband may have had a reason to kill him."

"A bigger motive is Blueberry Hill." Her tone grew sharp. "As she proved today, Cara won't allow anyone but her family to inherit. Given her reaction to my news, I'm afraid she may have killed her own brother to ensure that she would. Only how can I ever prove it?"

"But Cara would naturally assume Porter left everything to you. Until yesterday, she had no knowledge about the clause in his will that said you inherited everything if you and Porter had a child."

"Are you joking? Cara was with us at the lawyer's office in June when the new will was drawn up. So was Brody. She's been aware all summer that Blueberry Hill would be hers if Porter died without an heir." Sloane shook her head. "Apparently, Brody and Cara kept their kids in the dark. Wyatt didn't know anything about the will until I mentioned it to him last month."

I caught my breath. "Both Cara and Wyatt knew about the will before Porter died?"

"Yes. The only one who didn't know was Courtney. Now the whole town will hear about the will. I have to prepare myself for all the suspicion and gossip. It's not fair. It's been less than a week since Porter died. I've spent half of it sedated. The rest of the time I've been in shock. The horror of what has happened—the murder of my husband!—is only now sinking in. And now that I'm pregnant, it's even worse."

"Why? Don't you want the child?"

"Of course I do. But the entire Blueberry Hill fortune is mine. If Porter was killed because of Blueberry Hill, how do I stop the murderer from coming after me?"

Chapter Nineteen

A two-legged blueberry greeted me when I walked into the shop. With arms akimbo, the figure spun around. "How do I look, Marlee? Pat dropped off our costumes about an hour ago."

The sight of Dean outfitted as a blueberry wasn't unexpected. The Blueberry Blow Out's week of festivities ended with a downtown parade on Sunday. Many local business owners would be part of it, including The Berry Basket; the Cabot boys, Gillian, and I planned to march as giant blueberries. Because so much had happened this week, I'd forgotten about the parade. When murder and a broken engagement occur in the same week, everything else becomes a footnote. Thank heaven I'd ordered the costumes three weeks ago from Pat Wilkes, who also supplied costumes for the students of Miss Lana's Dance School.

"I love how the blue tights match the costume," I replied. "But there's so much padding, you resemble a big blue apple more than a blueberry. Maybe lose the headpiece."

"Marlee's right," Theo announced from the doorway that led to the kitchen and office. I was surprised to see my baker here. His shift ended hours ago. "It looks like an apple stem."

With a sigh, Dean removed the dark blue beanie from his head. "I thought it seemed a nice finishing touch."

"Told you the beanie was too much," Andrew said from behind the counter. "And I'm glad you're here, Marlee. I need to leave early to help out Oscar at Beguiling Blooms. He has to put together ten bouquets for the Nyhof wedding tomorrow. The bride asked for sweet peas, and they're tricky to work with."

"That's fine. I'll be here for a few hours, and Dean is scheduled to work until seven. So Mr. Blueberry and I can handle things. Only I need to leave in time to meet someone and then relieve Gillian at the fair by six."

A couple with two young girls walked through our open door. The children squealed with delight at the sight of Dean in his blueberry costume.

Dean held out his arms and chortled, "Ho, ho, ho, children. Welcome to The Berry Basket. And Merry Blueberry Blow Out."

While I admired Dean's enthusiasm, he needed to keep his holidays straight. Still, the family seemed pleased. The girls ran into Dean's embrace, which prompted the father to pull out his cell phone for a photo.

As Dean posed with the girls, I went in the back to put away my purse. Theo followed me. "I didn't expect to see you here," I told him.

Because Theo came to the shop before dawn to

do the baking, he often left by the time we opened the shop at ten. The past two weeks, I'd noticed Theo often hung around the store afterward. Albeit encouraging, it seemed uncharacteristic behavior for such a shy person. Theo had suffered a head injury as a child, which resulted in developmental problems that included social awkwardness. Last month I'd gotten to know Theo better as a result of the Blackberry Art School murder. We had even gone on a brief trip to visit each other's families, and he now viewed me as a sister. He'd also grown comfortable around Andrew, Dean, and Gillian. While it pleased me to see Theo emerge from his self-imposed shell, I didn't want him to spend all his free time at The Berry Basket, especially since I could only pay him for his baking hours.

"Andrew and Dean arrived before I finished the muffins, so I talked with them."

"I hope they kept you entertained."

"They're funny. They make me laugh."

"The boys *are* a hoot." I rifled through the pile of mail left on the desk in my back office. "But you've been up for hours. Why don't you go home and relax? I know you love to sit in your yard and watch the birds at the feeders."

"I stayed because I wanted to talk to you. Only I knew you were going to the church service for the man who died at the fair. That's why I waited until you came to the store."

This made me look up. He wore his usual grave expression. Even when the Cabots amused him, he showed little evidence of that, aside from a brief smile. "Is something wrong?"

"I heard you talk to Dean yesterday morning before I left. You talked about Ryan."

"Okay." I had a vague memory of the conversation regarding Ryan. Most likely, I'd mentioned that Ryan never turned his phone on while he was on his so-called fishing trips.

"You seemed upset because he didn't call. I thought you were worried something had happened to him. But it didn't. He's safe. I needed to tell you that."

Had Ryan stopped by the bakery early this morning? Having ended the engagement, I was in no mood for another scene with Ryan so soon after last night. "How do you know he's back? Did you see him in town today?"

He shook his head. "I saw him on the way to work. Ryan was in the truck with the Zellar name on it. The one he always drives."

This seemed odd. Theo came to work between three thirty and four in the morning. "Where was this?"

"On Huron Lane. Right at the corner where the Clay Café is. He came from the other direction, so he passed right by me. First, he stopped at the stop sign. Ryan had his arm out the window when he drove past. I don't think he saw me."

"Was anyone with him?"

"No. He must have been coming back from fishing. I just wanted to let you know he was home now. You don't have to worry anymore."

"Do you remember exactly what time this was?"

"Yes. I looked at the clock in my car after he drove by."

When he simply stared back at me, I prodded, "And what did the clock say?"

"Three forty-six."

Why would Ryan drive around alone in the wee hours of the morning? He left my house around ten thirty. Yes, he seemed upset at our conversation. And tooling around deserted country roads in the middle of the night would have allowed him to vent, let off stream, cry. But would he have done that for five hours? Unlikely. Maybe he went home to the Zellar farm, talked to his family, then realized he couldn't sleep and went for a drive. Or he visited a friend in the area for a sympathetic ear. If so, who? Theo said Ryan drove past the Clay Café, coming from the other direction. That road led farther out into the country. Who did Ryan know out there?

Let it go, I told myself. Ryan's whereabouts weren't my concern any longer. I had to stop trying to figure out what Ryan was doing and why. He held so many secrets, I couldn't even guess where he might have been that early in the morning. And did I really want to know?

"Thanks for telling me, but I saw Ryan last night when he came by my house."

"Are you okay?" Theo's gray eyes examined me even more closely than usual.

"I'm a little tired."

He appeared skeptical. "You look sad. Did something make you sad?"

If the Cabots had not been in the shop, I would have told Theo that I'd ended my relationship with Ryan. Theo possessed a number of admirable traits, including discretion and loyalty. He likely would be relieved; like Max, Theo was not a Ryan admirer. A shame I hadn't followed suit. But I didn't have the energy at the moment to also face any questions that would follow from Dean and Andrew.

Andrew breezed past my office, tossing his folded-up apron on a bench along the wall. "I'm taking off, Marlee. But we need to order more medium shopping bags. We're almost out."

"Thanks." I donned my own BERRY BASKET apron as Theo followed me out of the office. "Remember that everyone's pulling long shifts tomorrow, both here and at the fairground. Because of the fireworks Saturday night, there should be bigger crowds than usual."

"Got it." Andrew grabbed a blueberry tart from a rack near the oven. "Since you're wearing a dress, I assume you came straight from the memorial service." He took a big bite of the tart, smearing blueberry filling on his chin.

"Yep. I didn't want to waste time going home to change." I handed Andrew a napkin.

"Wait a minute." His attention shifted to my hand. "You're not wearing your ring. Did you lose it?"

Leave it to eagle-eye Andrew. "No. I gave it back to Ryan last night." I took a deep breath. "We broke up."

"What! You're kidding?" he mumbled through a mouthful of tart. "No way!"

Theo touched my shoulder. "Is that why you look sad?"

"Sad?" Andrew answered for me. "She should be relieved. Dean and I never thought he was the right guy. He was too jealous of any man who looked at you. And too close to the other Zellars. The whole pack of them live in a weird compound at their orchards. They're like Scientologists."

"You and Dean never said you didn't care for Ryan." Good grief, was I the only person who liked Ryan, aside from his family? Just how blind was love?

"There would have been no point in us saying we weren't crazy about him. You wouldn't have listened to us anyway." He swiped at his mouth with the napkin I gave him. "Okay, who ended it? Tell me it was you, not him."

"Yes. I was the one to break up with him. When he stopped by my house last night, I gave him back his ring. Ryan was upset, of course. He'd bought plane tickets to Vegas because he wanted us to fly off to get married in some wedding chapel his buddy told him about."

"This is incredible." Andrew looked toward the door that led into the shop. "Dean, get in here now!"

"What is it?" his brother shouted back. "I've got customers."

"Forget the customers. Marlee and Ryan broke up!"

Dean burst into the kitchen, his puffy costume scraping against the sides of the door. I never knew blueberries could move that fast.

When I arrived at Jacqueline's house at Blueberry Hill later that afternoon, a catering crew was packing everything up, while men took down the white tents on the lawn. No doubt Deirdre's Caterers had supplied a lovely luncheon for the memorial guests, but I was happy to have missed it. This whole week had been filled with far too many Gales and O'Neills—along with a boatload of speculation and gossip about my former fiancé. Now it seemed I was about to be privy to yet another Ryan revelation. But I doubted anything could surprise me now.

Because I'd only visited Blueberry Hill once for an outdoor charity event, I'd never been inside the house itself. Since I might never be here again, I took the opportunity to examine the two-story white house. The six tall columns, pediments, painted plaster exterior, and decorative transom marked it as Greek Revival. Unlike my 1890s home, however, this one had been built in the mid to late twentieth century. While attractive, it couldn't compare with the beauty and charm of my historic blue Victorian with its turret, gables, and third-floor tower.

As I walked up the steps to the front porch, I switched the wicker basket I held from one hand to the other. It felt like I'd packed half my store. But a gift of food for Jacqueline and the family seemed appropriate. I rang the doorbell and waited.

The door swung open. "Marlee, I'm happy you could meet with me," Jacqueline said with a smile. "Please come in. A shame you couldn't be here for the luncheon."

I hadn't expected Jacqueline to answer her own door. Due to the size of the Blueberry Hill fortune, I assumed a housekeeper would handle such mundane tasks. Then again, my experience with rich people largely involved Piper, who employed a staff of six. And that didn't include her gardeners. Certainly, Piper's five-story Italianate mansion on a bluff overlooking the lake far surpassed this one, both in size and splendor.

"I wanted to bring you something from my shop." I handed her the basket.

"How sweet of you. And it's so heavy. You shouldn't have given me this much. Thank you." She scanned its contents, which included berry-flavored wine, syrup, muffins, candy, and jam. "Let me leave this here so we can have our tea." She placed the basket on a wooden bookshelf in the foyer. Above it hung a four-by-four oil painting of blueberries nestled in leaves against an amber background.

"This is nice." I nodded at the painting.

"My late husband wasn't much for art, but he did love that painting. He told me he bought it ten years ago from a visiting artist who taught at the Blackberry Art School. A woman called Judith Sanford." She lifted an eyebrow at me. "Eric did not spend money on anything he couldn't find a use for, so he must have been impressed to purchase this. As far as I know, he never purchased another work of art. Everything else on the walls was bought by his first wife."

The foyer walls didn't hold any other artwork on its Wedgewood blue wallpaper, but a peek into the living room revealed a number of unimpressive, framed watercolors. And I glimpsed a framed painting at the top of the curving white stairway near the door.

"I asked the caterers to set up a tray for us on the terrace."

I followed her along the hallway through what looked like a study and into a glassed-in terrace at the back of the house. I found it a cramped room, filled with too much furniture and at least six potted plants too many. But the sunny space did look out over a colorful garden blooming with roses and lilies.

"Please sit." She gestured at a blue and white floral love seat. After I did so, Jacqueline sat at a matching love seat across from me. Between us sat a low table holding trays of tiny quiches, small crustless sandwiches, pastries, and a white teapot. "I hope you're hungry. I am. The luncheon stressed me out so much, I couldn't eat. Because I'm not from around here, almost everyone who came were strangers. I get anxious making small talk with people I don't know."

"I hope our conversation won't stress you out. You don't really know me."

"That's true. But I know all about you. Eric talked about everyone in the county who had anything to do with berries, and that includes Marlee Jacob, owner of The Berry Basket." She poured a cup of tea for me.

"I'm sure you heard what happened after you left the church."

Her polite smile vanished. "Cara couldn't wait to tell me. And not just me. She ranted to every guest at the luncheon. People were literally running to get away from her."

This sounded worse than I imagined.

"I don't know if I've ever seen anyone that angry," she continued. "Her daughter and son were so embarrassed, they left after only twenty minutes. Brody finally got her to calm down, but she started up again when Sloane arrived." Jacqueline took a sip of her tea. "At that point, I asked Cara to leave. I had no choice; she was making everyone at the luncheon uncomfortable. Everything went fine once she was gone."

"How did Sloane hold up?" Although I'd eaten a late lunch, the quiches looked too good to resist and I put several on a plate. "I drove her home this morning from the service. She didn't want to be near Cara."

"As soon as Sloane arrived at the luncheon, Cara began to yell at her. I sent Sloane into the house until I could convince Brody to take his wife home." She frowned. "I'm afraid everyone at the luncheon will be talking about it for some time. Including the caterers. When I planned the event I never had any idea it would turn out like this."

"No one expected Sloane to announce she was pregnant."

"I already knew."

"You did?" I asked through a mouthful of quiche.

"Sloane came to me yesterday. She said she'd taken several pregnancy tests since last week, all of them positive. But she wanted to make one hundred percent certain. Since I work at a clinic part-time, she asked what other tests she could take. I suggested a blood test and another urine test. And of course, a pelvic exam."

"Will she do it?"

"Why wouldn't she?"

"I don't know. And you can't blame Cara for being upset and angry. The same week Porter dies, Sloane discovers she's pregnant, which means she inherits all of Blueberry Hill. It seems a little convenient."

"Tragic too. A young man died in suspicious

circumstances. Now I feel bad that my stepson and I weren't close. He ignored me during the months I took care of his mother. And he disapproved of his dad marrying me. Understandable. A younger woman marries an older rich man, one in poor health. I'm sure everyone thinks I'm a conniving gold digger who seduced the dying Mr. Gale." She sighed. "If they only knew."

Although Sloane fit the gold digger profile, I had a hard time viewing Jacqueline as a scheming temptress. She seemed like those watercolors I'd glimpsed in the Gale living room: pale, limpid, washed out. A polar opposite to Sloane's vibrant glamour. And I had to agree with the disagreeable Wyatt: Jacqueline needed a makeover. If we were friends, I'd suggest she style her honey-blond hair in something other than a wispy pixie cut. And buy clothes that enhanced her figure, instead of hiding it. Even a little blush and mascara might do wonders.

"The gossip will shift to Sloane now," I assured her.

She shrugged. "It's nothing to me. I'm leaving Oriole Point."

"Where are you going?"

"Anywhere but here. There's no reason to stay. Eric left me enough money to start a new life. The house doesn't belong to me, which means I don't have to worry about selling it." She plucked a cucumber sandwich from the tiered tray. "Yes, I could live here until the day I died, but why would I want to? I'm all alone in this place, except on the days the housekeeper works. I haven't made many friends. And I hate living on the property. It's huge. Even though the farming operation is acres away, they're always hiring new people to work, which means more strangers coming on the property. I don't feel safe living here by myself."

"But Sloane lives really close." Because I drove her home that morning, I knew the house she lived in with Porter was no more than a five-minute walk away.

"Sloane and I hardly see each other. She thinks I'm dull." Jacqueline gave a sad laugh. "And I am."

"Don't take it personally. She probably thinks everyone over twenty-five is dull. But you may grow close now that she's pregnant. After all, it's only the two of you now on Blueberry Hill. Sloane told me that she'd like to leave as well, but that could be because of all the drama of this past week. If she stays, I bet she'd like you to remain. After all, she's going to have a baby. And she doesn't seem to have any family, aside from an older sister whom she misses."

"Let her sister move to Blueberry Hill to keep her company. I'm leaving. I should have done it months ago, but I've wrestled with depression since Eric passed away. I didn't have the energy to do much, except help out at the clinic now and then, and putter about here." She shook her head. "But I'm too young to live like a retiree. It's time I left Blueberry Hill and got on with my life."

Since this seemed a wise move, I didn't bother to dissuade her. "Will you stay long enough for the police to discover who killed Porter?"

Jacqueline shuddered. "Absolutely not. It's awful enough to have been here this past week. What with Sloane being upset, and the police questions, and not knowing who the murderer is. Another reason I don't want to stay in this house alone much longer. What if the killer has a grudge against the Gale family? That puts me in a vulnerable position. No. I have to leave. And as soon as possible."

Brushing quiche crumbs from my fingers, I sat back. "I have to leave soon myself. I'm working at the fairground tonight. Maybe we should talk about why you wanted to see me today."

"You're right. I didn't ask you here to discuss Sloane and my plans to leave." Jacqueline got up to retrieve a folder from an étagère by the door. Before she sat down again, she handed the folder to me.

I opened it up. "These look like legal documents. Loans."

"Some are copies of the paperwork my husband had drawn up when your fiancé borrowed money from him last September. Eric was in poor health at the time, and I can't help but think Ryan took advantage of him. The financial arrangement he brokered with Porter is in there, too."

I tried to examine the papers, but my hands shook. What had Ryan done?

She must have noticed my distress. "Those are copies of the originals. I'm giving them to you, Marlee. As his future wife, you should be aware of all this."

"I'll look these papers over later. But could you simply tell me how much Ryan borrowed from Eric and Porter?" I swallowed. "Exactly how much?"

"Four hundred and eighty thousand dollars."

I gasped. "That can't be true!"

Jacqueline looked regretful. "I dreaded having to tell you this. Ryan made it clear to Eric and Porter that these loans were to remain secret. No one was to know."

Fighting to get my breathing under control, I asked, "How many times did he come to the Gales for money?"

"As I said, he asked my husband for a loan back in September. A hundred seventy thousand dollars. Ryan made monthly payments on the loan, with interest. After Eric died, the money owed on the loan legally belonged to the Blueberry Hill estate, which meant Ryan made the payments to Porter. In January of this year, he borrowed more money, this time from Porter."

I felt dizzy and disoriented. Maybe I wasn't hearing her correctly. "Wait. If Ryan needed money, why did he go to the Gales? He hated Porter. Why not go to a bank?"

"I asked Eric about that. He said Ryan didn't want his family to know he needed to borrow money. That he'd do anything to keep them from finding out he'd gotten himself into debt. If he did it privately, he hoped to keep it private until the loan was paid off."

"But Ryan must have known Porter would make sure everyone knew."

"There's a contract in that folder that says if either Eric or Porter made details of the loan public, the loan became null and void. Ryan obviously insisted on such a clause. And it worked. Oh, Porter hinted around the family that Ryan had borrowed money from him, usually after he'd drunk too much beer. But no one knew exactly what he was talking about."

"Did Porter or your husband know how Ryan got himself into debt?"

She nodded. "Gambling."

I hung my head in despair. It all made terrible sense. Ryan had been addicted to crystal meth as a senior in high school; he spent months getting clean at a rehab center in Texas. I'd only learned this in June, and not through Ryan. When I had confronted him, he swore his drug problem was in the past. And apparently it was. However, he had replaced one addiction with another. No wonder he lied about those bi-monthly gambling trips. He probably hoped to win back enough money to get out of debt, but instead he only sank deeper. And he needed almost half a million dollars to get out of this hole.

This meant he must have gambled away the hundred and fifty thousand dollars that Ryan's dad gave each of his sons two years ago. I now understood why Ryan was desperate to keep this from his family. Their respect meant everything to him.

"I'm sorry to be the bearer of this news," Jacqueline said. "And I only found out the final details in the past few days. The family lawyers were at Sloane's house this week, going over legal paperwork regarding the estate. I was there, along with Porter's sister, when we learned the full extent of Ryan's debts. The lawyers strongly advised us to pass on this information to the police. Which is what we did. Since you're going to marry him—"

"I'm not. Ryan and I broke up last night."

This startled her. "I had no idea. You and Ryan were so affectionate with each other at Trappers Corner. Porter even told the two of you to stop being so lovey-dovey."

"A lot has happened since then."

Her eyes clouded over as she no doubt remembered that was the night Porter died. "Even though the police have these financial records, I don't think Ryan killed Porter over something like this. Why would he? Because he has assets to use as collateral, his family doesn't have to be any the wiser."

"I don't understand. What assets would Ryan use as collateral?"

"The assets he used this past May. When he couldn't make one of the payments to Porter, he put up the property he owns at Zellar Orchards as collateral."

If I hadn't been so shocked, I might have screamed. Ryan had not only lost all his money, he'd handed over the Zellar land bequeathed to him by his father. And he'd given it to his enemy.

Jacqueline may not believe Ryan killed Porter. But I did.

Chapter Twenty

I threw myself into work with such single-minded dedication, Ebenezer Scrooge himself would have given me a raise. And he wouldn't have needed any visits from ghosts to prompt it. Following my conversation with Jacqueline, I went straight to the fairground, where I operated my bounce house, worked at my vendor booth, then volunteered to judge that night's blueberry muffin contest after one of the judges called in sick. If they'd let me, I would have spun cotton candy and juggled. Anything to keep me from thinking about Ryan's gambling addiction and how he'd foolishly put himself at the mercy of Porter Gale. Which gave Ryan a powerful motive to murder him.

When I got home that night, I popped two Benadryl, which knocked me out quicker than a mallet to the forehead. Although it left me groggy the following morning, without their sedative effect, I'd have lain awake all night. Minnie certainly found me a sleepy companion the next morning at breakfast, and it took hours working with Gillian at The Berry Basket before I felt like I had finally woken up. By then it was time for me to return to the fairground for the last big day of the Blueberry Blow Out. Tomorrow, crowds could enjoy the downtown parade and the antique car show, but today we basically wrapped things up. And with a bang, too.

The fireworks for the Blow Out rivaled that of the Fourth of July, only these took place at the fairground, not over Lake Michigan. While the fairground had seen a record number of visitors this week, for me the Blow Out was a bust. The only good thing: Kit and I admitted our feelings for each other ran deeper than friendship. But we hadn't seen each other since our kiss at my shop. Given what had happened since then, I couldn't make time for this new romance. Especially since the last man I'd been involved with looked to be a murderer.

While I took tickets from the parents of their bouncing children, I kept thinking about Piper's Blueberry Fun House. That's what my relationship with Ryan had turned into: an experience that promised fun and excitement, but instead threw one unwanted surprise after the other at me. I felt like I'd been traversing a fun house with Ryan the whole time, from a distorting hall of mirrors where nothing was what it appeared to be, to a pit one fell into without warning, then had to struggle to get out of. Even a graveyard, where all my dreams of a future with Ryan died and were buried.

"You look too worried for someone at a carnival."

I glanced over to see Kit Holt smiling at me.

"Actually, I was thinking about the Blueberry Fun House."

"Is the fun house that scary?"

"Yes. I've been inside and have no wish to repeat the experience. Although I give Piper and Lionel an 'A' for sheer audacity."

He looked closer at me. "Is everything all right? I haven't seen or heard from you since Thursday night."

"Wait a sec while Rex and I change shifts," I told him as my carny replacement arrived. After exchanging a few words with Rex, Kit and I left the bounce house, the cries of delighted jumping children echoing behind us.

"I wish we had more time to talk, but I have to relieve Andrew at my vendor booth."

"I understand. I'm on duty, too." Kit leaned closer. "If I weren't, I'd hold your hand."

Despite my sad mood, I smiled. "Would you have kissed me, too?"

"I'll do that no matter what." He took me by the chin and kissed me. I kissed him back. "Thanks, Kit. I needed that."

"What's wrong?"

"Too much to talk about here. But I broke up with Ryan after I saw you on Thursday."

His expression revealed both surprise and pleasure. "I'm sure that was difficult for both of you. And I won't pretend I'm not glad, Marlee. You know how I feel about you."

"I know. Only I have a lot to sort out at the moment. Until that's all taken care of, I don't think I'd be the best company." *Especially if the police arrested my former fiancé for murder.*

"I'm a patient man. If what we have is real, we should take it slow. I'm sure you don't want to repeat a mistake any more than I do."

"Amen." I gave him another kiss, this time a quick one. "Are you working until close?"

"They called in added security from the sheriff's department. A suspect we're tracking may be at the fair tonight, so I'll be here until the end. But we should watch the fireworks together. I heard they're pretty spectacular."

"They are." I smiled. "The fireworks start at ten. And speaking of the Blueberry Fun House, why don't we meet there about ten minutes before? It's a good viewing spot."

"Sounds like a plan." Kit gave me a wink before heading off into the crowd on the midway.

Needing sustenance, I bought a blueberry lemonade and a large bag of popcorn to fortify me for my upcoming shift at the vendor booth. After six days at the fairground, I'd grown accustomed to the constant bells, whistles, and calliope music from the carousel. The carousel suddenly reminded me of the Zellar family, and I wondered which Zellar was running the attraction at the moment. Could it be Ryan? Or had Ryan been taken to the police station?

I peeked around the side of the stand selling nachos and pizza. The carousel spun twenty yards away, its painted horses bobbing up and down. Although his back was to me, I knew it was Ryan who watched the ride. Ryan, the man I had agreed to marry. The man I loved despite his lies and his weaknesses. But had he ever loved me? I didn't think so.

With tears filling my eyes, I left before Ryan turned around. It seemed painfully clear why Ryan had been interested in me. He must have been gambling long before I moved back to Oriole Point, his debts growing greater each year. And there I was with my million-dollar beach house. A single girl who had been through too many bad relationships must have seemed easy pickings. Despite all the time I devoted to my business—or maybe because of that—some part of me was ready to be bowled over by Ryan Zellar.

Little did I know he had borrowed money from Eric Gale last September. Needing more money by January, he next borrowed from Porter. It was also the month he proposed to me. I was his insurance policy if he got into more debt. Rather, my money from the sale of my house was his insurance. That's why he pushed so hard for me to sell the house, why he wanted us to marry sooner rather than later. And when I refused to sell, he had no choice but to put up his Zellar acres as collateral, hoping to re-claim them later when he convinced me to sell the house.

I felt like a clueless heiress in a gothic novel, romanced by a suave gentleman caller driven by greed, not passion. How could I have been unaware of what lay beneath Ryan's easy charm? Everyone from Piper to Theo to the Cabots was unimpressed by Ryan. Why was I fooled? My English literature professor mom often quoted from her favorite writers. I recalled one in particular from novelist William Makepeace Thackeray: "Love makes fools of us all, big and small." I was proof of that. And I qualified as one of the big fools, too.

* * *

I never thought to be going from tears to laughter within an hour. But I didn't expect Natasha to join me at my booth for the entire shift. Needing a place to sit, she convinced a portly man selling blueberry seedlings to let her borrow his folding hair. As she sashayed off with his chair, he regarded her with a stupefied expression. I suspected he'd go to bed tonight wondering if a shapely beauty in a white halter, lavender short-shorts, and gladiator sandals actually had appeared at his booth. Maybe he had dreamed it.

She greeted me with a flurry of kisses on both cheeks. "I am here to keep you company. It not good to be alone when heart is breaking over man. Even a man who does not deserve you."

"You're a sweetheart." I glanced up at the customer who waited to purchase a bag of blueberry coffee from me. "But I'm hardly alone."

She tossed back her gorgeous mane of hair. "Customer not same as friend."

"You're right. Thank you, Natasha." After making change for the woman, I turned my attention back to her. "Where's Old Man Bowman?"

"He says one night at fair is enough. Also his favorite TV show about Bigfoot hunters is on. So I come by myself."

"I'm surprised. The two of you have been joined at the hip since Cole died."

"Is not true. We spend much time apart, especially since I do not fish or hunt. And he does not like to shop. But I am fond of him. He is my *dyadya*."

"What's *dyadya*? A boyfriend? Lover?"

Her brown eyes widened. "*Ty sumasshedshiy*? Are you crazy? *Dyadya* is uncle. And Wendall was uncle of my dead husband. That make him my uncle, too."

"I guess that's true." I glanced down at her handbag on the ground. "It looks like a Yorkie is missing as well. Where's Dasha?"

"Carnival not good for Dasha tonight. There will be fireworks, and loud noises scare my little baby. I leave her home. But I tell myself to come to Blow Out so I can be with Marlee so she does not cry."

"I think I cried myself out the night I ended things with Ryan. But I'm glad you're here. It seems I learn more secrets about Ryan with each passing hour."

"Ryan sounds like my dead husband. Cole lies to me from moment he judges my beauty contest. I learn later I marry a liar and pig. One who hurts me, too. Ryan only keeps secrets."

"I'm afraid he's keeping more secrets than the KGB."

Natasha leaned closer, pointing at the man who examined my berry jams on the table. "Shhh. Do not say KGB name so loud. You do not know who listens." She sometimes forgot she no longer lived in Russia.

"Anyway, I've learned there's more Ryan has kept from me." I told Natasha what I had learned during my visit with Jacqueline yesterday. When I was finished, she nodded.

"Is sad Ryan not honest with you. My cousin Irina marry handsome man she meet during vacation on Black Sea. He says his father owns much oil in

Russia. Says family is so rich, they have houses all over world. Even Beverly Hills. Then she find out his father is drunken street cleaner in Strezhevoy. And that new husband Boris is, too. Irina angry. Never forgive."

"Did they divorce?"

"*Nyet.* She love him. But Irina tells her brothers to beat Boris up. They do such a good job, Boris has two broken arms. But it teach him not to lie to Irina."

This didn't surprise me; Natasha's anecdotes about Russia usually involved beauty pageants, bribes, or violence. Sometimes, all three. "I'm not interested in having Ryan's arms broken. And he has to find a way to deal with his gambling problem and his debts without me. But I am hurt that he proposed to me only because he wanted to sell my house for the money. How desperate Ryan must have been to get free of his debt to Porter Gale. I'm afraid he may have been desperate enough to kill him."

"Marlee, you are wrong. *Da,* Ryan not tell truth. And maybe he only want to marry you to get money from house. And if he did, I would break one of his arms myself. But I don't think he kill Porter."

"Sorry. I may only be an amateur sleuth, but it looks like Ryan had motive and opportunity."

"But house is worth million dollars. More than enough to pay Porter and get his land back. And you say Ryan never stops asking you to sell. He even asks this week. That means he thinks he can convince you to do what he wants. So why would Ryan kill the Porter blueberry man if he believes he gets all the money he needs when he marries you?"

She had a point. Why would Ryan rush to murder Porter if he still thought there was a good chance I'd finally listen to him and sell my house? After all, hadn't I said a hundred times that Ryan always got his own way, especially where women were concerned? Yes, Ryan was a gambler and a liar, but maybe I'd judged him too harshly.

The man interested in my berry jams ended up buying three jars. After he left, I sighed. "Let's talk about something else besides Ryan and Porter. I need a little distraction."

Wearing a wide grin, Natasha pulled out her cell phone. "I have distraction. My friend who was Miss Bulgaria text me last week to tell me about YouTubes I must see. You will love."

She was right. Someone had posted video of all the beauty contests Natasha had ever competed in throughout Russia and Europe. In the earliest contests, she was barely fourteen—sort of a Soviet version of *Toddlers and Tiaras*. We both howled with laughter at the dizzying makeup and costumes she appeared in over the years. Some contests had a talent portion of the program, which treated audiences to Natasha's attempts at tap dancing, gymnastics, magic, and ventriloquism. I found it "must see" viewing, particularly the Miss St. Petersburg swimsuit competition, when Natasha's right breast popped out of her bikini top.

It turned into a busy, enjoyable night as I sold Berry Basket products while taking every free moment to watch YouTube with Natasha. Eventually we had to stop. Both of our phone batteries finally died. And I sold out of every item I had brought.

"That's it," I said to Natasha when the last customer left my table. "We're out of battery power *and* stuff to sell. Now, we have an hour until fireworks."

"What we do until then?" she asked.

"How about if we take the cashbox back to my car, then you and I can find something delicious and unhealthy to eat."

"I am liking those ears of elephants."

"Our appetizers." I put the empty cardboard boxes in the recycling barrels provided, while Natasha cleared off the booth table. "And churros for our entrée."

"What is this churro?"

On the way to the parking lot, I explained the finer points of carnival churros, funnel cakes, and chili cheese fries. Natasha had just launched into a description of a Russian treat known as *plyushka* when I spotted Ryan in the parking lot. He was talking on his phone and didn't notice us. Farther up the lot, I saw his pickup with ZELLAR ORCHARDS on the side.

"Is Ryan leaving?" I asked Natasha in a stage whisper. "That's weird. His family not only sponsored the carousel here, they paid for the fireworks display. Whoever does that receives a plaque on the fairground stage right before the fireworks go off. All the Zellars planned to be there."

"Maybe he needs something from his truck."

But after Ryan got into his truck, the headlights came on.

"He's leaving," I muttered. "God only knows what he's up to now."

Natasha grabbed my arm. "My car is right there. We follow him. Like sloths."

"Sleuths," I corrected her. Ryan began to back out of his parking space.

"*Da*, let's be sleuths." Natasha pulled me to her vehicle, which was only three cars down. Like me, she had recently bought a new car; hers was a silver Audi.

I got into the passenger seat. Before I could buckle my seat belt, Natasha had already pulled out.

"He will not know we follow. I am good driver."

"Maybe we shouldn't do this," I told Natasha. "No matter how much you might doubt Ryan killed Porter, it's possible that he did. I don't want to put either of us in danger."

"We only follow. I stay far away from Ryan. Besides, I can protect us. Look in my purse. I have something in zipper pocket."

As we followed Ryan out of the parking lot, I rummaged around in Natasha's capacious handbag. Shocked, I pulled a gun out of her purse. "You carry a gun?"

"*Da*. Uncle Wendall tells you the other day. He gives me a gun so I feel safe. And I am good shot. Shark shooter, he call me. Don't worry. I protect us."

But I had a feeling nothing good would come of getting in a car with a "shark shooter."

Chapter Twenty-one

"You're good at this," I said in amazement as Natasha tailed Ryan's pickup. From the moment we left the fairground parking lot, Natasha drove far enough behind Ryan so he wouldn't realize he was being followed. Even if another car got between us, she kept Ryan's car in sight and always managed to catch up.

"I learn from man I date in St. Petersburg. He works in Ministry of Justice, but at night he sell *kontrabanda* on black market. Because he is government minister, he is followed—even when on dates with me. But they never catch us. Oleg is best driver. He teach me."

"Someone needs to make a movie out of your life."

"I would love such a thing. Selena Gomez should play me." She smoothly passed the van in front of us. Up ahead shone the rear lights of Ryan's truck. In the growing dark, we could barely see the outlines of his vehicle, or the fields and farms we passed.

"Where is he going?" I asked.

"Maybe to Zellar farm. We are in countryside."

"No. Zellar Orchards is in the other direction. But we are in fruit country. We drove by Janssen Blueberries a mile ago."

Ryan turned left. When we did likewise, I caught my breath. "Hold on."

Natasha briefly took her eyes off the road to look at me. "*Kakiye?*"

"We've just entered Blueberry Hill territory. See those bushes on either side of the road? This all belongs to Blueberry Hill. The long gray building on the horizon is where they process the berries." I pointed to my right. "The narrow road leads to the U-Pick."

Ryan's truck slowed, then turned up a driveway.

A feeling of foreboding swept over me. "That takes you right to the Gale homes. Is he going to see Jacqueline? Sloane maybe?"

Natasha braked when we reached the driveway bordered by two stone columns. One column held a street number; the other bore an elegant sign announcing BLUEBERRY HILL. "I turn off headlights now. Ryan may stop truck when we don't think and he will see us."

"You're safe to proceed. I was here yesterday. The property's huge, mostly gardens, tennis courts, a couple swimming pools, a lot of rolling lawn. Jacqueline's house is closest to the road, but you have to drive for about a minute to get there." I tried to see in which direction Ryan's truck went. "Sloane's house is a little farther past Jacqueline's."

With our headlights off and night falling, Natasha had to take it slow as we made our way along the winding drive. Ryan's rear lights disappeared for a moment behind a stand of Norwegian pine. After we made the same curving turn, we spotted him once more.

"Looks like he doesn't plan to visit Jacqueline," I said when his truck went past the Greek Revival house I had tea at yesterday. There were several lights on downstairs at Jacqueline's. "Not that I understand why he'd come out here to meet with Jacqueline or Sloane."

"I worry security people watch us and we do not know. Is Blueberry Hill family not rich? If this is Russia, guards would stand at gate. And cameras everywhere."

"This is Oriole Point. No one has security guards, including the banks." I touched Natasha on the arm. "He's parking at Sloane's house. You need to pull over."

Natasha parked the car behind a welcome screen of lilac bushes. "What we do now?"

"I'll wait until he goes inside, then sneak up to the house to see if I can hear anything."

"I come, too. And bring gun in case Ryan do something crazy."

"No. You and your gun stay in the car. I'll only be a few minutes, long enough to figure out why Ryan is here."

"Is good." Natasha took the handgun from her purse. "I be lookout."

"Just look out that you don't accidentally shoot your foot off with that thing." Holding a finger to my lips to caution her to remain silent, I turned off the car's overhead light to enable me to get out without anyone seeing. I left the door ajar; the slamming of a car door might alert Ryan.

Crouched like every cat burglar I'd ever seen in the movies, I made my way to the house up ahead. Hiding behind a privet, I observed Ryan ring the doorbell. Sloane opened the door.

I was close enough to hear him say, "Sloane, what happened to your face?"

"Oh, I didn't look where I was going when I got out of the shower an hour ago. Walked right into that stupid Greek column Porter put up in our bathroom. Gave myself a black eye."

Ryan looked over his shoulder. "I'm nervous about this. Why did you ask me to come here? We agreed not to be seen together."

"We have to talk," she said. "And please say you deleted my text message."

Once they'd gone inside, I raced up to the house. Luckily, Porter had built himself a contemporary home constructed of numerous floor-to-ceiling windows. Apparently he didn't feel the need to safeguard his privacy since none of the windows on the ground floor appeared to possess drapes or blinds. By staying in the shadows, I followed the movements of Ryan and Sloane as they walked through the dining room and a state-of-the-art kitchen. When they reached the back of the house, Sloane opened the sliding glass door to a patio.

Before they went outside, Ryan pulled Sloane close and kissed her.

I forgot my spy behavior and pressed myself against the window to watch. How long had *this* been going on? For a shocked second, I wished I'd brought Natasha's gun. Not to shoot them. But what I wouldn't give to scare the daylights out of the cheating pair.

At last, they stepped away from each other. Ryan followed Sloane out onto the back patio. The landscape lighting enabled me to tiptoe through the daylilies and reach the patio a moment after they did. I peeked around the corner of the house. Sloane and Ryan sat on a cushioned wicker couch. Despite the passionate kiss, she avoided his gaze.

It took every ounce of self-control not to jump out of the shadows and accuse them of cheating on their partners. No matter how betrayed I felt, I reminded myself to be cautious. If Sloane and Ryan were romantically involved, had they plotted to get rid of Porter? They each had a reason to benefit from Porter's death. Did Ryan hedge his bets in case I didn't sell my house and give him the money? Had Sloane—and all the money she'd inherit—served as his backup? It made me sick to think Ryan had turned his persuasive charm on Sloane. I wondered if he'd worked out a deal with Sloane that when Porter died, she would forgive his debts to the Gale family. Before this week, I would have sworn Ryan was incapable of such deception. Now I feared he might be capable of anything. Even murder. I had to get back to the fairground and tell Kit. Along with Greg Trejo and Chief Hitchcock . . . and everyone else in the county.

"How are you holding up?" Ryan asked. "I felt bad about leaving town right after Porter died. But I didn't see how I could have been of any help if I'd stayed."

Sloane reached over to smooth back his hair. "The Gales and O'Neills have been enough to handle. You would only have made things more stressful."

"I'm pretty stressed out right now. The police took me in for questioning again today. They said you and Jacqueline gave them documents detailing my loans from Porter. I never expected that information to come to light. What the hell happened?"

Because the house was out in the country, the only sounds competing for my attention were crickets. I could hear every word they said. But it worked both ways. Ryan and Sloane could also hear me if I made a wrong move.

"We didn't have any choice. The family attorneys went over all of Porter's papers because of the complexities of the will. They told us to give the information about the loans to the police." Sloane sounded defensive. "You did borrow a great deal of money from the Gales. How long did you think it could remain a secret?"

"They also know I put up my Zellar land as collateral."

"Be realistic. There was no way to hide it from the attorneys. Or the police."

"Sloane, do you know how bad this looks for me? The police learned I have a gambling problem. They have proof I owed your husband hundreds of thousands of dollars. And that I lost my property to him. You and Jacqueline have made my life extremely difficult. Earlier today the police searched my family's house at the orchard!"

"You shouldn't be surprised. The police suspect

anyone who had access to insulin. They searched my house, and Jacqueline's, and the O'Neills'. Why are you angry at me?"

"I'm not angry. I'm worried. Like Porter, my mom didn't use cartridge insulin pens. She took her insulin via a needle. They suspect I took one of her vials and switched the solution."

"The same could be said of me. Do you see me getting hysterical?"

"I'd feel better if you did. You're way too calm. And they're suspicious about why I left the fairground for a couple hours after the tug-of-war fight. I told them I only returned to the Zellars because I needed to get away and calm down after the fight. But the Zellars' farmhouse is where my mother keeps her insulin. The police asked me if I took this opportunity to empty one of her insulin vials and replace it with potassium chloride. And they have loads of witnesses to confirm I was in and out of that tent at Trappers Corner where Porter kept the damn cooler." Obviously frustrated, Ryan hit his hand on the couch. "I think they're about to arrest me for Porter's murder."

"They will if you act like this." Sloane stood up. "I don't need more problems this week. I've had quite enough, especially now that I'm pregnant. That's why I asked you here."

"Then it's true," he said. "You are pregnant. Is the baby mine?"

I let out a startled cry and fell forward, knocking over a metal watering can.

"What the hell was that?" Ryan jumped to his feet.

"Who's there?" Sloane asked in a harsh voice.

Heart pounding, I ran back to Natasha's car, this time far more noisily. I heard Ryan yell, "Get back here!" at my retreating figure.

"Drive." I threw myself into the car. "Now!"

Natasha pulled out of our hiding place. "Put on seat belt," she ordered.

"I think Ryan and Sloane murdered Porter. And Sloane may be pregnant with his child."

This so shocked Natasha she responded in Russian. I looked back, but didn't see Ryan's truck. Good. We had a head start.

Natasha suddenly braked, throwing me forward.

"What happened? Why did you stop?"

"Almost hit woman."

I looked out my passenger window to see Jacqueline dart in front of the truck. "Are you okay?" I asked her.

She hurried to my side of the car. "Marlee, what are you doing here? Your friend almost ran me down."

"Most sorry," Natasha said. "But we must leave."

"Jacqueline, go back in the house and lock your doors. I just heard Sloane and Ryan talking. I think they killed Porter. And that baby of Sloane's is probably Ryan's."

Jacqueline turned paler than usual. "What!?"

"Please get back in the house. Call the police, too. Our cell phone batteries are dead. And don't go anywhere near Sloane or Ryan." I bit my lip. "To be safe, why don't you get in the car with us. We're going straight to the fairground to look for a sheriff's deputy I know."

"Don't be silly, Marlee. I'm not going anywhere. And I'd like an explanation for why—"

Without warning, Natasha took off, leaving Jacqueline staring after us. "What are you doing?" I said.

"Getting away from Ryan. He is in truck behind us."

I looked out the rear window. She was right. "Step on it."

Chapter Twenty-two

Natasha sped along the country roads like a Russian Janet Guthrie. If she'd competed in the Blackberry Road Rally last month, she probably would have won. Grateful for her driving skills, I also gave thanks that at no point did I catch sight of Ryan's truck. I hoped that meant he couldn't keep up with Natasha.

"Here we are." Natasha squealed into the fairground parking lot. Every parking space was taken, so she drove onto the sidewalk and came to a stop. We both jumped out of the car and rushed up the long walkway leading to the carnival midway.

"Why we not go to police station in Oriole Point first?"

"Because of the Blow Out crowds, most of the police will be here," I explained. "Including Kit and Detective Trejo."

"How we find them?"

She had a point. The fireworks were due to start in twenty minutes, causing everyone to flock to the midway, the best place to view them. All I could see were throngs of excited people. Due to the music coming from the nearby fairground stage where a popular band from the 1980s was finishing their concert, the noise level had ratcheted up.

"I told Kit to meet me in front of the Blueberry Fun House at ten o'clock. But I hope to catch sight of him or Greg Trejo before then. I'm worried about Jacqueline. What if Ryan and Sloane do something to her?"

"Why would they? And she look like she not believe you." She frowned. "I tell you what I do. I know what the Trejo detective looks like. We met during murder case of my husband. I go search for him, and you look for the sheriff called Kit. Maybe we find them before fireworks. If not, I meet you at fun house."

I kissed Natasha on the cheek. "You're my favorite beauty queen."

She grinned. "*No konechno.* But of course."

As Natasha went off in one direction, I headed in the other. Although I hoped Kit would be at the fun house a little early, he was nowhere in sight. But if he planned to meet me here soon, he couldn't be far away. If only I could position myself high enough to scan the crowd. A chorus of screams met my ears, and I looked up at the Blueberry Hill Death Drop. I toyed with getting in line for the ride, but remembered how quickly it was over. Not enough time for me to search from my high vantage point. Also, I had no desire to be strapped into the same gondola that Porter had died in.

Frustrated, I wandered through the midway, looking for an alternative. The white and yellow lights of the Ferris wheel caught my eye. Perfect crowd viewing, especially since Wyatt O'Neill was not currently operating it. Eager to reach the ride, I nimbly dodged fairgoers. A little too nimbly, it turned out, as I tripped headlong into a man coming from the opposite direction.

"So sorry," I said, readjusting the messenger bag slung across my body. "I wasn't looking."

"Well, well, well. If it isn't Wonder Woman."

I recognized him as one of the two carnies who harassed Jacqueline the first night of the Blow Out. "Not you again. Is there no way to avoid you?"

"Sweetie, you're the one who almost knocked me down." He looked around. "Where's Honey?"

"Jacqueline isn't here, so you won't be able to chase after her like an insensitive baboon. Now move aside." I put my hand on his rock-hard chest and gently pushed. He didn't budge. "And you may want to stop calling every woman you meet 'honey.' Or 'sweetie' or 'babe' or—"

"Honey is her name. I worked with her five years ago in Philly. Called herself Honey Lynch." His sour expression turned gleeful. "Since you called her Jacqueline, you must be one of her marks. I get it. She's on the grift and you don't know you're part of it."

"Grift?"

He cocked his head at me. "Isn't this rich? Wonder Woman doesn't know she's being conned. Now it makes sense that you tried to protect her from us. Proves how simple you are. Honey Lynch has never needed anyone to rescue her."

"If you're accusing her of being some kind of a con artist, that's impossible. Jacqueline has lived here for two years."

He snorted. "If enough money's at stake, a good grifter will run a game that lasts for years. And knowing Honey, I bet she found herself a juicy game. Let me guess. She married some rich guy."

This brought me up short. "Yes. But she was his wife's nurse for months. That's another reason she can't be a con artist. She's a nurse. Jacqueline works for a health care agency."

He rolled his eyes. "Jeez. How do you think you run a game? You need to be on the square; that's how to fool people into thinking you're legit. Hell, I've known con artists that played at being school-teachers, priests, real estate tycoons, beauticians. A nurse would be easy for Honey. Back in Philly, she worked a con on some hotshot surgeon. I'm sure she picked up all kinds of pointers about doctors and nurses she could use one day." He chuckled. "Looks like that day has come."

I nearly believed him. After all, three Gales had died since Jacqueline's arrival. I'd been uneasy about that from the beginning. But except for a small cash payment from Eric Gale, she hadn't benefited from the deaths, leaving her no motive. Unless she was a homicidal maniac. Only she didn't seem the maniac type.

"A nice story," I told him. "But you're mistaking her for some other woman."

"Oh, no, she's Honey Lynch. Me and Tom knew it was her as soon as we saw her. Of course, she's made herself look like a real plain Jane. No makeup, cutting off all her hair, wearing ugly loose clothes. If you've never seen Honey all dolled up, you're missing something. She's damn sexy. Looks like that singer, Faith Hill."

I struggled to imagine Jacqueline all glammed up. "Why didn't she recognize you and your buddy?"

"She did. Even remembered our names. But she sure wasn't happy to see us. You see, Honey cut us out of that grift with the Philly surgeon. A grift Tom and me helped set up. When she saw us here, she got nervous we might still be angry with her. But we're not." He shrugged. "At least not as angry as we were. But we figured she was pretending to be someone she wasn't, which meant she's on the grift again. Honey was afraid we'd blow her cover. We only chased after her to have a little fun."

I tried to recall how that encounter had gone with Jacqueline and the carnies. I did remember they had called her "honey" several times, but I'd assumed they were just being rude.

"You're starting to believe me. I can tell by that worried look you got. Seen it on a mark's face every time they realize they've been conned."

"If she is playing a con game, it doesn't look like she's getting much out of it."

"Only because you don't know who else she's playing it with. Honey always had a partner." He tapped me on the nose. "And you should thank me for setting you straight, Wonder Woman. I might have saved you from being conned."

I watched him disappear into the crowd with dismay. Was he right? Was Jacqueline a con woman whose real name was Honey Lynch? And had she come to Oriole Point to find a way into the wealthy family who owned Blueberry Hill? What troubled me most was the last nugget the carny shared: Honey always worked with a partner. Sloane arrived on the scene within a year after Jacqueline. Both women came from somewhere else, both had little contact with their own families, both ended up marrying a man who owned Blueberry Hill. And while Jacqueline hadn't been left much when she was widowed, Sloane hit the jackpot when Porter died. Especially now that she was pregnant.

Whoever killed Porter had access to insulin vials and to Porter's own supply. Both Jacqueline and Sloane had access. And if they were working together, both had a motive. Whatever Sloane inherited would no doubt be split with Jacqueline. Jacqueline told me yesterday that she planned to leave Oriole Point. Sloane mentioned on the car ride from the church that she wanted to sell Blueberry Hill and make a new life for her and her child somewhere else. It looked like they'd already made plans for their escape once the money was safely in Sloane's hands. What a triumph if they could get away with it.

With a sigh of frustration, I scanned the midway, not recognizing a single face. The police needed to take Sloane and Jacqueline into custody as soon as possible. Along with the carny, who should be brought in for questioning. This time, I'd taken care to memorize his name tag: Pete Hensley. Kit had to be nearby. Greg Trejo, too. Only I'd never find them in this crowd, at least not while on the ground. Once more I set off for the Ferris wheel.

After buying a ticket, I settled into one of the passenger cars. The carny swung the restraining bar closed, then stood back with a bored expression. As the Ferris wheel rose in the air, I began to search the crowd below. The Ferris wheel afforded a sweeping vista of the midway, teeming with people and ablaze with colored lights.

On my third and final rotation, I was prepared to admit defeat. The ride moved too fast for me to see anyone on the ground clearly. However, the next time the Ferris wheel stopped to let someone on or off, my car happened to be right at the top. I took advantage of this to once more search the crowd.

"Yes!" I caught sight of Kit Holt speaking with another sheriff deputy near the Tilt-A-Whirl. I gave thanks for the bright neon clown face shining down on them. Without the sign, I might never have seen him.

"Kit!" I yelled, waving my arms. "Kit!"

The din of the carnival midway drowned me out. I had to get off this ride before Kit disappeared into the crowd. It felt like the Ferris wheel hadn't moved for about five minutes. Did the ride break down? I groaned at the thought.

I shouted to the carny below, "Please get the ride moving again!"

Another long minute passed before the Ferris wheel started up. However, the Ferris wheel did not stop at the bottom to let me off. Instead, it went up about ten feet and halted.

"Please, I want to get off." I looked down at the carny, only to see Wyatt O'Neill staring back at me. He must have switched with the other man during one of my rotations.

"Wyatt, let me off the Ferris wheel."

With a malicious grin, he started the ride again, making it stop once more at the top. "Wyatt!"

I'd been so busy searching for Kit, I didn't realize the rest of the passengers on the Ferris wheel had disembarked at some point. Amusement park rides stopped running before the fireworks show began. Years ago, someone became injured on the roller coaster when the carny operating it got distracted watching the fireworks. Since then, fairground attractions shut down during that time. Only Wyatt had no intention of doing so—not where I was concerned.

I leaned as far forward as I dared, which made my passenger car rock back and forth. If the ride hadn't been so tall, I might have considered jumping. If only for the possibility that I'd land on the smarmy little beast's head. "Wyatt, let me off this ride or I'll start screaming!"

"Go ahead," he yelled back. "Everyone will just think you're having fun!"

Maybe if I screamed his name, Kit would hear. But when I turned to where I'd seen Kit last, he was no longer there. Great. What if this idiot kept me on the Ferris wheel for the entire fireworks show?

Waving both arms, I bellowed, "Somebody help me! I'm stuck on the Ferris wheel! Police! Call the police!"

Mercifully, the Ferris wheel began to move. When I reached the bottom, a sullen Wyatt jerked the lever to stop the ride. "You're determined to get me into hot water with the police."

I couldn't exit the ride fast enough. "You're the one who keeps doing stupid things to attract their attention."

"At least Lucas has my back."

"If his dad has anything to say about that, he won't."

"What does that mean?" he asked.

But I had no time to calm the idiot's nerves. I needed to find Kit. Running about the midway in this crowd seemed futile. Kit promised to meet me in front of the fun house at ten o'clock. I might as well wait there. As I muscled my way through the crowd, I wondered if Ryan had followed Natasha and me to the fairground. Even if he hadn't recognized me as the person eavesdropping on him and Sloane, he knew something had gone amiss. By now, he must have spoken with Jacqueline. She knew exactly where Natasha and I were headed.

I winced to recall how I told Jacqueline that Ryan and Sloane were lovers and had probably murdered Porter. If I'd put the blame only on Ryan, I'm sure she and Sloane would be thrilled. But I also incriminated Sloane, which jeopardized their con game just as it was about to come to a close. Which meant I should steer clear of Jacqueline and Sloane until the police arrested them. But was Ryan a threat to me as well? Had Sloane seduced Ryan in order to convince him to switch insulin vials? Exactly how many people were involved in Porter's murder?

Despite the unhappy events of this past week, I prayed Ryan had not taken such a dark turn. Gambling, lies, addiction, infidelity: they paled beside murder. My heart would break if Ryan had killed a man over those miserable gambling debts. And it would destroy his family.

When I arrived once more before the garish walls of the Blueberry Fun House, a CLOSED sign hung on the blue picket fence Piper and Lionel had erected around the building. There wasn't a carny or fun house visitor in sight. Neither was Kit Holt.

I pushed open the swinging gate that led to the fun house entrance. If the carny was inside the fun house, I'd ask to borrow his cell phone. When I walked up to the fun house entrance door, it looked slightly ajar. Good. Maybe the carny was inside shutting things down. But when I swung the door open and stepped inside, only that monster Baltimore oriole greeted me.

"Is anyone here? Hello?" I listened for a response.

Nothing except the echoes of spooky birdcalls issuing from the wall speakers. Most likely the carny decided to enjoy the fireworks first, and lock up afterward. Might as well wait outside so Kit could see me. When I turned to leave, the fun house entry door swung open. I prepared myself to greet either Kit or the absent carny. But it was neither.

With a sinking heart, I said, "Hello, Jacqueline."

Chapter Twenty-three

"Hello again, Marlee," she said, shutting the door behind her. If Jacqueline found the giant bird that loomed over me a startling sight, she gave no indication of it.

"This is a surprise." Actually, it was a shock.

"Why? You asked me to come with you and Natasha to the fairground. I decided you were right."

"How did you find me here?"

She laughed. "I saw you on the Ferris wheel, waving and shouting at people. You were on the ride for a long time. Half the midway probably spotted you up there."

Unfortunately, none of them was Kit Holt. "What changed your mind about coming to the fairground?"

"Your accusation that Sloane and Ryan killed Porter. I realized we needed to talk as soon as possible about whatever you saw happen between them."

"I'll make it easy for you." I had to find a way to get her outside. This was not a conversation I cared to have in a darkened fun house. "They kissed. And he asked her if the baby was his. Obviously they're lovers. The question is for how long."

"Not long. Only since June."

"How in the world do you know that?"

"I let them meet at my house when Porter was on the property."

Despite my nervousness, I bristled. "You didn't think there was anything sleazy about helping Sloane cheat on your stepson? And my fiancé to cheat on me?"

She shrugged. "They would have gotten together regardless. Besides, Sloane needed my help. I didn't want to see her get shut out of her husband's will like I did."

"I'm guessing she needed help getting pregnant. Which Ryan conveniently provided."

"Sloane had little choice. She wasn't even in Porter's will for the first year of the marriage. His sister Cara was instead. Because they married so soon after meeting, Porter was reluctant entrusting his fortune to a woman he barely knew. But Sloane eventually convinced him to change his mind."

I gave a contemptuous snort.

"Oh, Sloane can be most convincing. And Porter was much more in love with her a year later, particularly since they were trying to have a child. That's why he changed his will in June. If he died without an heir, Blueberry Hill would be split between his wife and his sister. If there was a child, Sloane got everything."

"Is she even pregnant?" I asked in disgust.

"Of course she is. With this much money at stake,

a fake pregnancy would have been impossible to carry off. Cara would have seen to that."

"How lucky for Sloane that my fiancé was on hand to be her baby daddy. And that she got pregnant so quickly." I decided to play the aggrieved betrayed woman. It was safer than accusing anyone of murder. "I also suspect Ryan didn't get involved with Sloane only for the sex. He probably hoped she could influence Porter to cancel his debts."

"Maybe." Her sly smile suddenly reminded me of Sloane. Where did this self-assured Jacqueline come from?

"I don't want to talk about this right now. The idea of Ryan and Sloane together makes me ill. And I regret saying they killed Porter. I know Ryan. He may be a liar and a cheat, but he's not a murderer. I was just upset over what I saw at Sloane's house. I still am, so let's end the conversation. Besides, Deputy Holt is meeting me outside any minute and I have to leave."

"You're not in the right frame of mind to talk to him. Like you said, you're upset. And why wouldn't you be? You discovered your fiancé is having an affair with another woman. And that he might have gotten her pregnant. However, it may make you feel better to know Ryan is not the only possible father of her baby. Sloane has had several other flings this summer."

"Let me guess. The lovestruck Wyatt is one of them."

"Oh, please. Sloane wasn't that desperate. Besides, she couldn't risk having a red-haired freckled child nine months later. No way to pass that baby off as Porter's. But she did meet up with a few gentlemen on her so-called shopping trips to Grand Rapids and Chicago."

"I'm not in the mood to hear about the sordid love life of Sloane. Nor do I enjoy speaking with the woman who helped her in all this. That's between you and Sloane. Ryan, too, I suppose. All I want is to be left out of this whole disgusting arrangement."

"Too late." She unzipped her shoulder bag and pulled a hypodermic needle out of her purse.

"What is that?" I stumbled back, knocking down the monster oriole behind me.

"Ketamine. A common anesthetic, often used on animals. Some vets call it cat Valium." She pressed the syringe, sending a thin jet of liquid into the air. "There won't be any pain, Marlee. You could even find the resulting trance-like state pleasant. Although a few hallucinations may occur before you lose consciousness."

I balled my hands into fists. "Get out of my way or I'll scream this fun house down."

"Go ahead. Who will hear you? Listen. The fireworks have started."

She was right. Loud booms and explosions reverberated overhead. And the Blueberry Blow Out fireworks were always long, noisy, and dazzling. As much as I loved fireworks, it was the second time this summer they had put me at a distinct disadvantage.

I wondered how difficult it would be to wrestle the hypodermic away from her. Jacqueline was a decade older than me. Then again, she was a little taller, with a lean, toned frame. For some absurd reason, the line from *Julius Caesar* popped into my head: "Yond Cassius has a lean and hungry look. He thinks too much. Such men are dangerous." Being brought up by an English professor leaves its mark. Certainly, the dangerous Jacqueline had thought far too much about stealing the Gale fortune and how to get rid of anyone—including me—who stood in the way. I wasn't going to wait around to get injected with some damn cat anesthetic.

"Why do you need me unconscious?"

"So I can finish cleaning this mess up. You shouldn't have come to Blueberry Hill tonight, Marlee. Sloane and I had everything worked out, even to her black eye: self-inflicted, of course. When your friend almost ran me down tonight, I was on my way to Sloane's house, from where I would have alerted the police that Ryan Zellar—number-one suspect in Porter's murder—was threatening Sloane. I saw him hit her in the face."

"You're framing Ryan for the murder," I said with chagrin, but also relief. Thank God Ryan was not a killer.

"Who else was as desperate as Ryan? All that money he owed the Gales. Even worse, the Zellar land his father had bequeathed to him. Ryan's hatred of Porter was so great, he almost killed him after the tug-of-war contest. A few hours later, he actually did, and by using a vial taken from his mother's insulin supply. At least that is how the police will view it, especially after Sloane and I confirm that Ryan came to Blueberry Hill tonight to threaten Sloane. If she didn't cancel his debts and return the Zellar property, he'd kill her, too. Initially, we planned to put the blame on Wyatt. He's such a waste of space. But we decided your handsome fiancé would work out much better. And it has." She held up the syringe with a thin, vindictive smile.

I lunged for Jacqueline. "Kit! I'm in here! Kit!"

My weight threw her against the door, but she kept hold of the hypodermic needle. I squeezed her wrist to force her to drop it, but the woman seemed made of iron. "You won't get away with this," I said. "Although I can't figure out why you need to make me unconscious."

She pushed back hard, her hand inching closer to my exposed neck. "Because once you're unconscious, I'll set this place on fire. Even if they're able to put the fire out before it all burns to the ground, you'll be dead of smoke inhalation by then. There will be nothing to indicate you died of anything but that. No suspicion of foul play. They'll assume Oriole Point's berry girl simply got trapped in the Blueberry Fun House." Her eyes narrowed at me. "And Sloane and I will be free to set up another night to entrap the clueless Mr. Zellar. After all, you are the only person to know what went on between Ryan and Sloane."

"I told Natasha!"

"No one will believe her. That silly Russian can only repeat what you told her. And you won't be able to verify anything. You'll be dead." Jacqueline broke free of my grip and shoved me to the floor. Before I could raise my head, she plunged the needle into my bare arm.

Horrified, I felt as if I had been stung. "You bitch!"

She stood over me with a calm expression. "Relax. Let the drug take effect. It will end your misery. I don't like killing people. It's messy. But sometimes there is no other choice."

"You're insane."

"No. I'm a professional. I came here after months of researching the Gale family and the Blueberry Hill fortune. I knew Heather Gale was dying, and her husband Eric likely to be close behind. So I played nurse for as long as it took to make my way closer to being Mrs. Gale. Soon to be the widowed Mrs. Gale. And I didn't even have to hurry things along. Nature took care of that."

"You think you're clever," I said. "But I already figured out what you'd done, Jacqueline. Or should I call you 'Honey'? Honey Lynch. That is your name, isn't it?"

She stiffened. "How do you know that?"

"See, you're not so smart." I got to my feet, pretending to be weaker than I was. How long until the drug took effect? "I know you're a grifter and that Sloane is your partner."

"She's more than that." She gave me a cool smile. "Sloane is my kid sister."

I didn't have to pretend to stagger when I heard that. "Your sister?"

"I've been training her in the game since she was sixteen. She's almost as good as I am. And with the Blueberry Hill fortune now hers, she won't have to run any more cons after this. Neither will I. We arranged for Sloane to be at that fruit growers' conference where Porter first saw her. I knew the type of blond inflatable dolls that Porter preferred. And my sister knew how to become his fantasy. We were smart to make this a double game, with both of us working to marry a Gale. I didn't think Eric would be such a stingy pig to leave me basically nothing. But we weren't going to take the chance of Porter cheating Sloane the same way I had been cheated."

"As soon as the will was altered in Sloane's favor and she became pregnant, Porter had to die, didn't he?"

Jacqueline nodded. "Marlee, there's no point in standing up. You'll only topple over and hurt yourself when the drug kicks in. I suggest you lie back down. Because you're not getting past this door. And this is the only way out."

Her statement proved she'd never been through the fun house. Otherwise she'd know there was an exit at the opposite end of the building. It was my only chance at escape. And survival. I hoped the drug didn't overpower me before I reached it. "Sorry, but I'm not in the mood to take this murder attempt lying down," I snapped back.

Grabbing the giant stuffed bird behind me, I threw it at her. When she ducked, I raced into the hall of mirrors, where I immediately slammed my knee into one. Despite the blinding pain, I kept moving. The distorted mirrors showed an eerie image of an elongated figure close behind me.

"You'll pass out soon," Jacqueline warned.

But I'd already run into the shadowy chamber filled with black trees, almost tripping over the dummy of Benjamin Lyall on the floor. As I crouched down to avoid getting my hair caught in any of the branches, I felt a wave of dizziness. Oh, no.

"Marlee, this is pointless!" she yelled before emitting a tiny scream.

I glanced over my shoulder. The animatronic oriole that had startled me earlier in the week had come loose again and smacked Jacqueline in the face. It swung upside down from the branch repeating, "Nevermore, nevermore, nevermore . . ."

I ran into the next fun house chamber, causing strobe lights to flash on, followed by the air jets. My dizziness grew worse and I fell back against the wall. Pushing on, I hoped to avoid the release of the ping-pong balls from the ceiling. But I felt oddly removed from my body, as if I were a puppet whose strings were being pulled.

Thankfully, I exited the chamber just as Jacqueline entered. I took a second to enjoy the alarm on her face when balls danced about her head from the strong gusts of air from the floor. If only there was a way to lock the door behind me after leaving each room. But all I had to do was outrun her. I'd been in the fun house before. She hadn't. I had the advantage. That would feel more comforting if I also didn't have an anesthetic coursing through my veins.

With the sound of Jacqueline's footsteps behind me, I made my way down the connecting corridor. I avoided looking at the walls, which seemed to be pulsating. A metallic sound greeted my ears. Either I was hallucinating, or Ellen Lyall was about to make her entrance. When the mechanical doll emerged from the wall, she said, "Beware the blueberry bog."

Grabbing the life-size figure by the shoulders, I

shoved it toward Jacqueline. The robot seemed to fly on wheeled feet before hitting Jacqueline, who fell back.

I heard Jacqueline curse, followed by a crash. It looked like Ellen Lyall had another trip to the animatronic repairman in her future. The Blueberry Bog lay ahead. I remembered Piper's advice about taking the narrow walkway along the wall rather than wading through the ball pit.

"*Look to the right,*" I told myself as I reached the open doorway to the ball pit. "*Look for the walkway.*"

Without warning, Jacqueline grabbed my arm and I yelled. After a brief struggle, I spun Jacqueline around, then shoved. She fell backward into the ball pit. As she flailed about in a sea of giant plastic balls, I hovered in the entranceway. The balls now seemed to float in the air. The drug was winning. I had to get to the exit before complete victory occurred. I put my back against the wall and forced myself to traverse the narrow walkway to the other side. I knew if I looked down to monitor Jacqueline in the pit, I'd pitch forward and all would be lost.

Once I reached the other side, I fell against the wall, fighting back unconsciousness. I had to reach the room that held the swinging bridge. Not only was the exit in that direction, so was Cornelia's wolverine-hunting hatchet. By heaven, if I couldn't make it to the exit, I refused to go down without a weapon.

As I lurched across the swinging bridge, the taped voice intoned, "Welcome as we bridge the years from 1760 to the present." A swinging bridge was the last thing a person with rubbery legs should be on. I almost toppled over the side as the room swam. Spots appeared before my eyes. I couldn't pass out. Not yet. Gripping the roped sides, I pulled myself over to the Cornelia mannequin. Just in time. I felt the bridge sway even more as Jacqueline set foot on it. She must have seen how dizzy and wobbly I was since she deliberately began to swing it more.

The only good thing was that the knee I had slammed into the mirror no longer hurt. Apparently, the drug was also a pain reliever. "You won't make it out of here," Jacqueline said.

I had reached Cornelia and yanked the hatchet out of her hand. Even in my disoriented state, I saw that the hatchet was cheap plastic. Sometime this past week, Piper must have replaced the real hatchet with this fake. Piper never took any advice I gave her. Why did she have to start now?

As Jacqueline made her way to me over the swaying bridge, I threw the hatchet aside. Almost falling over the side of the bridge due to my disembodied state, I made several grabs for Artemus's rifle, finally snatching it when Jacqueline was only a few feet away.

"Keep back!" I held the rifle like a cudgel and swung it back and forth. "I'll bash your head in if you don't go back across the bridge."

She looked nervous, but only for a moment. That's when the rifle broke apart in two, and I was left with only half of what appeared to be a toy rifle. What an awful time for Piper to become this responsible.

"Sorry. You lose, Marlee." She gave me a sad smile.

"But you should be proud. You stayed on your feet much longer than I anticipated."

I hurled the rest of the rifle straight at her. "Well, I'm not done yet!"

As the world spun around me and the bridge rocked beneath my feet, I staggered to the other side and finally reached the Blueberry Burial Ground. If I didn't make it to the exit door, it would end up being my final resting place, too. The skeletons hanging from the ceiling danced all about me. And there seemed a lot more of them this time. Thirty? Forty, maybe. It looked like an army of skeletons filled every bit of space above me.

Not only was the vertigo overwhelming, I could no longer feel my feet. I stumbled to the ground. "Get up, Marlee," I said aloud. "Get up and get to the door."

If I had to, I would crawl. I was doing just that when two feet appeared before me.

"Give it up, Marlee," Jacqueline said. "You're about to black out. It's like going to sleep. It's easy. Do it. I'll take care of the rest. Go to sleep."

I pressed my nails into my hands. Any sensation to keep me awake. "I won't let you burn me in here." My mouth felt like cotton. I heard what sounded like drumbeats getting closer and closer. "And I won't let you frame Ryan for murder!"

"It's too late. You're going to die. And Ryan is going to prison."

With the last bit of strength I possessed, I pushed myself to a standing position. After a wobbly second, I reached up to grab the feet of the skeleton directly overhead. I gave a yank and sent the skeleton clattering to the floor around me.

"What the hell are you doing?" Jacqueline asked as I crouched down among the bones.

Thank goodness Piper had not removed the butcher knives she had supplied her skeletons with. I picked one up now, then forced myself to stand once more.

"Out of my way." I pointed the knife in her direction.

Jacqueline took a step back. She backed up even more when she tried to grab for the knife and I slashed at her arm. A red line of blood instantly appeared.

"You cut me, Marlee!"

"I'll do more than that. Move aside."

After an excruciating moment, she did. Refusing to turn my back on her, I brandished the knife while walking backward to the exit. I prayed I wouldn't pass out before then. Almost there, I repeated. Almost there. One more step. Two more steps.

A horrendous growl sounded behind me. Startled, I dropped the knife. Too late I remembered that stupid wolverine robot by the exit. Both Jacqueline and I reached for the butcher knife, but she got to it first. I was so dizzy and out of it, I could only slump to the floor.

"You're a fool to push me like this, Marlee. I helped Sloane kill Porter. Do you think I'd hesitate to gut you right now?" She stood over me, the knife's sharp tip pointed at my throat. "I swear if you try one more thing before blacking out, I'll plunge this into your heart. With luck, the fire will cover up any injuries I inflict."

A sharp noise rang out.

Jacqueline screamed and dropped the knife. As weak and disoriented as I felt, I saw that her hand was now covered in blood.

"Who shot me?" she cried out.

What was going on? As much as I wanted to know, I felt too weak to raise my head off the floor. I heard footsteps and voices. One of them was Jacqueline, wailing that she was hurt. Kit Holt's frightened face appeared above me.

"She wants to set the fun house on fire and leave me to die," I told him. "And she gave me a shot with a needle."

"Call EMS," someone ordered.

Spots swam before my eyes. I tried to grab Kit's collar to pull him close. "She killed Porter. Sloane did, too."

"Don't try to talk." Kit stroked my brow. "We need to get you to the hospital."

"Can they save people with cat drugs?"

He looked even more concerned by my question.

"Is my Marlee okay?" Natasha now appeared and kissed me on the cheek.

"Did I hear a gun?" I hoped I wasn't hallucinating all this.

"You sure did," a man said. It sounded like Greg Trejo. "Natasha shot the knife right out of Jacqueline Gale's hand."

I could barely see Natasha hovering over me

as I slipped into unconsciousness. "Incredible," I mumbled.

"Incredible?" Kit stroked my brow again. "If I hadn't seen it with my own eyes, I would never have believed it."

The last thing I heard was Natasha saying, "Why is everyone so surprised? I am shark shooter."

Chapter Twenty-four

I've never been so glad to see the summer season in Oriole Point officially come to a close. Given how perilous that season had been, I decided to celebrate with a rollicking beach picnic at the lake house. No one was more grateful to be sitting on the beach eating grilled hot dogs and corn on the cob than I was. I actually closed The Berry Basket for the day, even though Labor Day always resulted in healthy sales. But after my latest brush with death, I decided it was healthier to enjoy at least one holiday away from the demands of my shop. As I watched friends and family eat, swim, and play volleyball on the beach, I understood—maybe for the first time—why leisure time was as necessary as work.

"Here's another hot dog, baby girl." My mother placed a hot dog slathered with mustard on my cardboard plate. "And your dad wants to know if you'd like a hamburger, too. He just put them on the grill."

Because I had a mouthful of corn, I could only shake my head in response. Mom gave me a kiss and a hug.

She had been doing that a lot these past two weeks. So had my father. After I was rushed unconscious to the hospital following my misadventure in the fun house, Tess alerted my parents. They made the two-hour trip from Chicago in record time. Soon after I awoke from the anesthesia that Jacqueline had injected me with, they were at my bedside, tearful and relieved. Fortunately, I recovered quickly from the ketamine. But they refused to leave my side for the next two weeks, even coming in to work with me and Minnie. I had enjoyed every minute of being fussed over. But autumn was nearly here, which meant my parents had to get back to their life in Chicago. Mom had classes to prepare for, and the hotel Dad managed had several VIPs expected within the week. Time for life to return to normal for all of us.

I took a big bite of what was now my second hot dog. My last for the day. Otherwise, I wouldn't have room for the desserts Theo had baked for the picnic: blueberry lemon cake, strawberry tarts, and blackberry crumb bars. It made me happy to see Theo here. I only wished he didn't feel compelled to stand guard over the makeshift pastry table he set up on the sand. But I'd noticed him conversing—and even laughing—with everyone who stopped by his table. I also convinced him to take a break and toss Frisbees with Aunt Vicki, her boyfriend Joe, and Lionel. Who knew our mayor was such an expert Frisbee player?

I was just as surprised by the sight of Greg Trejo building sandcastles with his three children. Although I sent his family an invite, I didn't expect them to show up. It delighted me when they did, especially since his children were boisterous and his wife was a sweet, relaxed woman who reminded me of her brother Kit. Indeed, with her curly brown hair, large expressive eyes, and endearing smile, she could be no one else's sister.

As for Kit, he had spent almost as much time with me since the fun house incident as my parents. With the three of them hovering about, Kit and my parents had become quite friendly. He bonded with them in a way Ryan had never been able to. Then again, Ryan had no interest in any family except the one he had been born into. I feared that attitude was making his life even more difficult now.

After the police arrested Jacqueline and Sloane on suspicion of murder, they were taken into custody. The state police brought in Ryan as well. That's when he learned the two women planned to frame him for Porter's murder. Since I was in the hospital when this occurred, I didn't see his reaction. But according to Greg Trejo, Ryan was by turns shocked, outraged, and desolate.

I knew how great Ryan's desolation must be. He could no longer keep his debts and gambling addiction secret from his family. Their approval and respect meant everything to him. Because he refused to admit he needed help with his addiction, he had compromised his integrity, his inheritance, and his family's respect. He'd also nearly been sent to prison for murder. Of course, he had also lost me, but I suspected that didn't pain him at all, which saddened me.

We'd been together for over a year, and engaged to be married for over half that time. I had loved him. A part of me still did. But had I ever known the real Ryan Zellar? Perhaps I'd fallen in love with someone who never existed. A man who asked me to marry him only because he needed the money from the sale of my beloved lake house.

Just when I thought that was the most hurtful thing Ryan could do, I learned he had been sleeping with another woman. And for a reason as mercenary and cold-blooded as the one that prompted him to pursue me. I'd been a fool for trusting a single thing about Ryan. But as Tess and Natasha reminded me, Ryan was as skilled a con artist as Jacqueline and Sloane. By marrying me to get my inheritance, hadn't he been playing a long game just as expertly as they had with the Gales? Yes, his betrayal hurt. But I had stopped blaming myself. I'd been manipulated by a man long accustomed to deception.

It did help that a decent, honest, loving man had entered my life. Without the comforting presence of Kit Holt, I'd probably be licking my wounds over my relationship with Ryan for a long time. I might even have grown bitter and cynical about romance. But I refused to become disillusioned, not when I lived in such a beautiful village and had such wonderful parents and friends. And Kit.

I smiled as Kit sat down beside me at the picnic table. His plate overflowed with potato salad, a hamburger, a hot dog, two ears of corn, and a wedge of watermelon. "You know, you're allowed to take more than one plate," I told him.

"And call attention to my hog-like appetite? I don't think so." He took a big forkful of potato salad. "I'm counteracting all the food I plan to eat by swimming every thirty minutes."

"I'll join you. It's a holiday and I'm having as many of Theo's berry desserts as possible."

Although I hadn't yet gone into the lake today, I wore my bathing suit: a new orange one-piece, daringly cut. Maybe a little too daring for my parents' tastes, but Kit had not been able to keep his eyes off me. And I appreciated the sight of Kit in his dark blue swim trunks. But then, I simply appreciated Kit. Without him, the Ryan debacle would have caused me even greater pain than it had.

The Cabot brothers sat across from us, their plates piled with slices of watermelon.

"Is this some new fad diet?" I asked.

"Not really," Dean said. "A nutritionist in Ann Arbor claims that if you eat fruit before every meal, you'll lose weight. And all your snacks must be fruit."

"Sounds like a silly fad diet to me," I said.

Kit chuckled. "A fruity one, too."

Dean threw me an exasperated look. "Anyway, I'm trying it for a week so I can feature it on my blog. I'll let my followers know if it actually works."

I turned to Andrew. "And you're helping him with the experiment?"

He frowned. "No. I'm hoping it works. I've pigged out on Theo's desserts all summer. Now my jeans are too tight. And I can't allow that. If I put on just five pounds, I'll look like a blimp next to Oscar. Having a boyfriend with the body of a runway model has its downside."

I looked out on the lake where the aforementioned Oscar stood on his paddleboard. His lean physique didn't seem to intimidate another man on a paddleboard floating past him: Old Man Bowman. Although I had to admit that Old Man Bowman was in good shape for a seventy-year-old. Those regular hunts for Bigfoot kept him spry and fit.

"What's the latest on Wyatt O'Neill?" Dean looked at Kit. "Do you think he'll do any prison time?"

Four days after Lucas Hendriksen collapsed in front of the harvester, his father convinced him to tell the truth and admit that Wyatt had sold him the drugs. Kit and a fellow deputy went to the O'Neill Farm, where they charged him with possession and sale of a Schedule One drug. He was currently out on bond.

"He's a first-time offender, so he won't get the maximum sentence," Kit replied. "Five years is likely, along with a fine."

I sighed. "I feel bad for his parents. Cara must be inconsolable."

"Furious is how I'd describe her," Kit said. "She believes Lucas worked out a deal with the sheriff's department to receive probation. A deal that may see her son locked up. I have a feeling she'll spend a lot of Blueberry Hill money trying to keep Wyatt out of prison."

A volleyball landed on our table, smashing one of the open bags of potato chips. "Hey!" Andrew shouted. "Let's keep the ball away from the food."

Tess and David ran up to retrieve their ball. "What do you care?" David laughed. "You're only eating watermelon."

"Aren't you two going to eat?" I asked them.

"We need to finish the game first," Tess said. "I wish now we had picked Gillian for our team. She's the reason our games have been so close. Her team might actually beat ours."

Tess tossed the ball up and down, eager to get back to the game. In addition to being accomplished glass artists, Tess and David were volleyball fanatics. I suspected that after they finally broke for food, their fellow players would be faced with several more hours of blocking, jump serves, and top-spins. I had played volleyball enough times with the couple to familiarize myself with every aspect of the game.

After David and Tess ran off to resume playing, Kit asked me, "Do you normally have such large get-togethers?"

His gaze took in the more than fifty people currently enjoying my beach. Because I only had one picnic table, everyone else ate beneath cabanas and on beach blankets spread on the sand. Piper held court in the biggest cabana: one set up by her pool boy, who was also serving as her personal butler today. It didn't surprise me to see that Suzanne Cabot had claimed a place beneath that cabana. Knowing Piper, she welcomed it for all the gossip she would glean from the Cabot boys' mom.

"I usually work on holidays, except for Easter, Thanksgiving, and Christmas," I told him. "Closing on Labor Day is a big deal for me, so I decided to invite everyone. Gillian's parents are here, along with her brother and sisters. And her new boyfriend."

"His teeth are too big," Andrew remarked.

I ignored him. "Aunt Vicki invited half the volunteers of Humane Hearts. And Max brought along his two buddies from Riordan Outfitters. And they brought dates."

Because I still felt the tiniest bit guilty for breaking up with Max in high school, I'd been pleased to see Max arrive with a woman. They looked to be getting along wonderfully, too. Although he might regret volunteering for that volleyball game with Tess and David.

Looking out over all these people, I realized this gathering would never have occurred if I'd married Ryan. It would have been Zellars only, for every holiday, every get-together. Even if his betrayal hadn't occurred, at some point I would have called off my wedding to Ryan. I needed more people in my world than those who lived at Zellar Orchards.

"What's the latest with our pair of grifters?" Dean asked. "I love that we had actual grifters in town. It's like that movie with John Cusack and Anjelica Huston."

"Don't forget Annette Bening," Andrew said. "I love Annette Bening."

"Jacqueline looked a little bit like Annette Bening," Dean said between bites of watermelon.

"And I thought she had a Mia Farrow vibe. Apparently, she looks like a lot of famous people. The carny told me she resembles Faith Hill when she's not trying to make herself look so plain." I looked at Kit. "I know Sloane is out on bail, and that she got Jacqueline out, too. It seems unfair for Sloane to use her Blueberry Hill fortune to make bail for them."

"Innocent until proven guilty," he reminded me. "Although the prosecutor is trying to freeze her assets, for now she has access to the Blueberry Hill fortune. That's how she was able to pay the twenty-million-dollar bail for herself and her sister."

"Never dreamed the two of them were sisters," I said. "But Sloane did tell me the only person in her family she was close to was her big sister. I just never figured out her sister was literally close to her."

"Did either of them confess?" Dean asked.

Kit shook his head. "Not during the official interrogation. But Jacqueline admitted everything to Marlee in the fun house. Naturally, the defense attorneys will claim Marlee's memory was compromised by the drug."

"That's not true. She told me a lot of it *before* she stuck me with the needle."

"I know, Marlee. I'm only telling you what the defense is likely to say." Kit squeezed my arm. "Luckily, Greg, Natasha, and I were in the Blueberry Burial Ground when Jacqueline was about to use the knife on you. We heard her say that she helped Sloane kill Porter. When a state police detective and a sheriff's deputy hear you confess to a crime, it's difficult to talk your way out of it."

"They might buy their way out of it," Dean suggested. "With the Blueberry Hill money at their disposal, Sloane and Jacqueline could assemble one hell of a legal defense team." He looked behind me. "And here's just the man who might know."

We turned to see Chief Gene Hitchcock. As longtime friends of the family, I had invited him and his wife.

"If you're curious about the con artist sisters," he said, "they're wanted for a number of other crimes, including manslaughter. Pete Hensley, that carny who recognized Honey at the carnival, has been most helpful. We ran a check on him. He's wanted in two states for identity theft. In exchange for immunity, he's agreed to tell us everything we need to know about the colorful lives of Honey and Britney Lynch, which are their real names. Trust me, the two of them *will* go to prison."

Although relieved to hear this, I also felt sad. "What happens to the baby Sloane is carrying?"

"We've learned there's another Lynch sister; she's nothing like the other two. Joely Lynch Weaver is a thirty-five-year-old schoolteacher in Missouri with two children. Her husband is a firefighter. She hasn't seen or heard from her sisters in years. We checked her out. Her background is as clean as it gets. Naturally, she was upset to hear that her sisters were accused of murder. But not surprised. When we told her about the baby, she asked if she could apply for custody. There are so few Lynches remaining, she'd hate for this baby to suffer for the sins of her family. The court may very well agree to her request."

I couldn't help but wonder if the baby was Ryan's. "Will they do a paternity test?"

"Cara O'Neill insists on it," Hitchcock said. "If it turns out to be Porter's, the baby inherits Blueberry

Hill. And if that's the case, Cara will certainly fight Joely Weaver for custody."

"How ironic if the baby turns out to be Porter's and the court gives custody to Joely," I mused. "That would mean the only honest, law-biding Lynch sister ends up with access to the Blueberry Hill fortune."

Kit winked at me. "Crime doesn't always pay."

"But a few lessons at the gun range certainly does," Hitchcock added. "Here comes our sharp-shooter."

Natasha walked toward us, resplendent in a white bikini, white gauze cover-up, and a floppy white straw hat. On her arm hung a white straw handbag, with Dasha's little head peeking out.

"Excuse me," Kit said. "She's a shark shooter. And don't you forget it."

"I won't forget that I owe her my life." I ran to greet her, both of us exchanging air kisses and a hug.

"I forget to tell you about dream I had last night," Natasha said with obvious excitement. "I dream I am in fun house again. But now I am being chased, not you. It is big blueberries who run after me. They look like Dean in blueberry costume he wears in parade, but much bigger. And right before blue-berries catch me, I turn into peacock and fly away. Is most important dream."

"Why?"

"It means my new spa must be called after pea-cock. And I must pick building for my spa right away. This week. Before there are no more fresh blueberries left."

Because my friend took her dreams seriously, I did, too. "I think you're right. It's high time Oriole Point had a spa called Peacock."

"*Da!*" She hugged me again as Dasha gave a happy yap. "Now we must have blueberry dessert to celebrate."

We walked arm in arm over to Theo and his pastry table.

"They all look delicious, Theo." I intended to have one of each. Maybe two.

"I must have piece of blueberry cake," Natasha announced. "Because of my dream."

He placed a big slice of blueberry lemon cake on a plate and handed it to her.

"I think I'll start with blueberry cake, too," I said.

Theo appeared concerned as he handed me a slice of cake. "Are you sure, Marlee? A lot of bad things happened during blueberry season. I almost didn't bring the cake. I didn't want the blueberries to remind you of murder and Ryan and the fun house."

"Are you kidding? Boyfriends come and go. So do murderers and Blueberry Blow Outs." I took a big bite of the cake, savoring the rich batter and sweet fruit. "But blueberries are forever."

Recipes

Blueberry Coffee Cake

After Marlee and Kit share their first kiss, she sends him off with a pastry box filled with blueberry coffee cake. She tells Kit that her baker, Theo, got the recipe from his mother—who got it from Betty Crocker. Because the best bakers know better than to mess with a classic, here's the classic Betty Crocker recipe.

Crumb topping
½ cup granulated sugar
⅓ cup all-purpose flour
½ teaspoon ground cinnamon
¼ cup butter or margarine, softened

Coffee cake
2 cups all-purpose flour
¾ cup granulated sugar
¼ cup shortening
¾ cup milk
1 egg
2½ teaspoons baking powder
¾ teaspoon salt
2 cups fresh blueberries

Vanilla glaze
½ cup powdered sugar
¼ teaspoon vanilla
1–1½ teaspoons hot water

1. Preheat oven to 375°F. Grease bottom and
    side of 9-inch-square pan or 9 x 3-inch
    springform pan with shortening or cooking
    spray.
2. In small bowl, mix ½ cup sugar, ⅓ cup flour,
    and the cinnamon. Cut in butter with fork
    until crumbly. Set aside.
3. In large bowl, stir together all coffee cake
    ingredients except blueberries. Beat mixture
    with spoon 30 seconds. Fold in blueberries.
    Spread batter in pan. Sprinkle with topping.
4. Bake 45–50 minutes, or until toothpick
    inserted in center of cake comes out clean.
    Cool 10 minutes; remove side of pan.
5. In small bowl, mix all glaze ingredients until
    smooth and thin enough to drizzle. Drizzle
    over warm coffee cake.

Makes 9 servings.

BAKED BLUEBERRY FRENCH TOAST

When Marlee and Tess meet for breakfast at the
Sourdough Café, they order this delicious baked
French toast. Since Marlee produced cooking
shows during her TV career in NYC, she
recognizes the dish as a delightfully gooey
recipe by celebrity chef Emeril.

French toast
1 tablespoon unsalted butter
14 slices white bread cut into 1-inch cubes; crusts
   removed and discarded
1 cup fresh blueberries, rinsed and picked over
2 8-ounce packages cold cream cheese, cut into
   1-inch cubes
10 large eggs
2 cups half-and-half
⅓ cup maple syrup
¼ cup fresh squeezed orange juice
Blueberry sauce

Blueberry sauce
3 tablespoons cornstarch
1½ cups water
1½ cups sugar
½ cup fresh squeezed orange juice
1½ teaspoons orange zest
½ cup blueberries, rinsed and picked over
1½ tablespoons unsalted butter

1. Butter baking dish with a tablespoon of butter
2. Arrange half of the bread cubes on the
   bottom of the baking dish.
3. Top bread cubes with blueberries and cream
   cheese cubes.
4. Layer the remaining bread cubes over the
   blueberries/cheese cubes.
5. Whisk eggs, half-and-half, maple syrup, and
   orange juice in large bowl.
6. Pour egg mixture evenly over bread mixture
   in baking dish.

7. Cover with aluminum foil and refrigerate at least 1 hour, or overnight.
8. Remove dish from refrigerator and allow to come to room temperature, about 20 minutes.
9. Preheat oven to 350°F. Position rack in center of oven.
10. Bake the covered French toast for 30 minutes.
11. After 30 minutes, remove aluminum foil and continue baking another 30 minutes, or until toast is golden brown and puffed.
12. Remove from oven and let slightly cool, approximately 15 minutes.
13. After plating, ladle blueberry sauce over the French toast.

Makes 10–12 servings.

Blueberry sauce
1. In small saucepan, stir together over medium-high heat cornstarch, water, sugar, orange juice, and zest.
2. Cook until thickened, stirring occasionally, approximately 5 minutes.
3. Add blueberries and simmer mixture, stirring occasionally until berries burst, approximately 5 minutes.
4. Add butter. Stir mixture until melted.
5. Remove blueberry mixture from heat. Spoon or ladle over warm French toast.

Makes 3 cups.

BLUEBERRY MUFFINS

During the Blueberry Blow Out, Marlee steps in at the last minute to judge the festival's blueberry muffin contest. No matter how delicious the winning muffin may have been, it's unlikely that it beat the taste of this famous blueberry muffin recipe first sampled by the public in Boston's famous Jordan Marsh department store.

½ cup butter, softened at room temperature
1¼ cups granulated sugar
2 eggs
1 teaspoon vanilla extract
2 cups flour
2 teaspoons baking powder
½ teaspoon salt
½ cup milk
2 cups fresh blueberries, washed, drained, and
    dried, stems removed
3 teaspoons granulated sugar, for muffin tops

1. Preheat oven to 375°F. Place rack in center of oven.
2. Cream the softened butter and 1¼ cups of sugar until light.
3. Add one egg at a time, beating well to blend into the mixture. Add vanilla.
4. Sift flour, baking powder, and salt together. Add to cream mixture, alternating with the ½ cup of milk.

5. Beat for several seconds.
6. Place ½ cup of the blueberries in a small bowl. Mash with fork.
7. Mix mashed blueberries into batter. Gently fold in remaining whole berries.
8. Line a 12-muffin tin tray with cupcake liners. (Baking the muffins without liners may cause sticking due to the juiciness of the blueberries.) Even if using cupcake liners, lightly spray the liners and top of the tin tray with nonstick spray. Those delicious blueberries will spread.
9. Fill the muffin tins with batter. Sprinkle 3 teaspoons of sugar over the tops of the muffins.
10. Bake at 375°F for approximately 30 minutes, or until tops are light golden brown. Insert a toothpick in the center of a muffin to make certain it comes out clean.
11. After 5 minutes, gently remove from muffin pan. Place on rack to cool.

Makes 12 muffins.

Connect with U s

Visit us online at
KensingtonBooks.com
to read more from your favorite authors, see books
by series, view reading group guides, and more.

Join us on social media

for sneak peeks, chances to win books and prize packs,
and to share your thoughts with other readers.

facebook.com/kensingtonpublishing
twitter.com/kensingtonbooks

Tell us what you think!

To share your thoughts, submit a review,
or sign up for our eNewsletters, please visit:
KensingtonBooks.com/TellUs.